✝

A COUNTRY CALLED PHILADELPHIA

A COUNTRY CALLED
PHILADELPHIA

NATHAN MERRITT

1B2O
STUDIOS

ISBN: 978-1-7370799-3-4 (paperback)
ISBN: 978-1-7370799-4-1 (ebook)
The audiobook, narrated by the author, will soon be available.

Cover art and design by Nathan Merritt

Insert Painting: *The Vision of Saint Eustace, Other Scenes with Tests of His Faith Beyond* by Maarten de Vos, 1601

Previously published as *The Sodium War* by Nathan Merritt

Publisher website: 1820studios.com

Printed in the United States of America

1820 Studios, Utah
E15-260130

For Athena, who inspired this journey to change my heart.

A new commandment I give unto you,
That ye love one another;
as I have loved you,
that ye also love one another.

By this shall all men know
that ye are my disciples,
if ye have love one to another.

—Jesus the Christ

The Vision of Saint Eustace, Other Scenes with Tests of His Faith Beyond

Painted by Maarten de Vos, 1601

Preface

After the string of mass shootings across the United States in August 2019, Athena, a dear friend of mine, challenged me with writing a screenplay concerning the alarming rate of gun violence in America. She even had the idea of enumerating the casualties in the end credits if it were made into a film.

Over the next month of brainstorming, I realized that the story that I wanted to tell wouldn't necessarily be about gun violence but racism, which is a significant motivator for hate crimes. Instead of debating gun control and alienating either half of the country, I wanted to share a story that could inspire empathy and a love for others.

By December 2019, I had organized sequence notes for the entire story. At one point, the project consisted of a trilogy of screenplays, but it evolved into a novel with three parts. I felt the story was important enough that everyone should read it—not just a handful of film producers.

The real-life events of Covid-19, displays of systematic racism, political upheaval, and rioting eerily resembled plot points that I had already devised for the story, and these motivated me to persevere with the project.

I know that this is a controversial story. I am not proposing that white supremacy is as widespread as outlined in the book. It is regarded as a fringe movement, and my intention is that we stay vigilant in keeping it out of government and mainstream society. I do not support the racial slurs and ideologies depicted in the story. They are included as a means of creating awareness to the harm that they can cause.

The core of the story came from my personal struggle with helping others realize that racist speech hurts, and I know that I'm not the only one. If you hear racist speech, no matter how insignificant or harmless it may seem, please teach the person that it does cause pain and that it perpetuates division. Find a way to heal.

I have a deep love for the state of Texas and for the people that are there, my family, and my friends. This is a work of fiction. Places and characters are not based on real locations or people.

My hope is that this story may spread a little more love and peace. Please, be kind to everyone around you.

—Nathan Merritt

Part One

Chapter One

Imminent Storm

Rafe watched his young mother tape up the inside of their living room windows, even though his science teacher had told him it was a bad idea. Instead of shattering into smaller pieces of glass, the windows might fracture into large, deadly shards that could hurtle across the room.

"Whatever you do," the well-spoken black teacher, Mr. Fourier, had said earlier that day, "make sure you don't tape up your windows or stand next to a bulging door during the hurricane tonight. Doing those things can hurt you." He had even used illustrated overhead projections to make his point clear.

The small, seven-year-old Rafe looked around his living room and imagined a bloody, cracked windowpane lodged into the wall behind him. It was a frightening image, but he didn't dare mention the concern to his mother as she continued stretching the tape across the glass.

Unfortunately, he was bound by his Southern upbringing to *respect his elders*—the thought of correcting his mother was too terrifying. Tiny for his age, all he could do was watch the crime scene unfold and imagine how he might be a silent, powerless accessory to murder.

"Rafe," his mother, Edith, asked, "can you bring me another roll of tape? I believe there's one in the kitchen, in a paper sack." Even though it was 2003, his middle-aged mother seemed perfectly content living with all the norms of the 1950s. Her curly, blonde hair was short, and she wore a floral, pleated dress that came down to her knees.

"Yes, ma'am," he responded and dutifully returned, visibly anxious, knowing that the duct tape he was holding could be in the hands of the investigative police in the days to come. He stood next to her, immovable, like a robot that had been given conflicting lines of code to process, and he was afraid that sparks would soon fly from his ears. *At least that's what happens on TV*, he thought.

She applied another strip of tape and said, "Alright, I think we're just about done." It was then that she finally looked at the sweaty, pale boy and asked, "Are you okay?"

He nodded sheepishly, and his perfectly combed, blond hair didn't move at all. His mother frequently reminded him that she liked it that way.

"How was school today?"

Outside, dark clouds had already formed, and a few drops of rain began to fall. As the pecan trees swayed in the wind, Rafe thought he saw the wheelbarrow in the yard move just a little. Looking at the scene reminded him of something else the teacher had taught that day.

"Mr. Fourier showed us what happens when you light a balloon on fire."

"Really?" His mother quickly whipped her head around as if she had caught someone red-handed. "Did *that man* light a fire in the classroom?"

"No, we went outside this morning. It was sunny."

Deflated, she returned to inspect her work. "So, what happened? Did it pop?" she asked, closing the curtains. The deed was done, and there was nothing he could do to rectify the situation.

4

Now beside himself, Rafe sat on a small storage bench to watch his mother move furniture away from the windows. He wondered if that afternoon might be the last time he would see her alive because of the accident that was bound to happen. He tried to memorize every second of their final moments together.

"Did it pop, Rafe?"

"Yes," he replied, almost unsure of himself, "but the water balloons took a lot longer because the water *absorbed* all the heat." He liked saying the new word he had learned in class that day.

Lifting a heavy chair, she muttered, "I wonder why *that man* had you playing with balloons. Surely, there are other things to learn."

Rafe had to convey the storm's gravity, but he was still timid. "Mr. Fourier wanted to show us why we're having this hurricane. He said that the ocean is taking a lot of the sun's heat, and that's what makes bad weather happen."

"Oh, I see." She didn't seem fazed at all by the science teacher's lesson or remotely concerned about their *impending doom*.

For the rest of the night, Rafe kept vigilant in his duty to make sure nobody entered the potential crime scene. During dinner, he looked toward the living room every time he heard a crack of thunder, expecting the worst. The storm raged on, though, as the heavy rain pummeled their home.

RAFE AWOKE TO HIS MOTHER lifting him with his blanket out of bed in the middle of the night. A faint light came from the hallway, so he could barely see. He knew it was her, though, by the sound of her soft voice.

"It's okay, dear. We're going to sleep in my room tonight."

She quickly walked down the hallway, shielding his face from his father's flashlight, and made it to the bedroom. Being carried always strengthened his faith in her and the love that bound them.

For as long as Rafe could remember, there was always a plan in place for a hurricane. His mother's closet was in the middle of the house and the furthest away from any window.

"Is he okay?" his father asked in the dark.

His mother softly replied, "I think he went back to sleep."

As the thunder roared and the wind howled, they huddled on the closet floor. Since his mother was still holding him in her arms, he felt the door close with his toes. The final step of security, the faint sound of the latch, could barely be heard over the horrendous destruction outside.

"Is everything off?" she asked.

"Yeah," his father responded, "I checked the gas, electricity, and water. So, we should be alright."

"Mom?"

"Yeah, sweetie?"

"Are we going to drown?" He was petrified. All he could think about was the house being destroyed under the weight of the water outside, like the balloons popping in class. He thought about the taped windows cutting the walls and the doors exploding. And what made it worse was that the darkness of the closet amplified all of his fears.

His father's voice was low enough that Rafe couldn't tell where he was sitting. "Don't worry, Son. Everything will be fine."

It was then that his mother hummed the most beautiful song for him. He had heard it many times before, and he couldn't tell if she was humming just for him or the whole family. The love behind the angelic notes penetrated every fear and sank deep into his heart as he closed his eyes and drifted off peacefully.

Chapter Two

But a Sword

(16 Years Later)

All Rafe could do was watch Bri play with her curly red hair instead of focus on the task at hand. He even held the menu in front of him as a last-minute shield in case she happened to glance at him. After several months of dating, she was still that intoxicating.

Behind her, a lamp with the perfect color temperature gave her just the right glow, and Rafe moved in his booth seat a little to find the right angle to take a mental picture of her.

"Alright, I think I've got it," she said with a small chuckle. "You?"

It was then that she finally looked up, and he melted, completely smitten by her beautiful blue eyes and freckles.

"What's so funny?" he asked as an automatic defense mechanism.

She looked around at the small Mexican diner and admitted while leaning in, "Whenever I got a veggie burger as a kid, they always assumed that my mom had ordered it. I'm sure I've confused a lot of waiters in my day."

Rafe found her treasured menu item at the bottom of the page, and after checking to see if it was within budget, he joked, "Well, if I order the same thing, then the poor guy won't have to worry."

"Have you ever had one?"

"Nope. First time for everything, I guess." He quickly scanned a few side dishes on the menu should the vegetable atrocity not sit well with him. In his mind, it was downright un-American to eat such a thing. Right now, though, a side dish would be a luxury.

"Wonderful! They're amazing! I hope you like it!" She smiled in such a way that cemented the whole ordeal, and he couldn't resist it.

The little diner was crowded and noisy, so Rafe didn't hear his phone ring. Although they had reached an agreement about their order, the only way he could relieve his anxiety about the burger was to study the image design of Mexican paintings on the walls.

"Is that your phone?" Bri asked.

He reached into his pocket, looked at the screen, and declined the call as if nothing had happened.

She continued amiably, "Who was it? You can take it if you like. I don't mind."

"Oh, it was my mom," he responded, slightly bitter. For him, the mood had changed. Instead of being present with the love of his life, he was reminded of his mother's tendencies.

Bri sat up and genuinely asked, "How is she doing? I haven't talked to her in a while."

"The same as always, I guess—"

Across the room, a group of men at a table had grown impatient, and one of them shouted at the waiter, "Hey *beaner*, can we get some service over here?"

8

The sole waiter in the small diner was a slow-moving, elderly Hispanic man. "Yes, sir. One moment, please," he managed as he finished serving his current table.

Bri turned to Rafe as if she wanted to start a war. She wore her moral compass around her neck as if it guided every single action, and he knew that she couldn't let the racial slur go unchecked. They had been down this road before.

As soon as she edged toward the end of the booth seat, Rafe whispered, "Don't worry about it. Just let it go."

"I can't do that. That man needs to be called out."

"Why? It's not going to do any good. Just look at him. He's probably not going to change." The man across the room was a tall, rugged cowboy, and Rafe wanted to avoid any confrontation with him.

Bri stood up right away. "Sir, please apologize to the waiter." The noisy diner quieted down, and most of the patrons stopped to watch.

"Why?" the tall man asked. "Are you calling me a racist?"

Rafe tried to tap her foot, but she was too far away; talking about all of this was horribly awkward. But of course, if any of those gentlemen approached Bri to hurt her, that would be a different story. He understood that kind of fight.

"No, I'm just asking you to apologize," she responded calmly.

The waiter humbly interjected, "Really, ma'am, it's no trouble at all." He approached the new table with pen and paper in hand, ready to take the orders.

"Good! Because I'm not a racist," the tall gentleman declared.

"How you choose to identify yourself is your prerogative. I'm just calling you out on your actions. Why do you want to offend this person?" Bri asked. The duel was getting more and more awkward with each new volley.

"Well," the cowboy replied as he looked at the waiter, "it seems he doesn't take any offense, so it's not offensive—"

"I'm offended," she quickly rebuked.

The towering man then slowly walked up to Bri, and the closer he came, the tighter Rafe's fists clenched as he sat at the table. After all these years, Rafe still had a small frame, but he was very trim and athletic. He thought about running out the door with Bri in his arms to escape the situation, but he figured that they would inevitably return to a similar confrontation again.

The small restaurant was silent, and all eyes were on Bri and the rugged cowboy that approached her. If someone in the room were willing to fight against racism, they could now vicariously take up the mantle through her. Many phones were already recording and live streaming the standoff.

"But you're white," the man argued, now standing two feet away from her. At this, Rafe slowly rose with both fists seemingly glued to the table.

"I'm offended as a human being," Bri stated as she stared the tall man straight in the eye. A slice of the current state of America, the two squared off like a brewing storm.

Quickly breaking the stare-down, the cowboy noticed Rafe's white knuckles that were ready to strike. The man unexpectedly turned around to face the waiter and repented, "I'm sorry for what I said. There was no need for me to be mean. I'm sorry."

With that, the tall man tipped his hat toward Bri with a sheepish smile and returned to his table. A crisis was averted, and a different atmosphere fell over the diner. A few more *pleases* and *thank-yous* were heard, people smiled a little more, and the waiter stood a little taller.

WHEN THEY FINALLY REACHED the motel parking lot in his truck, Rafe couldn't ignore his error anymore. "I'm sorry about that back there. You were right."

Bri opened her passenger door and playfully asked, "About the burger or the guy who was very rude?" Before he could say anything, she closed the door, leaned through the open window, and teased, "Don't worry about it. I usually am."

Her smile was disarming, and in the moonlight, he could do nothing but admire her. He truly aspired to be more passionate and courageous like her but felt that he couldn't possibly attain that, even after several lifetimes.

As he offered no reply other than a chuckle, she asked, "So, tomorrow at 4 AM then?"

"Yeah, we need to head out early," he answered, looking at the New Mexico desert landscape with anticipation. "I appreciate you doing this for me. Hopefully, you can get enough sleep." By the time he had finished speaking, she had already set an alarm on her phone.

While scanning her texts, she returned, "Not a problem," and gave him a peck on the cheek. "It looks like the Townsend hearing was stalled. I may need to call in and help."

"It never ends, does it?" He no longer had her attention, and she was off on one of her crusades.

As they walked toward her motel-room door, she replied, "No, not really." Her tone was both disheartened and energized at the same time.

A few years younger than Rafe, Bri was a natural-born spitfire reporter. She had the uncanny gift of yanking out the truth and presenting it in a way that anyone could understand. This was her oxygen. You knew that as soon as she adjusted her glasses, she was trying to look past whatever you may have just told her and look right into your soul.

When he reached his own motel-room door, which was next to hers, he couldn't help but be inspired by her and her dedication to her craft. He watched her read the latest on the Townsend hearing, and he assumed it was political. To him, it didn't matter, but he knew it should.

"Well, goodnight then," he said as a reminder of his presence.

"Goodnight," she politely replied, not lifting her phone-bound gaze as she closed the door behind her.

Rafe couldn't close his door, though, as there was too much promise in the vast New Mexico desert, beautifully lit by the early winter moon. Everything was perfect.

Chapter Three

Under a Bushel

To the south, in a little town called Sodium, Texas, Rebah stood at her kitchen sink. She was content washing dishes, as it was a form of therapy for her. Although she was in her mid-thirties, the many years of being an elementary teacher had dragged across her worn-out face.

This was her time to unwind and think about the day, to assess if she could have done anything differently as a teacher.

She often muttered, "Yep, I need to look up the Spanish word for that" or "I've got to make copies of that worksheet." And the only way she could concentrate was by listening to church hymns on a little CD player that Jim bought for her many years before.

At times, Rebah would mention a boy's name in her planning, and Jim would bark out from the living room, "Who's Tomás?"

"Oh, he's one of my students," she would say, followed by an update with ecstatic enthusiasm. "He's actually reading now!"

Without another word, Jim would usually continue watching the crime-heavy news on TV and not pay her any more attention.

Unfortunately, the dishwashing session ended abruptly, and she removed her apron. There wasn't another item to clean in the kitchen, the CD had stopped, and it was time to move on. Rebah found herself peering into the dark living room, longing for something, as the kitchen was the only lit room in the house.

Holding a laundry basket, she walked down the upstairs hallway and knocked on her son's bedroom door. "Sam, are you hungry? I have your dinner on the stove if you're hungry."

Calling out his name again through the cheap wooden separator was fruitless. When she opened the door, she drew a heavy sigh—he had already left for the night. A quick scan of his room revealed dirty laundry and broken toys on the floor, trash strewn about, and an open window that let in the devastation of an evening downpour. She promptly closed it with a shiver.

From the outside, the tiny house on the outskirts of town was now dark except for Sam's room. As Rebah stood at the window on the second floor, she appeared like a beacon as blackness covered the landscape for miles.

After an exhale, the mother slowly dialed a number on her phone. "Hey, Jim—" she started, already broken.

The voice on the other end was loud and abusive, but she kept the phone to her ear.

As soon as there was a break in the senseless scolding, she meekly said, "I'm sorry to call you. Is Sam at your place tonight?"

The reply was equally berating, and she ended the call, thanking him for his time and watching Samuel. She then helplessly sank down into the puddle of water at the base of the window, consigned to another evening alone.

"Father in Heaven," she whispered, "please watch over my boy." Somehow, knowing her small prayer was at least heard was comforting.

14

Chapter Four

Placidus

The bullet pierced the flesh but missed the soul. As the body fell to the earth, the sky darkened, and it began to drizzle again. There was no intent for remorse or even a thought for any eulogy. No words were uttered. A father had just died—and the spirit lived.

BEFORE PULLING THE TRIGGER, Rafe had the mule deer's neck in the scope's crosshairs. He knew he wasn't skilled enough to shoot the head, especially with the deer's quick, unpredictable movements, and he wasn't positioned correctly to aim for the small target area of the heart.

There were limitations, though. If the shot were too low on the neck, the buck would probably take off and eventually die a slow, painful death.

Rafe looked up at the early morning overcast sky across the New Mexico desert and noticed that the wind was picking up. The magnificent animal would soon scamper away, and he knew that by just watching it graze, the deer could hear the second hand of his wristwatch move. It was otherworldly like that.

Through the scope, he marveled at its dark eyes, and he thought about how his father took him hunting when he was ten.

HOURS BEFORE SUNRISE, the only thing the preadolescent Rafe could see was the beam from his father's flashlight sporadically bouncing all over the grass. His father was looking for something. Unfortunately, the numerous tall trees blocked out the moonlight, and all the boy could think about was the howling wind and the creaking trees that seemed to engulf them.

"Okay, now get on up in this tree," his father softly commanded in a Southern accent. The small tree before them had low branches for climbing, and it would serve as a decent perch for the young hunter. "I'll hand you the gun when you're ready."

"Yes, sir." He reached for a few branches to hoist himself up and was annoyed at how his father's flashlight created shadows that made it harder to see where he needed to go. Finally, after climbing about eight feet from the ground, the boy said, "Okay, I'm ready," and reached down for the weapon.

His father had dark brown eyes and always sported a full graying beard. Rafe always thought it was because he was hiding a scar or something interesting on his face, but the truth never came out. More of a listener, his father only spoke up if Rafe needed guidance or help moving forward.

"Now, I'm fixin' to go this way," he said, "so whatever you do, don't aim in that direction. Okay?"

The boy looked in the direction his father had pointed, but it all looked the same. It was a dense forest at night. He quickly nodded with his eyes closed because the flashlight was aimed right below his face and resolved that anything to his left would be off-limits.

When he heard his father leave, he was finally able to open his eyes. "Bye, Dad."

"Yep," his father whispered.

All Rafe could see was the flashlight beam getting fainter as the silhouette of a man walked stealthily toward his own tree like a deer himself. Rafe was soon alone, holding a 20-gauge shotgun for his imagination.

Every sound was amplified like a choir of nightmares. The chirps, the howling wind whipping through the creaking branches, the soft footsteps on dry leaves below, and the incessant clawing on bark all took center stage in his mind.

After shifting around in the tree multiple times, trying to find any of these creatures, he found himself uncertain which way his father had gone. He didn't dare lift his gun. Shadows moved in every direction. Some were small and were probably branches or bushes, but others he couldn't make out.

Suddenly, he noticed a massive shadow that looked like a bear slowly approaching his tree. He couldn't move. He couldn't even blink.

In an instant, he closed his eyes, the darkness being almost no different than before, and he said the quickest prayer he could. When he uttered his final plea and opened his eyes, the beast was gone. The moon shone a little brighter on the ground below, and the little boy sighed in relief.

NOW YEARS LATER, Rafe looked at the deer's neck through the scope and wondered if what he had seen that one night might have also been a deer. Perhaps. There was no way of finding out.

He smiled, knowing that all those fears from his childhood were long gone, and he pulled the trigger. The great buck fell, and he imagined the sound of it.

Fortunately, Rafe was able to drive his truck right up to the magnificent animal. He was so excited that he flew out of the vehicle with his video camera, leaving the engine running and the driver-side door open.

As he danced around the dead animal, composing dramatic, handheld shots, Bri stayed in the warm truck, having leaned over and closed his door as soon as he left. He could shoot still-life objects for hours, continually searching for an image design that spoke to him, but he knew that he could only have his girlfriend for a short time. She had to get back as soon as possible.

Somehow, remembering that night with his father brought out his Southern drawl, and he called out to her, "It's fixin' to rain. We gotta do this."

When she finally arrived at the corpse, carrying the camera tripod and audio equipment, she shook her head with a chuckle at how easily he had slipped into his old manner of speaking. "Fixin' to, huh?" she teased as if to confirm an apparent return to his childhood.

"Well, some things just remind me of my dad." He admired the deer and wondered what a hunting trip with his father would be like now. *What kind of conversations would we have? Would my dad be proud of me?* Questions and fantasies swam around his head as he stared at the bloody scene.

Bri surveyed the rocky brush terrain near Placid, New Mexico, surrounded by misty mountains in every direction. "Alright, so where do you want me?"

"It's all about the background," he replied as he glanced behind himself. While pointing at a flat rock in the ground, he proposed, "So, how about over there?" Already kneeling next to the deer, he imagined how the whole story would edit together.

18

She then moved the camera and tripod toward the desired location and made a few manual adjustments. Rafe was never comfortable in front of the camera, but somehow holding the head of a dead deer by the antlers put him at ease.

"I'm thinking a zoom out from the head to a medium-wide should be good," he said, brimming.

Without realizing it, Bri glanced at the overcast sky to witness the unavoidable signs of what was to come and tucked a few strands of her curly red hair under her sweater hood. She had survived without any online communication for almost four hours and was now visibly eager to return to civilization. "And after this, we're done, right?"

"Yep. This is the last shot," Rafe confirmed, turning the animal's neck so that it was facing the lens.

Bri looked up from the viewfinder and protested, "Don't you want to close its eyes? It's freaking me out!"

"No. I think they'll grab people's attention."

After a few more camera adjustments, she said, "Alright, I'm rolling."

Ecstatic that his video ended with an actual kill and that he documented the whole hunt successfully, he began the final segment.

"And so, to sum up, we had a couple of things going for us." Rafe held up his gun and taught, "We had top-quality optics, we found some tracks near this small pond, and we relied on the rut, which is a time when the mule deer acts abnormally and is less cautious."

It was then that his mind wandered off. He thought about the weight of the whole ordeal and how he might hoist the magnificent animal onto his truck. *It's a burden, but it's worth it*, he thought to himself.

"Well, folks," he continued, "that'll have to do for this week's episode, so remember to plan, be patient, and keep your eyes peeled. This is Rafe Davidson. Until next time!"

As soon as they had packed the camera and hunting gear, it started to rain, and he tried to lift the deer but couldn't. "Would you be willing to help me with this?" he asked Bri, realizing he couldn't handle the cumbersome task alone.

She had already turned on her phone to engage in the morning's headlines, texting with one hand and using the other to shield the device from the sudden downpour. Her current crusades were so vital that she was unaware of how soaked she had quickly become. "This rain is something else, huh?"

While Rafe hastily shifted some of the equipment toward the cab to make room for the new burden, he noticed Bri standing in the rain, seemingly unaffected, as she continued to text. "Alright, do you want the head or bottom?" he inquired.

She pocketed the phone. "Which one's lighter?"

"It's all the same."

"Well, I'm not touching that head," she declared.

The mule deer was unnaturally heavy, but they finally managed to hoist it onto the bed together. Unfortunately, Bri came away from the ordeal with blood smeared across her chest.

Disgusted, she shrieked, "Gross! Now I need to change my sweater."

"If you wait long enough, the rain will wash it out," Rafe said as a sincere and practical gesture. But as soon as she gave him a smirk, he backpedaled. "Of course, you can wear my jacket that's in the cab if you want—"

"Nope, I'll be fine. I came prepared for anything, including being bloodied-up, apparently." The rain continued to fall, and she quickly flew into the cab to find a suitable remedy.

As Rafe moved the buck closer to the cab so that he could close the gate, he found himself transfixed by the animal's dark eyes, as if he were staring into a beautiful night sky. There was a connection and an overwhelming feeling of peace, even while standing in the cold rain, that he couldn't wrap his mind around.

Bri opened the cab window and asked, "Are you okay?"

"Yeah," he finally returned, coming out of a trance.

Engrossed in her phone, she continued voraciously consuming a massive amount of information and responding to texts. Suddenly, she exclaimed, "My phone's blowing up!"

Chapter Five

Unhinged

S amuel, Rebah's only child, knew what he was doing was right; *It's what God wants*, he thought. He couldn't figure out why he was still sweating, though.

He approached Columbia Elementary like he did every morning, unkempt, marching down the same sidewalk where his mother used to hold his hand on the way to school, and they would converse openly. Of course, he didn't need to hold her hand now; he was 11.

His stringy, dirty blond hair hung over his eyes, which looked like they hadn't seen a dream in years. He wore a death-colored ball cap, which was against the school dress code, and it only pushed the strands down further, creating an eyeless enigma.

Samuel removed the cap once he arrived at the schoolyard, though, as he felt that everyone should obey the rules. There was an order with everything in his life, and it required strict adherence.

He observed the chaotic groups of children running and playing on the grass as he charged toward the front entrance. Their antics and over-hyper energy always annoyed him. *Stupid little kids—they're all the same,* he silently judged.

OCCASIONALLY, REBAH DID GET A GLANCE from Samuel as he passed her first-grade classroom, but there wasn't even a break in his stride that morning. Her heart had been beyond broken for many months.

Without realizing it, she had wandered into the middle of the hallway among a sea of children to watch the last glimpse of her only child disappear around a corner. Suddenly, without warning, he turned toward her at the last second and gave a faint smile. She didn't know that her eyes were wet.

"Mrs. Jarik, are you okay?" a bright young girl with black hair asked Rebah as she took her hand.

Her default teacher facade then took over, and she responded, "Yes, Isabella, everything's fine." She put her arm around the softhearted girl, and they both walked into the classroom. "How's your dog feeling today?"

As the door closed behind them, Isabella shared, "He told me that he's really sad that his mother was picked on."

LATER THAT MORNING, IN HIS SCIENCE CLASS, Samuel learned about different insects from a slideshow presentation. Because the lights were off, the boys around him kept making distracting noises.

Coming to the end of his short fuse, Samuel spun around in his desk to look at the boy directly behind him, Mario Sanchez, and blasted, "What do you want?"

After a chuckle and a confirmation glance toward his friends, Mario snickered, "Nada."

Samuel wanted to reach out and punch Mario right in the jaw. He had no idea what the boy said, and for all he knew, it could have been an

24

insult. Staring at Mario's long, frizzy, black hair in the dark, Samuel envisioned scalping him like a Civil War soldier from one of his military books at his father's house. For the young white boy, those were the only books worth reading.

"Boys, settle down!" commanded Mr. Lorenz, the only adult in the room.

Samuel turned back around to continue studying the pictures from the slideshow. He counted their legs and noticed the thinness of their dead wings.

Stupid little bugs, he thought to himself. *Why would God want these things anyway? What purpose do they have other than food? They all look the same—annoying little bugs.*

The lights flickered on, and most of the students found themselves caught in the act of something, either still giggling, sleeping, or just being 11 years old.

"Alright, y'all come up here and see what I have for you," invited Mr. Lorenz. The class gathered around the table at the front of the room, which displayed many of the same insects from the slide presentation, only now they were suspended by pins on little foam boards.

There were cockroaches, beetles, grasshoppers, butterflies, and many other specimens that caused a few children to utter their disgust at the display. But despite their disapproval, they pulled in closer, as if they were rubbernecking the scene of a small insect Armageddon.

Unfortunately, Mario was small for his age and couldn't see the table from behind everyone, so he went around looking for a spot to fit in, but there was no room. At last, he moved in close to Samuel, merely brushing his arm. And without any hesitation, Samuel landed a pent-up blow right on Mario's face, sending him to the ground, spread out like one of the dead insects for everyone to see.

Annoying, little bug, Samuel thought.

25

The children chaotically gathered around the new real-life display on the floor, accidentally bumping the table. And before Mr. Lorenz could prevent the inevitable, one of the dead butterflies took flight and crashed onto the ground with a severed wing.

"That's enough, Samuel! Get yourself to the principal's office now!" the teacher demanded. The choice had been made, and the consequence was now set.

Samuel didn't care. He walked out of the room with his coat and backpack as a few boys helped Mario to his feet. There was blood on the floor, and like the plague, everyone scurried away from it.

Mr. Lorenz soon ordered a nearby boy to run a clean rag under the classroom faucet. "Everyone, get back to your seats!"

He quickly walked Mario to his desk and examined his bloody nose and the back of his head, which had received a small cut when he hit the floor. Thankfully, his thick, dark hair had helped to soften the blow.

"Here," the fatherlike teacher said softly to Mario, handing him the wet cloth, "hold this to your head. Everything will be alright."

His eyes now wet, the towering man stood up and addressed the children as if it were his last lesson. "This has got to stop!"

As the teacher approached the table at the front of the room, he considered shoving it a few inches out of pure frustration and righteous anger, but he slapped it like a heavy gavel instead. The students jumped.

"Please, for the love of God, just be nice to each other!" he implored. "I don't care what your dad does or what your mom says—we're all God's children!"

All of their eyes were on him, and he wondered if he had frightened them or if he had pierced their hearts enough to make a difference.

He soon approached the classroom door, defeated, knowing that every parent would probably find out about his outburst and demand his resignation. There was nothing that anyone could do; the racial hatred in the town was too deep and widespread for redemption.

To his astonishment, the troublemaker obediently sat on the bench outside the principal's office at the end of the hallway, so the teacher returned to the class, pulled out his phone, and dialed for assistance.

WITH HIS HEAD COCKED TO ONE SIDE, Samuel found himself studying the red brick wall by the office. The bricks were staggered, never forming a straight, vertical line. It seemed like the whole mess worked against itself, but then he saw it:

A single jagged, cement line in the wall formed a staircase from the floor to the ceiling, and he marveled that such a symbol was there among the chaos the whole time. It spoke to him. Not only was he trying to do the will of God, but there was also an order to all things.

Once Mr. Lorenz's door finally closed, the echo shot across the hallway, and Samuel bolted further into the school.

Chapter Six

No Words

A few months before, Samuel received a book assignment from his English teacher, Ms. Beauchamp, and he returned to school with a letter from his father describing his unapologetic disdain for the book's subject matter.

The letter demanded exclusion from the exercise and that he would lobby to have the book removed from the school grounds, regarding it as irrelevant, unnecessary, and downright offensive.

The impressionable boy was living with his father more by then. And because his father beat him with a belt until his backside bled and yelled at him with curses to kingdom come so much that his ears frequently rang, the poor boy always did as his father told him.

One evening, though, in an act of defiance, Samuel read the introduction to the *infamous* book for the assignment, and it included an anecdote about Abraham Lincoln. When the president met the author, he declared, "So, this is the little lady who started this great war."

He smiled at the implication that someone like a small woman could start something so grand as a war. He hoped he could equally be of use.

SAMUEL MADE HIS WAY DOWN THE HALL and into the school library, where a kindergarten class read a board book with a librarian. The children sat on the floor, mesmerized by the book's vibrantly colored animals from around the world, and they happily repeated the text after the librarian. "Stupid, colored animals," he mumbled.

After a desperate, heart-pounding search, he finally came to the same *offensive novel* from the book assignment—and it stared back at him on the shelf. It hadn't been removed yet.

The various lengths of book spines surrounding the novel created a jagged, unorganized mess. *Why couldn't they be the same? Why are there so many different colors and sizes?* he wondered.

He violently grabbed *Uncle Tom's Cabin*, the object of his father's loathing, and held it open on the shelf with other nearby books, just like the insect display from class. Without a second thought, he reached into his backpack for his mother's old cigarette lighter.

After just one strike, he laid it right in the middle of the book and stood back. At first, the blinding flame ascended without any consequence, but soon the metal shelf above it started to brown, and the two exposed pages from the book turned black.

Samuel admired his creation. His eyes were transfixed as if he were a two-year-old looking at lit candles on a birthday cake. In his mind, he was crossing a fiery bridge to manhood.

He soon walked away, though. No one saw him enter, and nobody knew he was there; he was already a ghost.

Within seconds, Samuel made it to an unlabeled maintenance door in the back of the school. There was nothing for it now; he had to follow through. He reached into his backpack again and pulled out a small key on a chain.

The hallway was empty, and as he opened the heavy door with the key, the sound echoed in both directions. For a moment, he felt like he was on a stage at his church, and the echo sounded like an ecstatic ovation. It had been a year since the last time he wore a genuine smile.

The circular stairs in a dark corner of the maintenance room had a high pitch, and he felt as if his heart was coming out of his chest as he climbed. Every step toward heaven was getting harder and harder to attain, but at last, Samuel emerged onto the roof.

Maneuvering between a maze of air ducts, he quickly located a black bag he had stashed several weeks before. He looked up at the sky to admire how the clouds moved, how predictable the times and seasons were. *Every single atom in nature obeys God because He is obedient*, he reminded himself. *He is a god of law and order.*

By now, the fire alarm rang throughout the school, and the small children began to file out slowly by their classes. There were a few raindrops here and there—the last remains of a morning shower.

Samuel recognized one of the third-grade classes and their teacher below. The children shoved each other, and the teacher couldn't control them—the line had become a mess. One small boy left the group and studied the grass as he moved his foot from side to side across the lawn. The wet blades bent ever so slightly and slowly returned straight once his foot went past.

Several other classes had congregated, and Samuel watched them all from above, like a god. It was then, with a fit of pent-up anger that he could no longer control, as if something otherworldly had taken over his body, that he took aim with the gun from the black bag and shot the boy playing with the grass until he fell to the ground, lifeless.

31

Holding the trigger down, Samuel moved the barrel to a small six-year-old girl that he thought he knew. She didn't belong where she was standing, and she fell, her blood soaking the wet grass.

As he reaped with the gun from side to side, much like King Herod, the horror showered countless little innocent children with a quick, piercing pain that sent the babes into a warm and welcoming heaven.

In an indescribable scene straight from hell, children screamed and ran in every direction. Samuel watched them scatter like mice, like the cockroaches he thought they were. *Brown, black, dead.*

No words could convey the shriek of those left behind, as if thousands of years of tormented mothers and fathers screamed from the ground and held out their hearts for God to help them.

Mr. Lorenz did everything he could to keep his students safe, but Mario and his friends were among the first to fall. In an instant, when the tall teacher stood up and spotted Samuel, he calmly shook his head at him. Instead of a plea, it was a condemnation. What he taught died along with him.

The rain was heavier now, and Samuel walked along the roof wall like a lost boy, powerless to something he couldn't see, something he didn't understand. Sound faded away, and all he could think about was the power he wielded as he wreaked havoc in a heartless slaughter. He was seemingly a god with command over life and death, and yet something controlled him.

On the other side of the school, his mother and her first-grade students ran toward the parking lot. Samuel approached the wall above them with his head cocked again, witnessing his mother flee from him as if she didn't know him, and he let his finger off the trigger.

She's not supposed to be here, he thought. He hadn't realized that she would have to leave the inferno as well.

Chapter Seven

Heaven's Tears

The downpour was now unavoidable, and the morning sky had become too dark to drive without headlights. Rafe even leaned forward in his seat to see the road, catching only glimpses between the windshield wipers.

His mind wandered, recalling a few more childhood memories with his father. He missed him dearly. Although the rain sounded like metal pellets ravaging the roof of the truck, it seemed very distant and almost another world away to him.

Suddenly, a heart-wrenching gasp from Bri pulled him back into reality. Rafe slammed on the brakes, causing the truck to slide uncontrollably on the wet pavement, and they came to an abrupt stop on the highway.

He leaped out of the truck to see what might have caused her reaction—perhaps, she had noticed something he hadn't.

Luckily, they were alone on the desert road. Thoroughly drenched, he realized that he hadn't passed another car for at least an hour, so he leaned into the cab and asked Bri, "What's wrong?"

He was so immersed in remembering his father and navigating through the deluge that he forgot that she was in the middle of a phone call with her news producer. Visibly shaken, she motioned for him to sit down.

"There's been another mass shooting!" she answered him.

"What?" Rafe had been so wrapped up in his little world and drowning in other preoccupations that his bubble just burst. It wasn't necessarily because of what had happened but because it affected her so dramatically.

Bri could barely talk. "It was at an elementary school, in a place called Sodium, Texas," she relayed to Rafe. She couldn't control the tears that were sliding down the side of her cheek.

After a few nods, she solemnly told the producer over the phone, "Okay, will do." Her voice was that of a frightened girl who was on the verge of hiding from the world. She ended the call and placed the phone on the dashboard as if their fate was lying in front of them.

Having never seen her cry before, Rafe wanted to grab her phone and throw it out the window just to take the pain away, but he couldn't. "Where's Sodium, Texas?" he asked.

"It's a little south from here, and since we're so close, they want us to report on it."

He went straight to production logistics—it was a safe place. "Alright, we have a few cameras and several mics, so we should be okay." As she shook her head in a fit of incredulity, all he could see was her curly red hair bouncing across her skin.

"Did they catch the shooter?" he probed, almost removed from the situation. He just wasn't ready to process the story on a personal level.

"I don't know," she sobbed as if she were about to shut down to keep out the horror.

"An elementary school, huh? I hope they shoot the guy. It's always a guy—I don't know why."

34

Nothing. Rafe knew that there wasn't anything he could say that would make the situation better. All he knew was fumbling man-speak.

Suddenly, Bri wiped her face, picked up the phone, and dutifully searched for directions to Sodium, Texas.

† † †

REBAH LAY FLAT ON THE GROUND with her hands clutched over her head like a prisoner. The screams echoed in her ears, and she glanced at her six-year-old babies crying around her.

She looked up again at the roof, and just before the dark figure moved out of sight, she thought she recognized him. The moment seemed like something from a dream, and without knowing why, she felt a surge of uncontrollable pain in her heart. Without reason, she felt that everything was her fault.

SAMUEL HAD ALREADY LET GO OF THE TRIGGER, and it was then that a sharp pain ravaged his back and chest. Before he fell to the ground, he watched his mother lying on the wet grass. Even though she was very far away, he could see in her eyes the tender care of a loving mother.

He studied the way she moved her head to locate the children around her and marveled at how much she loved them. She reached out and pulled several of them close to her like a hen gathering her young. No matter how much power he was holding between his hands, it couldn't overcome the love he knew he always had right at his fingertips. Reaching out from the ledge, he felt his mother give him one last embrace. He then closed his eyes, thinking only of her and how she loved him. Everything else faded away.

Chapter Eight

Angels

The rain had let up a little when Rafe and Bri arrived at Columbia Elementary in his truck. Sirens blared as EMTs, parents, and countless volunteers rushed to encircle the little ones strewn across the lawn. Because of all the prayers being cast, fire trucks seemed to blast the school with a sanctified deluge.

The place now felt like a hallowed site, as if no more harm could be done. Ambulances flooded the streets, many wept uncontrollably, and the embraces between strangers were life-giving.

Rafe and Bri quickly gathered their camera gear and walked over to what they figured was a command post.

Captain Charlie Merlot had already seen them approaching and ran toward them while talking on his two-way radio. "Can I help you?" Merlot asked them in a rushed manner.

His weathered face had a thick graying beard, and he commanded attention with his piercing green eyes. Decades of service had shown him every horrid display of humanity, but this had pushed him to the verge of hopelessness.

"Yes, we're with KOLB-TV, out of Gulf Haven, Texas. Can you tell us what happened?" Bri managed, trying to convey as much comfort and brevity in her voice as possible. They didn't have a company vehicle, so their station jackets had to talk for them. Luckily, Rafe had stashed a few in his truck.

"Yeah, go ahead," Merlot spoke into his shoulder radio, followed by indecipherable crosstalk. "Okay, okay," he replied. "Oh, no!"

"What's wrong?" Rafe asked while setting up the camera.

The captain returned, "Look, I only have a second!"

As soon as Rafe nodded, Merlot took a deep breath and relayed, "A fire started in the school library, and as classes were leaving the building, a shooter opened fire. At this time, we don't know if the incidents are related, but the shooter has been neutralized." At the tail end of the report, he held back tears and shook his head in utter disbelief.

After more crosstalk, he shouted into his radio, "Alright, I'm on my way!" An ambulance with a deafening siren then wailed right by them.

"What happened?" Bri questioned the captain as he turned to leave.

"Another mass shooting at another elementary school! It's like 9-11 all over again!" he replied.

Rafe and Bri looked at each other—the situation was now bigger than them both. Something was happening in Sodium, Texas, and there was no turning back.

"Sir, can my colleague, Rafe, ride with you to the other scene while I work here?" Bri proposed as she surveyed the catastrophe. She was already crying.

Merlot looked Rafe over. "Yes, come with me."

BEFORE HE KNEW IT, RAFE FOUND HIMSELF SPRINTING behind the officer to the patrol car. The storm-ridden morning sky had darkened even more, and the red and blue lights oscillated on Merlot's face as he opened the driver's door. Rafe tried to gauge him but couldn't.

Unfortunately, this was a first for him; he had never been on an assignment. He spent his days shooting endless rows of couches and cars, making TV commercials for clients, but this was reality. He wasn't supposed to sell something—his job was to share the depths of humanity.

He looked out the patrol-car window and noticed that Bri was already sobbing with a mother. Now behind glass, the whole scene was framed like a film, and he felt removed from all of it.

"What's your name again, son?" Merlot probed, pulling Rafe out of his trance.

"Rafe Davidson."

"This is stupid. How could *he* do it? I've known him—" Merlot couldn't finish and just shook his head.

"You know the guy who did it?"

"Yep, but I can't disclose that right now."

Rafe didn't know the protocols for being on-assignment, so he figured he should document everything. "Can I shoot you as you drive? I mean, can I record you?"

"Yeah, sure."

Rafe adjusted his camera and slid a microphone onto the officer's bullet-proof vest. "Okay, here's a mic. Can you tell me your name and position, please?"

"Captain Charlie Merlot, Sodium P.D."

"Okay, what can you tell us?"

"Today, around 9:55 AM, a fire started in the Columbia Elementary School library. The cause is still under investigation, but it is believed to be arson. A separate incident followed involving a shooter opening fire from the roof of the same school."

The police radio chimed in with instructions for different units as two fire engines raced past the patrol car. The whole town was in a state of crisis.

Merlot continued, "At this time, we are unsure of the casualties from both incidents as first responders are still at the scene. The shooter has been neutralized. Currently, I am en route to Crow Elementary. Dispatch has reports of a similar incident there. One officer is down—"

The police radio continued with crosstalk of what seemed to be an army of units coming to grips with the situation.

"Sorry. There's a lot going on. Can we kill it for now?" the officer asked as an ambulance flew by at top speed.

"Yes, sir." Rafe thought that was a weird phrase, given the circumstances. He then pointed the camera at the streets as they drove past to gather as much cover video for their story as possible.

The homes and storefronts were empty, forgotten, and appeared sickly. They collectively seemed like a man on his deathbed confessing a life's worth of sins before being lowered into a hole in the ground. Such was the spirit in Sodium.

Merlot glanced over at Rafe as he drove. "We're about to pass over the Morrah River. The bridge is a little bumpy."

"Okay, thank you." Rafe wanted to ask something but couldn't.

"Sodium's not much to look at these days. Business has been bad for a while."

As they approached Crow Elementary, Rafe noticed that the smoke from the school was almost as dark as the stormy sky.

Homes in the neighborhood appeared to only house ghosts, as every structure seemed to have been robbed of life. Everything had been ravaged by time and racism long before the hands of fiery hatred had taken what was left of the community's soul.

Suddenly, there was crosstalk over the radio. "Repeat, the shooter is still active. They have not been apprehended."

"Stay in the car, son! Stay down!" commanded Merlot. As he shut the door, the loud sound of metal hitting metal made Rafe jump.

Sirens and screams from the wretched nightmare filled the smoky air, and only a thin pane of glass separated him from the onslaught of gross inhumanity.

All he could do was record it. The threat couldn't reach him.

It reminded him of a surgery that he shot for an orthopedic surgeon's training video. As blood and tissue filled the frame, he focused on how well the image was balanced and how the depth of field allowed for an intricate rack focus from the cut bone to the peeled-back flesh.

The content of the shot faded to the back of his mind as he concentrated on the image design of the frame. It saved him from getting sick.

And that's when he saw him. Standing only 40 feet from the patrol car, a five-year-old black boy shook uncontrollably with fear and screamed for his mother.

Rafe zoomed in with the lens for a close-up of his face. His dark brown eyes streamed a painful flood of tears, and his mouth was open as wide as it could be, imploring a host of heaven to come to his aid. His prayers were utterly heart-wrenching.

As he watched the boy in his viewfinder, his heart began to swell and ache. He wondered how he could remain so removed from this fight for life. This was bigger than a news story and more important than the perfect shot. This was no longer about manipulating the viewer or explaining the dire need for help.

He leaped out of the patrol car like a winged angel, a bolt straight from above, and he scooped up the boy. Rafe thought he heard gunshots, but the only way to survive was to drown it all out.

The angel flew back to the oscillating red and blue beacon with the boy in his arms, and they hid on the ground by the driver's side of the car.

"Don't worry! You're okay! I've got you!" Rafe assured, but the boy continued to cry without sound.

Chapter Nine

813

That night, Rebah poured another bowl of cold cereal, making it her fifth. She had pulled all the covers off her bed and now sat on the floor entombed in them.

There was no consoling her. She had tried to wash the dishes earlier, but her hands kept shaking, and the scalding water burned her at one point. She retracted her hand and stared at the reddened skin—she was still alive, unfortunately.

That's when she turned off the kitchen light, which was the only light on in the house, and decided to cry it out in her tiny bedroom in the dark.

The top of Jim's dresser was adorned with a half-dozen framed pictures of Jim and prominent men in town, several awards, and trinkets from his various clubs and associations. Unfortunately, Rebah had allowed dust to cover them over the past several months.

The storm had now passed, and a bright moon found the top of the other dresser, which was cluttered with mending to be done and papers to grade.

She thought about going over the papers to get through the night, but right now, eating cold cereal on the floor and cradling a photo album was all her heart could manage. She turned a page and moved her fingertips slowly across several pictures of her broken family.

Samuel is still here, she thought. *Just like every night, he's reading in his room until the early hours of the morning. He never really liked going to Jim's house. He's my baby.*

Her mind raced and rattled, giving her a headache, and yet she couldn't stop the barrage of self-deprecation.

Jim would probably blame me, though. I'm in charge of teaching him everything. Where did I go wrong? Why did he stop talking to me? Why did he—

Suddenly, as if to see if anyone else was in the house, she launched the bowl of cereal right at Jim's dresser, knocking over his framed pictures. Milk flew across the room, splattering all over the floor, but she didn't care.

Finally, she belted out a mother's agonizing scream and buried herself in her blankets, not knowing if she would ever come out. Her boy was gone.

† † †

THOROUGHLY EXHAUSTED, RAFE AND BRI checked into separate rooms at a hotel. From the second floor, Rafe could hear the restless town below. Although the massacres flooded Sodium with hell many hours before, sirens still wailed, and an occasional helicopter flew over.

They had spent the rest of the day in a mad frenzy, producing multiple video packages for various news networks, including their own TV station.

Now running on fumes, Rafe lay on his bed alone, talking with his mother on the phone and cycling through national TV news channels with the volume down. They each ran the same horrid story, some turning it into a well-trodden political war, and others were intent on healing. More than anything, he just wanted to put the day behind him.

"No, Ma, I'm fine," Rafe reassured his mother on the phone.

She had aged well. Her curly, blonde hair had turned gray, but it wasn't from reading or seeking wisdom.

Now that his mother was alone, her house had become a living manifestation of online chatter and noise to keep her company. Her daily mental diet consisted of a never-ending barrage of different radio and TV programs that spoon-fed conspiracy theories, biased news with doctored footage, and beauty products. She even needed the noise to sleep.

"I'm so glad that Jesus kept you safe. It looks like those people had it coming, though," his mother pronounced like a judge and jury. "They probably have gun shops and liquor stores on every corner. I can't blame them; it's in their nature. Where's Sodium anyways?"

Annoyed with her condescending speech, he replied, "It's on the west side of Texas. I never heard of it either."

"Well, your shots looked pretty good on the tube. You got there just in the nick of time. Too bad you didn't get a shot of the killer. One of the shows I watch every night, *The News with Quentin Koresh*, always shows the killers. Did you ask to shoot him?"

Rafe thought that was a weird thing to ask. "No, the suspects' names haven't been released yet."

"He's probably one of those Mexicans, all drugged up," she declared in an uncontrolled, racist rant. "They don't obey any laws anyways, and they come here thinking they won't get caught—"

"Ma, are you okay?"

There was a little sniffle and a whimper. "I'm just scared, that's all. What if something happened to you?"

"Everything's fine, Ma. Don't worry—"

"Still, you be careful, ya hear!" she commanded. "I hope you get an award or something for your camerawork on this one. Maybe you can get a better-paying job; they hardly pay you anything at that place!"

"Well, I enjoy what I do," he returned humbly but still annoyed.

"Were any other TV stations there?"

Rafe smiled a little and exclaimed, "No, there aren't any in town, and we just happened to be nearby. This is pretty much an exclusive story."

"And Bri did an excellent job, too, with all of those interviews. You know, when you two go to places like that with *those* kinds of people, you should probably wear police jackets or something."

At this, he shook his head and turned off the TV with the remote. He had enough of the day and the whole situation. He was frazzled. "Okay, Ma, it looks like they need me for something. I gotta go."

"Oh, alright, sweetie! Love you! Tell Bri I said, 'Hello,' and give her a big hug for me!"

"Will do. Love you."

Rafe let go of his forced smile and tossed the phone on the bed. There was no way to handle his mother except to let her talk and just nod. Call it his upbringing or something ingrained in him that he couldn't go up against, but he was unable to correct someone older than him, no matter what they said. Bri never really understood that.

As he stared off at the moon in a second of peace, his phone rang again. It was Bri.

"Hey. How are you feeling?" he asked.

She rattled off more information, seemingly unable to turn off her need to investigate and analyze the situation. "I now remember what the

EMT muttered. She said, 'Yeah, it figures. He was wearing an 8-13 shirt under his sweater.'"

Half-interested, Rafe returned, "8-13. What's that?"

"You're going to *love* this."

He knew where she was going. Anytime she mentioned the word *love* about anything news-related, it had to do with politics or dogs. It was usually dogs, and her favorite assignments were reporting feel-good stories about them, but she had a special place for the government.

She explained coldly, "It has to do with Hitler."

"Hitler?"

"At one point, there were groups that used the symbol *88*, which stands for *HH* or *Heil Hitler*. H is the eighth letter in the alphabet, and the 13th letter is M."

"What are you saying? You know I'm tired, right? I'm fixin'— I'm about to go to sleep."

Finally, she declared, "Heil McKendrick. That's what it means."

"Are you serious?" Rafe gasped as he sat up in his bed.

Chapter Ten

McKendrick

T he Sodium Police Department barely had a skeleton crew. As the small town's funding and resources dried up over the years, many of the best officers left for better opportunities elsewhere. Most of the businesses had also suffered the same economic plague.

Having already been awake for 30 hours straight, Merlot was beyond tired. The investigation, processing of data, and helping the community with the tragedy kept going throughout the night and into the morning.

Since he was the only officer in the small town with experience in a mass shooting, the police chief tapped him to oversee the operation as soon as the emergency calls came in.

That *experience* was the reason for his transfer from Atlantis, Texas, almost two years before. Despite all the effort he put into cleaning up the streets, going door-to-door sometimes, promoting afterschool activities and community youth programs, that city seemed destined for utter ruin. Now, Sodium was on the same path.

Samuel Jarik was pronounced dead at the scene. At the other school, Crow Elementary, an 11-year-old named Michael Haman was found in a classroom lying on his stomach with his hands behind his back. His weapon was at his side. There was no emotion in the little boy's eyes —no trace of empathy or remorse.

As Merlot filed paperwork about the boys in his cramped corner at the police station, his desk phone suddenly rang. He recognized the extension, picked up the receiver, and firmly said, "Yes, sir."

Merlot nodded a few times, exhaled deeply, and ended the call. This was the last thing he needed.

† † †

THEY HADN'T SLEPT MUCH THE NIGHT BEFORE, but the news never sleeps. Bri scanned the news feed on her phone as she fixed her hair in the passenger-seat mirror. While driving through downtown, Rafe reached into the back seat of his truck to make sure he had brought the camera gear. It was going to be one of those days.

As they passed a house, two boys chased each other with water guns in the front yard, shouting threats and blasting each other in the face. "I shot you! You're dead!" the younger one trumpeted as if on a battlefield. Rafe didn't know how to react; the whole situation seemed hopeless. Even after the massacres, the town hadn't learned anything.

"Check this out," Bri started as she read her phone. "McKendrick has already visited the mother of one of the suspects. How did he find out so fast?"

She read the caption next to the picture. "Mother of the deceased shooter, Rebah Jarik, meets with President McKendrick, and he consoles her." In brutal honesty, Bri commented, "He's all smiles as if he just cured cancer, and she looks as if she's lost the world. I feel so sorry for her. It wasn't her fault."

Rafe looked up at the overcast sky, and it began to rain again.

THERE WAS A PARK JUST OUTSIDE OF SODIUM that had escaped the rotting of downtown. It had green trees, a playground, and a dog park. It was a picturesque backdrop for the president of the United States to give a speech.

By now, all the networks had sent correspondents to cover the story, and many other local news networks, reporters, and rubberneckers had descended upon Sodium. The chaos had echoed around the world.

Every production team had set up at the park and was now giving their latest update. It was an audio pandemonium of reporter-speak.

Fortunately for Rafe and Bri, their TV station sent mobile broadcasting equipment to facilitate live reporting. Because of the story's magnitude, management chose a production assistant to drive nearly 11 hours across Texas to hand-deliver it to them, and she was now sleeping at the hotel. Later that afternoon, she was to return. Such is the broadcast industry.

Holding an umbrella, Bri nodded to the camera and began her report. "I'm Bri Gilchrist for KOLB News-TV, and here is the latest on the Sodium Massacres. At least one shooter has been identified, an 11-year-old boy who was a student at Columbia Elementary, a predominately Hispanic school. So far, 22 people, including 18 children, have died, and 12 others remain in critical condition. The other mass shooting at Crow Elementary killed 25 people, including 24 children, and 4 remain in critical condition. The students at this school were predominately African American. The only hospital in Sodium, Saint Raphael Hospital, is now caring for those in critical condition. Two people have been airlifted to nearby El Paso. As both mass shootings happened at the same time and appear to be similar in nature, authorities believe that these incidents were planned together."

It was then that President McKendrick and his entourage filed out of the nearby RV, and as soon as he gave his campaign-trail smile and a stadium-size wave, the massive crowd behind the reporters clapped and roared.

Just before he opened the door, one of his aides rolled out a red carpet with hand-knotted gold fringe. The president's self-designed logo, a demanding black M on a white circular field and a small black heraldic eagle, was imprinted all along the bright blood-colored path. It was a carryover from being an artist at his advertising agency.

Of course, he was the only one allowed to utilize the carpet as his aides and associates flanked him on both sides, always just a few steps behind him. He told reporters that he didn't like getting his working-man shoes even dirtier than they already were. He was a *Tireless Fighter for the Everyman*, but he always required his presidential podium with a step to separate himself from the taxpayers.

He disapproved of prepared speeches, so he always went with *whatever ramblings that popped in his head* (as the headlines read), but he did so with such colloquial charm that it smoothed over any quarrel or situation. McKendrick was portly, not like a mall Santa Claus but a butcher—bald and sweaty, as if he had just taken off his blood-soaked apron and was ready to push his weight around.

"Good morning, Sodium, Texas!" The greeting was all he had to give for the several hundred spectators to erupt with thunderous applause as if they were addicted to him. The sky miraculously cleared for him, and he smiled as he closed his umbrella.

"I want to thank the good people of this beautiful town for inviting me to grieve with you, to mourn with you, to lift, and console you. I am

52

your brother, and I'm here for you." He preached in a melodic manner, finding persuasive strength in his dramatic pauses. It was always a show.

"Some of you would probably point out how old and bald I am—and I don't blame you—so you could just say that I'm your ugly older brother."

The crowds always liked that one, and of course, they fell for it that day with a widespread roar of laughter. With that relationship contract secure, he could take the conversation anywhere.

"Honestly, folks, I'm here for you. Lay your pain on me, and I'll carry you!" He waited for the applause for his Christlike generosity.

"I just spoke with a beautiful woman, Rebah Jarik. She's the mother of a brave little boy, Samuel Jarik, who was battling mental health issues and depression from his parents' recent separation. I was the first to know of it as Rebah trusts me.

"She lost that dear boy because he had succumbed to the violence in video games and attacked the kids who hurt him, who made fun of him, who hated him. I know many of you are grieving today, but don't forget that she is also in pain. Welcome her into your arms, and let us all mourn together.

"Let's remember the men in uniform, those brave soldiers in the community who help us keep it safe." McKendrick raised his arm in a welcoming fashion toward Merlot, who was performing additional security detail behind him.

He then exclaimed, "Captain Charlie Merlot, c'mon over here and let me give you a hug!" Merlot walked toward him, and McKendrick grabbed him with an awkward, overbearing hug, immobilizing both of his arms.

"Captain Charlie, I hear you were the one who neutralized the threat."

"Yes, sir." Merlot was in a delirious state of grief and exhaustion.

"What kind of weapon did you use?"

"Heckler and Koch, sir."

"German? Good choice!" McKendrick couldn't help raising his umbrella and firing an imaginary bullet of excitement into the air with it. He was that brash and irreverent, and his supporters loved him for it.

"Yes, because of Captain Merlot's unwavering oath and duty to protect you, he saved you from any more harm this poor boy could have caused. Guns save people!"

As the crowd chanted *Guns Save People*, Merlot stepped back from the spotlight, and a few tears escaped.

The portly preacher continued, "My new proposal for Congress allows for a Nobel-prize solution for this. Do y'all know what it is?" He looked over the massive crowd with his bigger-than-life smile, which was slightly upturned on one side.

"How many fire hydrants do we have? A couple on each block, right? We need to take care of a fire anywhere one pops up. We don't want Ol' Mrs. Leary's cow kicking over another lantern, right? We don't want to burn down the whole country. Imagine how much water that would take!

"I propose that we have cops, both retired and active, and plain-old good citizens patrol the streets. Every inch of the country could be safer with gun-wielding angels looking over us. Millions of people would volunteer to keep you safe."

He had tried this same bit out a few times before and was still gauging its traction. By the sound of it, Sodium was on board, and the president basked in the cheers and adulation. He was a storyteller, though, and there was more he needed to deliver on his stage.

"Another boy, Samuel's best friend, Michael Haman, was also going through a tough time. Right now, I can't tell you everything, as he's going through some counseling, but from what I hear, it's pretty traumatic, even for you and me."

Merlot cleared his throat for others to hear, but the president kept going.

"He's a good boy who got caught up going down a wrong path, but what did Jesus say? '*Until 70 times seven.*' Let's work through this together and help him recover. He didn't mean to cause all this harm."

At this, one of the reporters asked, "Sir, are these names officially released now?"

"Yes, I've released them so that we can all heal, and the families can heal."

Bri only had one question, and as the president took in what seemed to be a dramatic, grieving pause, she went for it. "Sir, do you have a comment about the fact that one of the boys was wearing an 8-13 shirt?"

Caught off guard, he returned, "What station do you work for?"

"KOLB-TV, Gulf Haven, Texas."

The president then demanded, "Turn off your camera. I don't like your station."

Appalled, Bri exclaimed, "Sir, you would rather defend the Second Amendment over the First?" Of course, Rafe didn't turn off the camera and caught the exchange for all to see.

He tapped Bri on the shoulder and quietly commented, "He doesn't get paid to defend the First Amendment."

Smiling, Bri whispered, "Touché."

The president ignored her and continued, "My heart goes out to everyone affected by this tragic loss, and I will talk to Congress about fast-tracking my changes for the sake of all our lives."

On dramatic cue, it began to snow, and the president pulled out his umbrella again. "This is some crazy weather we're having! '*Though your sins be as scarlet, they shall be as white as snow.*' The Lord's healing y'all, and I want to thank you for letting me be a part of it."

"Sir, are you planning on visiting the families of those in critical condition?" Bri inquired loud enough for everyone to hear.

Another reporter followed up on the question. "Yes, there are reports of 16 people in critical condition. What are your plans for them?"

The president took a long, dramatic pause, appearing to be thinking of each person one by one. He managed to allow his eyes to moisten and get choked up.

"You know, I reached out to your hospital, and they were completely ecstatic about me coming. I could hear the nurses in the background clapping and cheering. The administrator on the phone says a little boy smiled when he heard. I wanted to be there and help them through this.

"But you all in the front changed my mind," he continued, pointing to the reporters and cameras. "I didn't want this tragic loss to become a political debacle. I could imagine the headline: *President McKendrick Turns Massacre into Political Stunt for Votes.* Shameful, absolutely shameful.

"Think of the children I could have helped. Think of the families that I could have mended. Instead of fathers and brothers fighting with swords, I could have brought peace." The crowds always liked the way he interwove biblical passages.

"Peace be unto you, and may God be with you."

And almost with one accord, the crowd behind the reporters responded, "And with you."

President McKendrick escaped back into his RV with a waddle. His entourage followed, and the same aide rolled up the red carpet. The show was over, and the town returned to its tragedy.

Chapter 11

Shaking Off Ashes

It was now mid-morning. Bri sat next to Rafe in his parked truck and studied the crowds scattering as the mix of rain and snow descended on the unsuspecting masses. Wind rattled trees, and children shivered.

With a few last keystrokes on his laptop, Rafe announced, "Alright, the new McKendrick video is now uploaded. We'll see what happens."

Although she was curious to know what reactions might follow such a controversial speech from the United States president, what held her attention was everyone's sheer terror as they ran to their cars while covering their heads. The weather was not wanted.

The scene reminded her how excited she would become after an overnight snowstorm when she was a preschooler. Clothed with her snow pants, coat, and boots, she would fly out into the winter wonderland while everyone slept to make as many snow angels as possible.

After countless angels surrounded her home, she would carry out a little pink table and chair with painted flowers to eat breakfast and watch the glistening snow come down. Her peanut-butter-and-snowflake sandwich always made her smile. Sometimes though, she would have to brush off a few snowflakes.

Bri then speculated, "I wonder if more people would have died if it hadn't rained yesterday."

"What?" Rafe returned, not really paying attention. Instead, he summarized an article he was reading. "McKendrick just published a book called *Struggle: My Life as a Minority*. It's what he calls his *perfect solution to our racism-ravaged country*. I didn't know a sitting president could publish a book."

She didn't respond. The reporter was still taking in all the life around her: the rain falling on concrete, people suffering from the day before, and car tires sliding on patches of snow and ice.

Across the way, Rebah pulled into the parking lot entrance in a faded scarlet truck and backed up next to a dumpster. Still wearing pajamas and slippers, the grieving mother exited the jalopy and yanked at the tailgate, but it wouldn't budge.

"Hey, I believe that's the mother of the kid," Bri observed.

"Maybe." Rafe glanced at the earlier post about the president and confirmed, "Yeah, that's her. What's she—"

Bri had already left the truck and was walking in the rain toward her. "Ma'am, do you need any help?" she asked with a smile. As if on cue, the rain let up, and the sun came out a little.

Rebah's truck had a camper with a missing window in the back, and after one last tug, the tailgate finally came down with a clang. The grieving mother then reached in and retrieved a box full of Jim's framed pictures. "No," she answered bluntly.

Rafe approached the truck, and they both watched Rebah carry the load toward the dumpster. Unfortunately, she slipped on a small patch of ice, and she fell to the ground.

As Rafe flew to her rescue, Bri asked, "Are you okay?"

"I'm fine. I'm fine." It was an automatic response even though she was clearly in pain.

"Here, let me help you." Rafe pulled the grieving woman to her feet and picked up the box. "Were you throwing this away?"

Rebah came to herself and spoke more softly, "Yes, I'm sorry. Thank you."

Bri glanced at the back of the truck and discovered that there were several other boxes of clothes and other things. "Did you have anything else to throw away?"

"I'm sorry. Yes, everything that's all up in there. Thank you, sweetie."

The two foreigners quickly pulled a few boxes toward the tailgate, and Bri noticed that the whole bed was covered with ash—some even fell on her shoe. It was part of the hallowed school remains from the day before, and it would always be with the poor mother wherever she went.

As Bri carried a box to the dumpster, she replied, "I'm Bri Gilchrist, and we're with KOLB-TV News."

"I know who you are. I'm sorry my son did all this, but you'll have to go."

The reporter knew that she couldn't leave without the story and felt that she needed to peer into the mother's heart to learn more. "Why? What's wrong?"

As Rafe carried the last two boxes to the dumpster, Rebah offered some advice. "I know you mean well, but everyone here loves McKendrick. As soon as he said something against you, he painted a target on your back. Go home. Tell everyone my son shot all those people. Nothing will ever change."

"I'm sorry, ma'am," Bri managed. She wanted to hug her, but the distance between them seemed like miles. Rebah climbed into her truck

59

and drove off just as it started to drizzle again, leaving the foreigners speechless.

"SO, WHICH ONE SHOULD WE DO?" RAFE ASKED as they both looked at the row of houses across the street from Crow Elementary. One of the residents was bound to have an insight regarding the massacre and would probably provide quality soundbites for them to use.

Bri picked a gray, weathered house covered with decaying vines, which could have easily been the first structure built in town. The front yard had brown overgrown weeds that concealed several random objects, and the sidewalk leading up to the porch was barely visible. Rafe was sure the door frame was slightly crooked.

Before Bri had even touched the doorbell, an ancient man with stringy, gray hair charged at them, pointing a rifle right at Bri's face. His eyes were on fire, and his skin was red with over-boiled anger. His hatred was older than most.

"Get off my property!" he screamed with what seemed to be all the forces of hell. He then took his aim at Rafe and continued, "All you reporters lie like the devils you are!"

Bri shrieked and flew in retreat as Rafe fell over backward in horror. No one had ever pointed a gun at *him* before. He quickly scrambled to his feet, picked up the camera, and ran away, knowing that safety might not be reached.

As the man watched them flee, he brought his rifle back to his side, shook his head, and noticed that a small trace of ash was left on his porch. He looked up at the gray sky in disgust and swept the rebuke off his porch with his foot.

AS RAFE FLEW DOWN THE STREET IN HIS TRUCK, he glanced over at Bri in the passenger seat—she appeared ghostly pale and clammy.

60

"Pull over!" she wailed. She couldn't take it anymore.

Rafe slammed on the brakes right in the middle of downtown, leaving skid marks on the street. Barely holding herself together, the shaken reporter fell out of the truck and threw up on the sidewalk.

"Why are we even here?" she groaned with agony, kneeling on the cold pavement.

He couldn't bear to see her in pain. His heart sank as he went to her and held her trembling soul. "Do you want to go home? We have enough footage. They can all figure it out on their own!"

"No," she whispered as she shook her head. "There are people here that need us. We have to find out what happened."

Rafe noticed a few pedestrians had stopped to watch them, and he feared the whole town had put a black mark on their heads. He imagined someone in a window staring down the barrel of a gun to take either of them out as they bent over on the sidewalk.

Immediately, he recalled that President John F. Kennedy was shot in Dallas, which wasn't too far from Sodium. Fragments of the president's skull and brain covered the rear interior of the car, and Mrs. Kennedy placed her hand on his head en route to the hospital so that more of his brain wouldn't seep out.

"We could go to the hospital as you said. Someone may talk to us there." He felt that the whole situation was out of control and that they were steering a sinking ship.

Chapter 12

River Morrah

After the gray house incident, Rafe decided to leave the camera in the hospital hallway, right outside the patient's room, just in case. Now feeling unwelcome in the town, what drove him forward was the need to protect Bri and her curiosity for the truth.

They purchased an oversized teddy bear as a gift for a six-year-old girl who had been wounded, and when they came to her room, she was breathing with a ventilator and sleeping. The sight was overwhelming.

The little girl's mother, Naoma, a tired and frazzled Hispanic woman, smiled at the bear, knowing that her daughter would surely love it.

Bri softly greeted her, "Hello, ma'am. I'm Bri Gilchrist, and we just wanted to share this with you and your daughter. How is she doing?"

"Thank you. She is doing better, but she's in a lot of pain."

"Is there anything we can do?" Rafe asked sincerely.

Naoma had already noticed their TV-station jackets and politely responded, "No, but I'm thankful you came by. No one else did."

"I'm sorry about that," Bri returned. "We'll be in town for a few days, and if there's anything we can do, just let us know. We just want to help." She then handed her a business card with their hotel information and started for the door.

"Actually," Naoma said desperately, "if you want to help, could you pray for her, please? She's in *His* hands right now."

It had been many years since Rafe had prayed. Watching the young girl have oxygen pumped into her little body reminded him of his strained relationship with God. The closest he came to thinking of Him was reading Christmas cards.

Bri hugged her without hesitation and confirmed, "Yes, I'll pray for you and your little girl. What's her name?"

"Isabella. Mrs. Jarik is her teacher," she answered, but she was on the verge of tears as she whispered, "I don't blame her, though. It's this stupid town!"

Intrigued, Rafe asked, "Why do you say that?"

"With all the layoffs of white people in this town, it's no wonder they want us all dead. You hear of someone being shot occasionally, but there's never been something this—" She stopped herself and looked up at the reporters. "I'm sorry. No offense."

"Don't worry. Do you or your husband have a job?" Bri questioned.

"Yes, he works for the solar salt processing company in town, just like most people here, and he's working at a quarter of regular pay. With all the rain we've been getting over the last decade, the town has really dried up. Most people have left. We're the only ones that will work dirt cheap, and they hate us for it."

Bri took Naoma's hand to comfort her. "I'm sorry this is happening to you."

"Why don't you just move?" Rafe decided to succumb to his manly fix-it tendencies, seeing that the scenario had an obvious solution, at least in his mind.

In response, Naoma stared at him and stated coldly, "Mexicans are hated everywhere in America. There's nowhere for us to go."

"What about going back to Mexico?" he returned without thinking. Despite knowing better, his mother's tendencies seeped out of his mouth, and he knew he couldn't reverse the damage.

Bri then shot him a look that he took as a possible end to their relationship.

NIGHT HAD FALLEN, AND THEY WEREN'T SPEAKING. Bri reached for the truck dashboard radio to break the silence as they were bound together by duty to move forward. Rafe glanced over at her, but she had already turned to watch the downtown streets out of her window.

As if they couldn't escape the tragedy, the radio announcer reported, "And more on the Sodium Massacres: two more children have died as a result of their wounds, and the father of one of the victims was found dead in their home. Authorities are still investigating—"

Rafe turned off the radio and uttered, "Look, I'm sorry. I don't know why I said that; I wasn't thinking." She gave him nothing, so he continued, "It's just been a hard couple of days and—"

Infuriated, she quickly turned the radio back on, and *Black Mare* by Candice Vivian was playing. By now, she couldn't hide her anguish and started to sing along. The music was calming, and she closed her eyes to concentrate on it:

> *You heard me alone on the stormy shore,*
> *Kicking up sand 'til morning light.*
> *Can you see me from your front door?*
> *A black mare in the middle of the night.*
> *A black mare at night.*
> *A black mare at night.*
> *Beautiful mare not in sight.*

That is the plight.
You sought my beauty on the stormy shore,
Wrestling the world 'til morning light.
Will you rescue me? I implore.
A black mare in the middle of the night.
A black mare at night.
A black mare at night.
Beautiful mare without right.
That is the fight.

After the first verse, Rafe turned off the radio. "Hey, I'm trying to apologize and—"

That was the last straw. Bri turned on the music again and raised the volume. She then lowered her window, thinking that if only she could sing it to everyone in town, they could heal. They could all heal together.

She belted out the song as loud as she could, but it came out sounding damaged and battered. She was broken and sobbing, but it wasn't for anything that had happened to her—it was for all the mothers and fathers who were asking God for help.

"Are you crazy? We'll get shot!" Rafe quickly pounded the radio button off.

"Stop thinking about yourself for once!" she reprimanded. "Don't you see how racist this town is, how this whole country hates people of color?"

"That's not true."

She couldn't even look at him. "Yeah, it is. How close are we to kicking everyone that's not white out of this country?"

"What are you talking about?"

"You even said it yourself—'Why don't you go back to Mexico?' It's a whole mindset. You may not think anything of it, but you're just as bad as the shooters. You're murdering them with what you say."

"They're just words—" he returned defensively.

Suddenly, she boiled over in a rage, but it was closer to Christ cleaning the temple to teach. "Did you know that Hitler blamed the declining German economy after the War and the Great Depression on the Jews? He was able to bend a whole country to his racist views and ordered their expulsion and extermination. Have you ever wondered how German Christians could be willing to slaughter a whole race of people? Mob mentality exists!"

"Well, we're in the 21st century. This is America. That couldn't happen again. We're too smart for that."

"How do you know? We could be repeating history."

As they both returned to silence, she prayed in her heart, *Dear Father, please help Rafe understand. Help him see the light.*

THE AIR WAS STIFLING, PERMEATING EVERY DROPLET in the atmosphere like a cancer. None were spared from the sickness that enveloped the small town.

Rafe knew that he was in the wrong, but he couldn't figure out what to do. As he looked through the viewfinder at the dozens of mourners on the riverbank, he observed how the candlelight softened their sad countenances. Each candle had a small wooden plank affixed to the bottom, and even Bri had one.

He set up the camera by his truck, far enough to not interfere but close enough to record with a telephoto lens. There were tears and hugs— friends and strangers held each other close. They raised their voices in solemn hymns of comfort and prayed in silence.

And then, one by one, they each gently placed their floating candle in the water. It wasn't until Rafe zoomed out and captured all the tiny lights floating down the river that he marveled at how peaceful it seemed.

REBAH WATCHED THE CANDLELIGHT VIGIL ALONE on top of a small hill by the riverbank, and she noticed Bri's heartfelt sincerity as she cried with the mourners. The winter wind blew through her hair as she sat on the cold ground, and it seemed like her only comfort was a melting candle by her side.

"Dear God," she whispered. "Please forgive my boy."

Her heart ached as the tiny lights all stayed afloat and moved slowly, touching both banks. It could only be described as a massive heavenly finger amid the darkness that seemed to come down and touch everyone there.

It was as if by releasing their sorrow into the Morrah River, they could feel the scourge melt away from their souls.

Chapter 13

Healing in Their Wings

E ven after midnight, Rafe couldn't sleep. Agitated and anxious about the last few days, he found himself thumbing through a small *Gideon's Bible* that he located in his hotel-room nightstand. He remembered how he enjoyed looking at the lively pictures and reading about his heroes as a young boy.

One of his favorites was David, who fought Goliath with a slingshot and a stone. After Sunday school, young Rafe would try to swing small pebbles with his necktie, but they would undoubtedly slip out and fall to the ground next to him. Rafe always felt like he could never be a hero or any use to God.

Suddenly, a loud crash came from the adjoining hotel room, followed by Bri's haunting shriek. Rafe quickly jumped up and opened his door, but she was already there in the hallway with outstretched arms.

"What happened?"

Still in shock, she answered, "I don't know! Someone just threw a brick at my window and—"

"Are you okay? Are you hurt?"

"No, but can I stay with you?" She tried to say something else, but she only mouthed words.

Rafe held her close, and that's what she needed. He carried her to the bed, and she curled up in a ball under the covers, frightened.

Quickly dialing the front desk, he reported, "I'm sorry it's late. Someone just threw a brick into my girlfriend's window. Yes, room 224. No, she's in my room now for the night. Okay, thank you."

Not really knowing what to do, he asked Bri, "Do you need anything from your room?"

She responded as if she had been violated. "Could you bring my purse and my bags? They're all together by the window." She couldn't close her eyes, and suddenly she blurted, "Watch out for glass!"

"Don't worry," he said as he picked up a camera battery, which was the closest thing he could hurl if needed.

He walked into her room, and there was indeed a sizable hole with cracks in the glass. Outside, it was raining hard, and because the lights in the room were still off, he could see the moon when the clouds parted a little.

In the parking lot below, rain splattered on the cars and pavement, bouncing like hail. There wasn't anyone in sight, so he exhaled as he pocketed the battery. Although the glass was shattered, he could make out a reflection of his face, and it scared him a little.

His cell phone buzzed, and he looked at it with another full exhale. As he brushed off the glass from Bri's bags at his feet, he wondered why someone would want to harm her so severely.

The clouds had covered the moon again, and it was too dark to find the brick or whatever smashed the window. Someone else would soon look at the room and clean everything up, so he gathered her bags and left.

"Joseph just texted me," he reported once he returned to his room, "and he wants us to go to a regional rally in Beararm, Texas, tomorrow night. McKendrick—"

Somehow, Bri had fallen asleep, and he smiled as he approached her lying in his bed. They had both been through an intense handful of days, and he was grateful that she felt safe and comfortable around him enough to rest from the trauma.

He brushed a few red curls away from her eyes and pulled up the covers around her. In the soft moonlight, she appeared beautifully at peace, and he silently vowed to keep her safe as he watched her sleep.

After a few minutes, he retrieved a small blanket from the closet, curled up on the sofa chair as best he could, and finally bid the events of the day goodnight.

By the time the gym doors were open the next day, Rafe had already brought out a dozen baskets of hot rolls and venison platters for everyone. Instead of keeping the magnificent beast for himself, he felt the deer from Placidus would better serve the townspeople in their time of healing.

Bri had just finished adding the last few spices to her massive pot of soup, and many other volunteers were tending to their soups, sandwiches, and other snacks in the food line. It was a feast the small town of Sodium needed.

Everyone from all corners of town seemed to file in. Some sat down at the tables, and others hugged and cried with one another. The gym was soon full of people caring for each other, and a line started to receive the prepared food.

The recent events the town had gone through had amassed an immense outcry from around the country concerning gun control and reform. Support groups and volunteers flooded Sodium to help those both affected and not affected by the massacres.

It seemed like TV-station cameras were on every corner of town, capturing every emotion possible. It was as if the townspeople were specimens in a fishbowl, and it had a negative effect. Camera operators who had set up their equipment in the gym to record everyone turning up en masse received dirty looks.

Rafe observed one of the operators, and he thought about how the mourners at the river vigil were at peace together, singing hymns and praying. He no longer wanted to be separated by several elements of glass, impartial and peering into the lives of others. He and Bri were there when it happened, and although they were still gathering information about the incidents, they were grieving and healing just like everyone else.

"You're one of those reporters!" an elderly woman yelled at Bri behind the food table. "May you die a hundred horrible deaths!" she cursed, and she threw her hot bowl of soup at her.

People close to the incident turned to watch it play out, but as soon as the bowl and spoon were on the ground and the woman had stormed off, they all turned back to what they were doing.

Rafe rushed over to Bri, who was shaking. They had decided not to wear their TV-station jackets that day, as it clearly had become a trigger for some people. The only cause for such an outburst was that Bri had asked the president a question. *Is he that untouchable?* Rafe wondered.

Why is there so much hostility? Whatever happened to 'love thy neighbor?'

Chapter 14

Racism Sells

O nce they were inside the massive stadium, Bri pronounced, "Welcome to an unholy land." Rafe nodded in agreement.

Crowds of thousands yelled and whistled as a 50-foot United States flag lowered into place from the rafters. Men removed their McKendrick *M* hats, and mothers helped their toddlers fold their arms as a man approached the pulpit.

"Dear Father in Heaven," he prayed. "Please bless our dear President McKendrick and his unyielding arm in our fight for Thee. Bless him as Thy steward of justice against the blind and those that have lost their way. Bless him so that he may always be our president. In the name of Jesus Christ, Amen."

After the crowd agreed in unison, Rafe leaned over to Bri and commented, "I've never heard anything like that before. I thought Jesus blessed and healed the lost and blind."

"It's all a matter of perspective," she declared, studying the rally attendees around her. There was a particular glaze in their eyes as the president stepped up to the pulpit. He was a god to them; he could do nothing wrong.

"Evening, folks!" McKendrick greeted the massive crowd with both arms stretched out as if he were blessing them. There was thunderous applause, and a few men passed out as if they were at a famous Crying Tanks concert from the 1960s.

After 30 seconds of deafening adulation, he continued, "I want to start this out right. Thank you to my friend, Paul White, for the invocation, and thank all of you for being here tonight."

ONE COULD EASILY WRITE ENOUGH VOLUMES to fill a library about the man McKendrick. He admitted in an interview in 2013, right after his inauguration, that he threw his hat into the ring for the United States presidency on a whim to increase publicity for his advertising agency. But of course, by that time, his voter base was so enamored with him that they glossed over what others called his insincere patriotism.

It was a gift he had. Throughout his years in the advertising business, he had learned how to work a boardroom so that each member would feel at ease. His pitches were flawless, and his artwork seemed to speak directly to their souls. He knew the campaigns and images that would convert anyone into a customer.

Between the time he applied for the most powerful position on earth and his first public appearance as a candidate, he underwent a sort of transformation. For months, he studied Southern slang, memorized biblical stories and verses, and practiced giving speeches to his massive room of portrait paintings.

After each practice stump delivery, he would pass through his Caravaggio Hallway and stop at the painting of Christ's body being carried away. He would focus on the nail-driven hands and feet, the puncture wound in the side, and how the body was reverenced. Without fail, he would always rub his hands together and quickly leave.

He immersed himself with every nuance of Southern culture and belief system, and the reinvention was startling. By his first debate, he had molded himself into a wealthy, punching-bag preacher that would fight the establishment for the church-going working class. He had his eye fixed on that demographic as a supporting base and the political party with which many of them affiliated. And they loved him for his refined, comfortable, and religious McKendrick-speak. Of course, they also believed that wealth and wisdom went hand-in-hand.

In his research, he discovered which tribe of the culture war to pit himself against for the most votes, which fears to peddle, and which commercial lobbies were most profitable. He found out how to puppeteer electoral college delegates, persuade super delegates, and infiltrate religious councils to bind members into allegiance and faithful support. The magician learned the spells to ensnare the very elect and manipulate the legal loopholes of a broken government that had long ago become stale with gridlock and infighting.

"I WANT TO SEE YOUR HANDS," the sweaty and portly president commanded at the pulpit, "your beautiful working hands—as high as you can stretch them. Some people want to put me out to the slaughter. They want to call my presidency a disgrace—a sham! They want to pee on the Constitution and all over our beautiful flag and call me a liar! I won't have it. I'm not a disgrace!"

The scene was like a profane atrocity right out of the Bible. Everyone in the stadium held their arms above their heads, like the Israelites praying to Aaron's golden calf. Embarrassed, Rafe started to lift his arms as people were looking at them, but Bri quickly pushed them down, shook her head, and rebuked, "In the world but not of it."

75

"Raise your hands and let me hear your beautiful voices," the idol continued. "Repeat after me: I love my dear president, and I'll support him until I kick over. He is the epitome of American values and is God-fearing. He lives only to serve God and the good people of this nation who belong here. President McKendrick is bound only by God's laws, not the laws of man. He is the only one who truly knows the will of God and will singlehandedly root out corruption across this nation and make it Zion."

Everyone but the two reporters repeated the twisted oath.

"Alright, that'll do just fine," declared the president as if he were Peter at the Gate. "Thank you, kindly!"

McKendrick pointed out a little girl in the front row who was still giggling at the line *until I kick over* and commented, "This girl right here thinks I'm funnier than a bear slipping in honey. Bless your heart, dear."

"Did he just solicit a pledge to defend him to the death?" Bri quietly asked Rafe. Neither of them had been to one of his rallies before as there always seemed to be someone shot or bloodied in the parking lot.

It was on the taxpayers' dime that McKendrick enjoyed hosting these rallies every weekend since his administration had started. Whenever a city asked the White House administration to pay the rally's security detail bill, he would tell his supporters not to spend money in that city again, and the very loyal would relocate. After the first year of rallies, cities stopped asking to be paid.

The president continued, "I ask you truthfully: Can you sleep at night, knowing that there are people high on drugs, usually from Mexico or Africa, that climb ladders to get into your windows? They're looking for things that you've worked hard for that they can then sell on the corner to other people from Mexico, Africa, and even India. Just call me a liar if it's not true.

"And what if they stop and hover over your bed to look at your wife? What if they brush some of her hair away from her eyes? Could you sleep knowing that these are people that live in the town that *you* built?

"Crime is most rampant in cities with blacks and Mexicans, as expert studies show. They say as much as 93.8%. Now, that's a number that I can get down to 7.5% with my *Resolution 77*, which I'm currently drafting."

Rafe leaned in toward Bri and questioned, "What is he *even* saying?"

"All he has to do is throw in a few numbers to sound like he's very knowledgeable about something. People fall for numbers," she explained.

"My book, *Crime in America, Your America*, gives a detailed account of how immigration has been the downfall of our nation since the 1980s," the president continued. "And you know what? Every God-loving family here is going to receive a free copy here tonight!"

That really won the crowd over. Bri witnessed one mother right beside her shout so hard that she went hoarse. As if in a trance, another screaming woman took off her shirt and threw it at the president.

"I guess that's why entry donations are $75," Rafe commented as Bri shook her head in sharp disapproval of the whole ordeal.

McKendrick grinned sinisterly as his subjects acted like animals, chanting his name. "But I'm sure most of you already have that book. Am I right?"

IT DIDN'T MATTER WHAT MCKENDRICK WAS SAYING or what he was pushing; they were committed to the man, whole heart and soul. For years, numerous analytics tried to figure out the devout loyalty of his voter base. It was beyond psychological comprehension, and any debate with an *M-Head*, as they were called, was futile.

At every rally, a line of followers formed to receive the official *Little M* tattoo. It was painfully etched on the forehead, just above where a brim would sit so that it could be hidden by a hat. They called it the *blood line*.

His supporters only believed whatever he told them; everything else was a lie. Recording the president in any way without his express permission had become illegal, per se. When he decided to make an appearance that wasn't camera-approved, M-Heads were planted in the crowd to destroy any visible camera or cell phone. He had a very controlled public image, and his camera-approved speeches were edited for the sake of scrutiny.

RAFE GLANCED BACK AT THE STADIUM ENTRANCE, where one of the security guards had taken his camera gear, and he wondered if it would be returned to him. Apparently, they had chosen the wrong rally to cover.

He felt ill, and he didn't know why. His mom loved McKendrick and listened to his daily White House radio broadcasts. *Is she just another victim of the Pied Piper?* he silently asked.

"So, tonight, I'm unveiling a new book. Are you ready for this?" the president piped, and the thousands of spectators almost ripped their heads off with excitement. Of course, all of his speeches, texts, and books were regarded as holy scripture. They were analyzed and broken down into actionable phrases that each of his followers took to heart in their own way.

BRI ONCE READ THAT SOME MEN DEFECATED THEMSELVES when they heard Adolf Hitler speak at his rallies. His orations were so powerful and intoxicating that people couldn't control themselves. She never really believed that it could be possible until that night.

78

"This book has so many secrets that I can only give it away at my rallies," the president teased. "My advisors said that if I put it in stores, the mainstream media would tear it to pieces. All my hard work would go down the drain. They wouldn't understand. They don't know God's will like I know it. Do you want to know God's will?"

By then, the crowd was drunk with the president's voice. Bri looked over at a toddler who had fallen asleep in her mother's arms and wondered what she was learning at home. More than anything, she wanted to grab the child and run out the door with her. Knowing that she could have saved at least one person was worth any jail sentence.

"I'm just going to come out and say it," the piper piped. "We're here in the privacy of my home, my really *big* home." The crowd roared with undeserved laughter. "Let's just call it a huge sacred temple, and you are all my friends. No one is recording us, and the other side can't reach us here. PC culture is the death of freedom of speech, and they're not about to take that away from me." They clapped and cheered in accord.

He smiled and then waited for the crowd to die down to make his next point loud and clear. A pin drop could be heard as if the world were about to end, and this was the last calm before the storm.

"I really *hate* black people. I *hate* brown people. I *hate* the yellow ones and the red ones; whatever-color-from-the-rainbow kind of people are out there, I *hate* them—and you should too!" President McKendrick admitted.

"In fact, I know you do! They are all lazy. They steal to support their drug habits, and the other side just wants to cuddle them. I don't want my taxes supporting them anymore! They are the curse of humanity. God has cursed them because of their wickedness, and they are our footstool to do with them as we please!"

Rafe looked over at Bri and whispered in utter shock, "I wish I could have recorded that."

It was at that point that they started to back away slowly. Hand-in-hand, they turned around, afraid for their lives, and they walked toward the exit.

"Even if we had, they would dismiss the video as being fake or cry foul for recording without his consent," she reasoned with a faint voice. Journalism had just died. She could feel the grasp of the devil pulling at her voice.

They were more afraid of the thousands of ravenous wolves that had been given permission by their Messiah to hate, and they walked out of the gates of hell. Outside, the rain fell hard, and it was a welcome wash from the filth inside.

RAFE STARED AT THE ROAD AHEAD. It was pitch-black except for the headlights from his truck, and he felt very alone.

"You know how parents always say, 'Because I told you so' to everything," Bri asked, breaking the silence. He was on board with whatever she was going to share, as it was a welcome voice of comfort from a real human being.

"We're taught to accept what we're told, and eventually, we leave and question everything," she reasoned. "It's how we become who we are."

He quickly joked, "Yeah, who wants to be like their parents?"

She chuckled a little, and it was just the sign he needed to realize that their relationship wasn't doomed and that he could eventually be forgiven for his insensitivity the day before.

"I saw a little girl in there," she continued, "and I wondered if she'll ever question what her mother teaches her. Will she become a person who thinks for herself, who makes decisions based on some sort of moral compass?"

"I don't know. I'm losing faith in humanity after what I just saw."

80

"But that's just a fraction of people, right?"

Rafe glanced at her and said with a sigh, "His poll numbers are extremely high in many states, unfortunately."

"He's what they want. It's as if it doesn't matter what he does or what he says—the end justifies the means. He could burn down a church, and they would say that he's on God's errand, no matter how many people he might have burned. Any wrongdoing is permitted because they feel it's right," she angrily added.

She then stared forward for a while. "How do you change something so incredibly wrong if it's what most people want?"

"Pray, I guess," he uttered without actually believing it.

A minute went by before she folded her arms and said a prayer to herself, mouthing the words.

Rafe wondered what she asked.

Chapter 15

Peacemaker

Trying to get comfortable in his hotel-room sofa chair, Rafe studied the *Gideon's Bible* that he had found, and he paused to check on Bri. She had fallen asleep on his bed a few hours before, but he didn't want to go near her. He respected her, and more than anything, he knew she trusted him.

He looked down and started reading in Matthew:

Blessed are the pure in heart: for they shall see God.

Blessed are the peacemakers: for they shall be called the children of God.

Blessed are they which are persecuted for righteousness' sake: for theirs is the kingdom of heaven.

Blessed are ye, when men shall revile you, and persecute you, and shall say all manner of evil against you falsely, for my sake.

Rejoice, and be exceeding glad: for great is your reward in heaven: for so persecuted they the prophets which were before you.

Ye are the salt of the earth: but if the salt have lost his savour, wherewith shall it be salted? It is thenceforth good for nothing, but to be cast out, and to be trodden under foot of men.

Ye are the light of the world. A city that is set on a hill cannot be hid.

Neither do men light a candle, and put it under a bushel, but on a candlestick; and it giveth light unto all that are in the house.

Let your light so shine before men, that they may see your good works, and glorify your Father which is in heaven.

It had been many years since he had been to Sunday school, but he remembered studying those same verses countless times in his youth.

When Rafe was eight, he made a chart with construction paper and different colored crayons, and he showed it to his mother. On the left, he had written all the things he needed to do according to the Sermon on the Mount, and on the right were all the blessings he would receive.

"WHAT'S THIS?" RAFE'S MOTHER ASKED. She had to dry her hands with a kitchen towel before viewing his latest creation, but he didn't mind.

"I decided that I need to do things for God," the young boy affirmed, holding the simple contract for her to see. The matter was no longer about faith but fact, like the Capernaum centurion who knew his servant would be healed by Jesus speaking the word only.

"I need to be pure in heart," Rafe read, and then he continued with his explanation. "I don't smoke or anything, so I think I'm okay. According to this, one day, I'll see God. I haven't seen Him yet, but I guess I need to climb a mountain or something. He only lives in high mountains."

She chuckled. "What do you think He looks like?"

"I don't know. He has to have a beard and sandals, though. When was the last time you saw Him?" It was a sincere question from a boy that considered his mother perfect enough to have conversed with the Heavenly Being face-to-face many times before.

Her radiant smile and the sunlight behind her made her appear like an angel. "Well, He has fiery eyes and skin as white and brilliant as the sun! His arms are always outstretched, wanting to help us, and He sits in His throne high in the heavens!" she explained as she pointed out the kitchen window at the beautiful skyline.

"But most importantly," she continued, "He's always watching over us and protecting us from bad things and bad people."

He absorbed her sermon like a sponge. "So, how do I become a peacemaker?"

The young mother beamed at his earnest endeavor to be like Christ. "To be a peacemaker, you have to stand up and talk to angry people. You have to be kind and firm. Show them that you love them and help them through what they're feeling."

"Okay, that sounds easy," the student surmised. He was well on his way. "And what does it mean to be persecuted?"

She stopped to formulate an answer and then taught, "When bad people hurt you, and you know you're right, God will help you."

"Are there a lot of bad people?"

"Yes, they're everywhere."

The boy turned around to see if he could spot someone out the window, but there wasn't a soul.

SITTING IN HIS HOTEL ROOM, RAFE SMILED at the warmth the memories brought back. It felt as if he had rediscovered an old friend in the book he was holding. He put it in his pocket, chuckled a little, and said, "No, I probably shouldn't do that."

He reached up to turn off the nightstand lamp, and the darkness allowed him to view the streets below. It was raining a little, and something prompted him to pull at the lamp cord again. He followed this by turning the light off and on a few more times.

There, in his tiny hotel room, he imagined his little lamp was like a lighthouse for the people of the town. "Salt of the Earth," he whispered. He then shook his head and realized the connection. "We're in Sodium, Texas."

VOLUNTEERS NOW CAME IN DAILY to assist with counseling, food supplies, and other services the town needed. It seemed like everyone had shut down. Even those that didn't have a family member injured from the shootings appeared to be in a trance. Many had stopped eating.

After much debate, the city council decided to hold a joint funeral at the chapel with the highest capacity. On the appointed day, thousands of supporters from around the country came to be with the families as they ached over their lost loved ones. The small church they chose could only handle a few hundred mourners, and the rest held hands in a massive gathering around the block.

Dozens of protest groups flooded the scene. Some carried gun-control signs, and others implored their Second Amendment rights. A few groups wanted school security reform, and others had their own demands. Although it was intended to be a moment of reflection and remorse, it had turned into a powder keg of an unruly crowd and a media circus with TV crews trying to make sense of it all.

What was once thought of *as just another mass shooting* had become a national crisis. Politicians, celebrities, and social media pundits all tried to weigh in on the *racism dilemma*, as some called it. For days, Americans were glued to the TV, all digesting the same horrible footage.

Later, a national headline ran that captured the essence of the chaos, *The Sodium Butterfly Effect: Racist Massacres Echo Across the Country*. The United States had finally decided to open the wound as wide as it could to heal.

CAPTAIN MERLOT HAD TO CLIMB ONTO A PLATFORM to survey the warzone-like pandemonium outside of the chapel. The entire police department had been dispersed throughout the massive crowd as strategically as possible, but he knew a minor incident could cause a catastrophic eruption at any second.

The tired old man stood on the platform and teared up as one of the protest groups by the chapel doors chanted, "The Second Amendment kills. Reform or more blood is spilled!" The officers were grossly outnumbered and ill-equipped for the event.

"ARE YOU SURE WE SHOULD DO THIS?" BRI ASKED Rafe, not certain that they should even be in the town anymore. They had parked close to the church entrance hours before the funeral to watch the events unfold, but by that

87

time, there was no escape; the gathering around the chapel was beyond control.

He looked over at her from the driver's seat and resolved, "Yes, we need to say something. The nation needs to be aware of what's happening here. We need to fix this."

Gathering the last bit of courage that she had left, she climbed out of the truck and put on her TV-station jacket, determined to be a beacon of truth. With all the misinformation clouding the judgment of so many around the nation, she had to do something. She knew that because her message was true, it would shine brighter than the sun, and someday, wayward ships might come to a shore of understanding and brotherly love.

Rafe handed her the microphone and said, "Here's your bullhorn. Make a change."

She took a deep breath and spoke as if the future of the country depended on that one single story. "Good morning. I'm Bri Gilchrist for KOLB-TV News, out of Gulf Haven, Texas. We're standing right outside St. Gabriel Church in Sodium, Texas, where the town is mourning the recent mass shootings, which have now claimed the lives of 104 people."

When the devastating number left her lips, she closed her eyes, still in a state of incredulity. "The majority of the deaths happened after the massacres, as a result of and in response to the shootings."

A sudden loud noise made her jump, and she was caught off guard, but she pushed through. "Including Columbine in 1999, there have been 307 school shooting fatalities in the United States. As of yesterday, there are now 358."

She pointed at the gathering of people around her and continued with a deep exhale, "Thousands of supporters from across the country have come to celebrate the lives of those lost too soon in a joint funeral." It was hard to speak above the volume of the protestors and mourners.

Rafe panned the camera to view the massive crowd holding hands and singing hymns around the entire church block.

"There are also demonstrators here, who have taken this opportunity to reach out to the nation to solicit change," she informed as she approached one of the protestors carrying a sign.

"Ma'am, how do you think people will respond to your efforts today at the funeral of these mass shootings?"

The elderly woman looked right at the camera. "I want this nation to realize what we are doing. Instead of being reactionary, there should be prevention. Guns don't save people; they are the wrong tool to help those that are suffering. It's like withholding a vaccine and treating people only after they're sick."

As the crowd became louder, the woman brought the microphone closer and continued, "Do I know how people will respond? This country is divided on gun laws, and both sides feel that they are right. Both sides have legitimate reasons for their positions." She stopped as if out of breath from shouting over all the commotion.

She then preached, as if one of the founding fathers spoke through her, "This nation was founded on compromise. Opposition and reasonable debate create a better environment that will benefit everyone."

Even though the interview was longer than she had anticipated, Bri asked, "What do you think we should do as a nation concerning gun laws?"

"Well, for one, I think we need to stop hating the other side and work together. Instead of hiring or soliciting volunteer cops to patrol schools, they should figure out how to have dozens of counselors in every school who talk with each student weekly about their ambitions, life at home, their friends, and whatever else is on their mind. We can discover and fix a problem before it comes to violence."

Bri observed the enormous crowd and the different emotions that were on full display and asked, "Do you think that talking to people could be a better solution? Look at all these people. Can hostility be prevented with just talk?"

The little lady took out her marker and wrote on the other side of her sign: *Diplomacy is always better than war.*

It was right then that it happened. As the prophetic woman went back into her protesting circle outside the church, a group of men erupted from the crowd, yelling and throwing rocks at the protestors. She was dead within seconds from a fatal wound to the neck—her voice had been silenced.

In horror, Bri watched the bloody martyr fall. She thought about rushing to pick up her sign like the painting *Liberty Leading the People* and imploring freedom from the stale gridlock of American politics, but she turned to the camera instead.

With tear-filled eyes, she asked, "Is it possible for Americans not to hate each other? Can't we—"

She was so focused on reaching everyone on the other side of the lens that she didn't hear the screams around her.

It felt like a little pinprick, right at her temple. Bri moved to the side in response to a stone hitting her head, and she recalled a memory of her little brother. As she closed her eyes, she remembered him repeatedly poking her in the head to get her attention when she was a teenager.

"IF HE'S ANNOYING YOU, JUST DON'T GET ANNOYED," BRI'S MOTHER said to her as she read the newspaper on the couch.

Bri didn't receive a satisfying reaction from her mother for her grievance, and she couldn't believe it. She was the one who was attacked by the little instigator, and now she was being instructed to disregard it.

"Mom, that's so stupid. Stop trying to teach me something with everything you say. Life is so annoying!"

As the teenager stormed off and slammed her bedroom door, her mother returned, "Your emotion is your choice."

Bri always hated the fortune-cookie-style parenting. The cold phrases seemed hollow and lacking in any personal experience that would've explained why her mother believed in them.

A DOZEN PEOPLE DIED AS THE ROCKS AND STONES CONTINUED TO FLY. The crowd that was once holding hands scattered to their cars in retreat. Other TV-station cameras captured the action, and many people stood motionless, not knowing how to react to the sudden barrage of hate.

Rafe flew down to catch Bri, but the cold ground was quicker, and her blood splattered across his arms. In a temple-cleaning rage, he picked out the man from the crowd that had thrown the offending stone and exploded toward him. According to Rafe, the man had made the house of prayer into a den of thieves.

In his mind, he reluctantly repeated, *Blessed are the peacemakers.* His target already had missing teeth and was grossly underweight, but Rafe drove toward him like a diesel. *His plight is his own fault*, he silently judged.

And yet, the lesson echoed in his ears. *Blessed are the peacemakers: for they shall be called the children of God.*

Rafe's fist connected with the man's jaw, and the skeleton-like man crumbled to the pavement without dispute. As he lay on the ground, the gash on his face seeped blood, and it barely covered the stones that had fallen from his bony hands.

Right behind Rafe, Merlot drew his handcuffs. In no time, he overpowered Rafe, forcing him onto the ground so that he lay next to the man and his stones as equal criminals.

"Son, why did you do that?" Merlot asked Rafe.

"He hurt her!"

"'*Vengeance is mine,*' *saith the Lord. Violence only begets violence,*" responded the authority as he helped Rafe to his feet.

First responders arrived and quickly assisted the many victims strewn across the lawn in front of the church. From those pelted by rocks and stones to those who were trampled on by the frenzied crowd, the scene appeared like an all-too-familiar war zone.

Rafe looked back toward Bri as her body was lifted on a stretcher into an ambulance. The doors closed, and he didn't know if he would see her again. He had chosen this path, and she was gone.

"C'mon, son. Get in the back," Merlot commanded as they approached the patrol car. It had only been a few days before that Rafe sat next to him as a passenger, and now he was a criminal in the back seat.

"Look," Merlot explained from behind the wheel, "I'm doing this to protect you. This town is getting—"

Right then, a nightmare of screams and heavy gunfire from inside the church pierced the cancerous air. The front chapel doors were closed, and the bell above the spiritual fortress began to ring in distress.

Before he could even close the patrol-car door, Merlot leaped up in a rage and rushed toward the sanctuary as if the last shred of humanity in the town were being ripped apart.

Rafe could do nothing as he sat on the plastic seat in the back of the car, handcuffed and trapped. Through the wire mesh and glass, he witnessed more of the horror that would soon become known across the country as the Sodium War.

Chapter 16

Children of God

There was no way to escape through the locked and barricaded chapel doors. After the initial terror echoed against the brick walls, everyone inside quickly ducked below the wooden pews, but the bullets wreaked havoc on those holy wooden shields. Unsuspecting mourners soon joined their lost loved ones as lifeless bodies gathered on the floor.

Before the apocalyptic assault, the four men in the back had each dipped their hand in holy water, made the sign of the cross, and whispered, "In the name of the Father, and the Son, and the Holy Ghost. Amen." Their ankle-length white robes were offset with red sashes at the waist, and they each wore a golden cross necklace.

As their Hispanic and African American victims disappeared into the pews, they took aim underneath, stealing any hope of survival. Pain and screams tortured the sanctuary as the devils parading as Christians walked up the aisles, sending each person one by one into the next life.

They were untouchable, unchecked, and the law would not find them. By the time they made it to the front, many of the small caskets were full of holes, and the flowers on top had been dashed beyond recognition.

The clouds parted, and the sun pierced through a stained-glass image of Jesus holding a child in his lap. Warm hues spread across the floor, enveloping the chapel, and then Merlot shattered it to send all four men to follow their victims.

As Merlot holstered his weapon, he could no longer stand. He was pale and fell helplessly to the earth. EMTs, officers, and volunteers rushed in chaotic madness to the mourners' aid, but Merlot had peeked inside the hell. There were none alive.

RAFE WATCHED HIS FRIEND CRY. Another officer helped Merlot to his feet, and they hobbled toward Rafe's camera and tripod, which had fallen to the ground. After looking over the camera, Merlot carried it to the patrol car and sat down in the driver's seat again.

There was something Rafe admired about the captain, and he wished that he could be like him. He would follow him to the very end if he could.

"Thank you for getting my camera," he said finally, soliciting any kind of response.

"I hope it still works." He started the car and drove out of hell.

Rafe still had the image of Bri being hit in the side of her head burned into his brain. He played it over and over in his mind as if to ramp up his rage again. "We were broadcasting live with my mobile backpack, so everyone witnessed it."

"I'm sorry that she was—" The whole scene seemed to have penetrated the officer so profoundly that he no longer looked bulletproof.

Being the video person that he was, Rafe's imagination produced a shot of her head bouncing on the wet pavement in slow motion. It repeated in his mind over and over. Rubble and water from the ground flew up as her skin touched the cold, hard blackness.

"God, I hope she's okay," Rafe belted as tears started to stream.

"I'll have someone check on her."

"Thank you, sir." Somehow Merlot's voice was comforting. "What are you going to do about everyone in the church?"

"I don't know. I should have stayed and helped with processing, but I needed to get out of there. They'll understand."

Merlot's patrol car was the only one leaving the crime scene as they passed an onslaught of emergency vehicles. Rafe stared out the metal mesh window, and the raindrops pelted the glass so hard that they sounded like another barrage of bullets attacking them.

† † †

BRI FINALLY AWOKE IN THE BACK OF THE AMBULANCE just as it pulled into the hospital. Her eyes opened slowly, and she felt someone holding her hand. She knew the woman looking down at her was someone familiar, but she couldn't place her because she was wearing a medical mask.

Outside the ambulance, it was pouring rain again, so before the nurse covered Bri with a blanket, she assured her, "You're going to be okay." Even though her soft smile was hidden, her eyes showed her Christlike compassion. Bri smiled as she realized it was Naoma, the mother of the girl in the hospital.

The rain came down on Bri as she lay on the gurney, but all she could feel was the warmth of the blanket as they wheeled her toward the haven. She thought about Rafe, the woman protesting violence, and the countless children who were murdered. They needed to leave Sodium, Texas.

Father in Heaven, she prayed in her heart. *Please help us!*

Chapter 17

The Least of These

T hat night, Rebah sat in her faded scarlet truck with the engine on in the hospital parking lot. Unfortunately, she had been there a while.

As soon as Bri exited the hospital entrance, Rebah slowly pulled up next to her in the truck and asked, "Can I give you a ride?"

"No," Bri said politely. "The hotel is just a few blocks from here. I'll be fine. Thank you, though." With a tired smile, she started to walk away, but Rebah inched along with her in the truck.

"I'm sorry about everything," Rebah barely managed.

Bri was determined to leave, and all she could offer the grieving woman was a sympathetic acknowledgment. Too much had happened, and now the story and reporter needed to part ways.

Finally, Rebah mournfully stated, "I have something to show you."

Bordering on frustration, Bri responded, "Really, it's okay. I'm going to find Rafe, and we're going home. Don't worry about it."

"I have to tell somebody," Rebah whispered in agony.

Bri stopped and looked at her for the first time. The mother was pale and exhausted. "You don't look so good. Can I drive you home?" Of course, she herself was wearing a bandage around her head.

Rebah agreed with a nod, and she moved to the passenger side of the truck cab so that Bri could drive. "I saw the two of you today at the funeral. I'm so sorry for what you both have been through here."

"Thank you. Would you happen to know what happened to Rafe?" Bri turned on the headlights and noticed that only one worked.

"He's okay. Don't worry," the mother replied.

As Bri entered Rebah's humble home, the Texas winter seemed eerily amplified, as if the heater hadn't run for weeks, and she shivered. Rebah turned on a light to reveal an empty living room, save for an easy chair and a single lamp.

"I'm sorry, it's cold. I usually walk around with a blanket." She handed Bri a folded gingerbread house quilt and added, "I don't have much to eat. I can offer some homemade pumpkin bread if you like."

"That would be fine. Thank you." Remembering how pale her host was earlier, Bri asked, "Is there anything I can do for you?" The kitchen was remarkably spotless and very bare.

Rebah opened the fridge to reveal very few contents and retrieved the only container of milk. "Would you like some milk?"

"No, I'm fine, thank you."

The poor mother pulled out a chair at the small breakfast table in the kitchen for her, set a huge slice of pumpkin bread perfectly centered on a plate, and poured her some milk anyway.

"Thank you," Bri said. "Are you eating?"

"Oh, I'll eat later, dear," she replied as she went into the living room to turn off the light.

"Here," Bri insisted. "Have a piece of mine. You need to eat."

"Actually—"

Rebah abruptly left the kitchen mid-sentence and disappeared down a dark hallway, leaving Bri to contemplate what was next. Glancing at her phone out of habit, she noticed that the house didn't have Wi-Fi. She wanted to go. She wanted to leave town.

Several hand-washed dishes were air-drying on the counter, and she went over to the sink to see if there was anything that she could do. She needed a distraction from everything, and standing over the spotless sink, she was reminded of her mother and her neighbor.

"BRI, WOULD YOU BE WILLING TO HELP MRS. SUAREZ NEXT DOOR?" her mother asked through Bri's closed bedroom door. "She says her dishwasher broke, and her mechanic can't come until next week."

"What does she need me for?" a young Bri shot back in response.

"She needs someone to wash her dishes. She's elderly, and her hands shake so much."

Grudgingly, she agreed, "Okay, whatever."

"Thank you, Bri."

"I'm not doing it because I want to, so don't thank me."

Her mother then teased through the closed door, "Your well of compassion is showing again." After a few seconds, she continued, "Mrs. Suarez will be so happy. Thank you for serving her."

The 13-year-old Bri sat on the floor with her stuffed animals and cried, making sure she didn't make a sound. The rebuke had cut her heart.

Outside her second-floor window, there was the sound of metal rattling, and Bri stood up to see what it was. Unfortunately, Mrs. Suarez was having trouble opening the gate to her backyard, but after a solid push with all the weight of her tiny frame, she managed to get through.

The young girl watched her neighbor kneel painfully at her garden to weed with her small shaking hands. Every careful and concentrated movement in the dirt took an excruciating amount of time and effort, and the angel whispered a prayer for her, "Father in Heaven, please bless Mrs. Suarez."

Without another thought on the matter, she crawled out from her perch and onto the roof, and when she reached the edge, she flew down to help the poor woman. And this she did day after day, year after year, until they held hands for the last time.

Bri had changed that day, and she would often return to the memory to recalibrate. When she was at her very lowest, she thought of Mrs. Suarez clinging on to the last years of life and pushing through with all her might. It didn't matter what Bri was going through; someone else always had it worse. Enormous challenges became quaint trivialities when she helped others. It was the main reason she became a reporter—to love her neighbor.

BRI NOTICED A PICTURE FRAME THAT WAS OVERTURNED on Rebah's counter. She promptly flipped it over and saw that it was a photo of Samuel swinging at a park. The president had made him infamous across the country, and now Bri saw how emotionally lost the little boy was in the image. The glass was cracked in several places, and without hesitation, she turned over the frame to remove the picture and broken glass.

She looked at him for the first time without any horrible story attached, and she threw away the shards of glass that covered him. He had a faint smile and looked straight at the camera with eyes that were begging for love. The way he sat on the park swing looked like the person taking the picture was next to him on another swing. Bri then realized that this is how his mother saw him.

On the back, Samuel had written in his best cursive, *Happy Mother's Day! Love, Samuel.* Further below, Rebah had added, *Age eight. Family vacation to Grand Canyon.*

Rebah returned to the kitchen with a box and explained without reservation, "That was right before my husband left for good. So much for trying to—" She shook her head and put down the box as if she still hadn't recovered from the failed marriage.

"He already had an apartment outside of town that I didn't know about by then," Rebah shared openly. "He'd come home after work and then take off after I had fallen asleep. He didn't want to be with me anymore."

There was a silence, and Bri wasn't sure where to take the interview. "How long were you married?"

"Oh, we still are—going on 13 years now. You know, I used to be a horrible person. Jim saw something in me that was worth redeeming, and he helped me. As soon as I had his baby, I told the Lord that I would never go back, and I named him Samuel."

"That's a beautiful name," Bri commented, trying to offer some support.

Rebah sat at the table and ate some of the pumpkin bread. "Come sit down, dear."

The reporter quickly obliged with a consoling smile and took a bite from her piece of bread. The medium-sized box between them was old and had been repackaged many times. It was a moving box with *Samuel's Room* written on the side.

"I've been going through a lot of things, throwing out anything having to do with Jim, looking over Samuel's old school assignments, and trying to memorize his drawings. Do you have any children?"

"No, I'm sorry, I don't. But I'm sure it's been so hard for you."

"Thank you, dear." She stopped and looked down for a while as if in a confession. "I guess I should just tell you," she barely uttered.

Rebah reached into the box and pulled out a small medallion on a cord. "I found this in Samuel's room this morning, right before the funeral.

101

I went to the church and stood outside, knowing that I wasn't welcome, and I held it in my hand the whole time."

She gave it to Bri to look over. The round medallion was the size of a half-dollar. One side contained a Christian cross with curved lines connecting each of the four points, making a protruding diamond. The other side had an inscription, which Bri read aloud, "Honorary Sodium Spartan, Stoddard Haus."

"Jim didn't like that I taught at Columbia, which has Hispanic children. When I talked about my students, he'd say something like *'Better watch your purse'* or *'Don't teach them too much—they're not going anywhere.'* He didn't always talk like that—he changed."

Rebah shook her head, tearing up. "Several years ago, I started taking Samuel there because it was easier, and eventually, Jim blew up and left me." The mother snatched a piece of the bread and just held it.

"At first, Samuel spent time with him on the weekends. He told me that they would go to a place called the Stoddard Haus on Sundays. Later, I found out that it was the old Chapel of Love church just outside of town for people that wanted to elope. It was an in-and-out kind of place. As soon as you paid, they'd already have someone playing the organ."

Bri tried to process everything. She had no idea where everything was leading but figured that listening to her was helping her heal.

"I was thinking I could take you there in the morning if that's okay."

"Sure," Bri responded politely, "if you really need me to come."

As if out of life, Rebah at last stated coldly, "That's the place where they were training my boy to shoot people."

Chapter 18

American Dream

Rafe sat in a jail cell by himself. It was already dark outside, and the harsh wind repeatedly blew a tree branch against the window, tapping sinisterly against the glass like a sickle. He couldn't sleep, feeling that at any moment, some other tragic episode might transpire anywhere around him. He was on edge and exhausted.

"Mind if I join you?" Merlot asked while opening the cell door. Rafe didn't say anything, figuring that Merlot wasn't following the book that day, and he watched the officer sit down next to him on the bed.

"Bri's fine and was discharged earlier today. Small concussion," Merlot informed him, fulfilling his promise.

"Thank you." Rafe was downtrodden and just stared at the floor.

"Your video that you shot today has made an impact. Everyone is up in arms about seeing a reporter attacked on-camera. It seems that everyone knows about our little problem here."

"Am I in trouble, sir?"

"No, I put you in here for your protection. This is the safest part of the facility, and honestly, I don't know what else may happen."

"Why is everyone so mad at us?"

Merlot exhaled deeply and uttered, "I don't recognize America anymore."

Rafe studied his friend, who now held a hand over his eyes as if he couldn't bear any more of what life was showing him. The strain of sleepless nights, hopelessness, and grief were pulling him closer to his demise.

"It's going to be okay," Rafe assured, not knowing from where this courage was coming. "There's a reason for all of this. We can't see it, but it's there. We just have to trust God."

"Trust God?" the officer snapped back. "Trust God with all this hell on earth we're witnessing?"

"I don't know," the prisoner stated humbly. "He allowed all those children in Bethlehem to be killed by King Herod. He let Jerusalem be destroyed and Jesus to be crucified. There's a reason for everything."

Rafe stopped as if he were trying to listen more intently to an earpiece that wasn't there. "And sometimes, it's so there's a testimony against those that have chosen not to listen to Him, or it's some profound way to teach us something."

He spoke as if he were reciting a distant Sunday-school lesson from the recesses of his memory or doctrine that he didn't even know was inside of him.

Merlot turned his head as if to debate him but stopped. And unable to contain it longer, he protested, "It's never right to slaughter children."

"You're right. I know that God is taking care of them now, though, and we just need to move forward."

Merlot stood up, and for a moment, Rafe thought he would storm out and slam the cell door closed. Although the prison cell was relatively small, Merlot was able to pace back and forth, like a caged lion, ready to pick a fight. "You know, I shouldn't even be here. I'm the one who shot Sam."

Clearly, he had found something in Rafe that allowed him to speak openly, to excuse any form of correct police conduct or protocol. "I shouldn't even have this badge!"

"Yes, you should! You shot those men in the church. You're a hero." Rafe meant it. Although he was incarcerated, he respected and admired his jailer.

"But I've been helping Rebah and Sam for a couple of years now. They were like family!"

Rafe let him pace. There was no way to argue with guilt. He didn't know if Merlot was looking for sympathy or just needing a sounding board.

Suddenly, Merlot left the confinement and barked, "Come here."

As instructed, Rafe followed him cautiously as if he were walking on thin eggshells in a hen house. He didn't know if he was innocent or if he was being released. Just like his entire stay in the town, he was taking one second at a time.

The officer went to his desk and retrieved a framed black and white picture to show him. It was of a parked hay truck from the 1920s, and on the tailgate sat a poor couple in their early forties with their two young children, both under ten.

"This is my granddad," the officer said, pointing to the man. "He came to America shortly after the Kristallnacht in 1938. As a Jewish egg farmer in France, he could barely provide for his small family. He and my grandma were so afraid for their lives that they saw America as the land where they could escape the nightmare that was Nazi Germany. Although France had not yet been attacked, they feared what politicized hatred had become.

"They left along with many other Jews at that time because America was more than an idea. It was a hope that had been realized. It was a sanctuary, a place where a man could live without fear of a tyrant. All a poor man needed to do was plant seed in the fertile soil, and God would bless him and his family with the fruits of his labor.

"As soon as he saw the Statue of Liberty, he decided to change our last name from Merl to Merlot so the SS could never find us."

The old man stopped in his tracks and sobbed like a baby, "And now today, the plaque on the Statue of Liberty has been altered! After months of talk, they have shredded American values with their racism!"

He picked up a newspaper from his desk and quoted the desecrated *New Colossus*.

> *Give me your industrious, not your poor,*
> *Your huddled masses yearning to breathe free,*
> *The pure, rich salt of your teeming shore.*
> *Send these, the self-sufficient, hard-working to me,*
> *I lift my lamp beside the golden door!*

Rafe looked at him, wanting to understand his frustration, and asked, "What did it say before?"

A pathetic sigh left the old man's heart. "This means that my granddad couldn't have come to America if the current immigration code were in place. He was a poor Jew. It means that this country is no longer a beacon to the world, a refuge for those who are abused or without a penny to their name.

"It's as if America crucified Christ again and murdered the Good Samaritan. We are a nation of immigrants. We *all* belong here!"

At first, Rafe searched for something to console him, but all he found was his mother's racist rhetoric vying for the captain's analysis.

"My mom says that there's no more room for immigrants in the United States."

Merlot didn't say anything. He just looked directly into Rafe's eyes as if they were locked into an awkward staring contest. Rafe couldn't move.

At last, Merlot swiveled his seat around, and he retrieved another newspaper clipping from his small filing cabinet. "Did you know, son, that only three percent of the United States land is developed?" he asked, pointing to an article that backed up his claim. "There's plenty of room for anybody who is trying to escape their country with their family!"

There was nothing Rafe could say.

Chapter 19

The Iniquitous

Although it was mid-morning, the sky was dark, and the shooting range could barely be seen across the field. The whole compound was imprisoned with overgrown bushes and noxious weeds, almost hidden from the world.

"I can't go in there," a frightened Rebah mumbled to Bri in the driver's seat of her truck. "Unfortunately, I've known about Jim being this way for a while. He spent a night in jail several years ago for a fight he had in a bar. Apparently, he said some things he shouldn't have. Serves him right!"

Rebah was worked up, but at the same time, she was also visibly fearful for her life. "Anyway, if you want to go in, it should be vacant right now."

"No, I think—"

"Here's the key."

Bri watched it dangle from a cord in Rebah's hand for a few seconds, and then she suddenly snatched it like a lottery ticket. It could go either way: all up in smoke as a deranged conspiracy theory or a newsworthy development to one of the biggest stories she had ever covered.

The truck's only functioning headlight aimed right at the white chapel. Tiny snowflakes glistened in the beam, but they evaporated as soon as the stony ground rejected them. As she descended from the scarlet truck, Bri wondered if Rebah would take off and leave her there alone, but there was something about her smile that comforted her.

Bri soon discovered that there was no Wi-Fi signal or cell service available on her phone, but she kept pressing Rafe's quick-dial button anyway. The device had become dead metal and plastic. As she approached her shadow on the chapel door, she thought about Rafe and why he hadn't called.

It was then that she started humming *Black Mare* again, and there was something about it that helped her move forward. Like an anthem coming from her trembling heart, it parted the encroaching darkness.

The white building still said *Chapel of Love* above the door, but nothing else about it backed up the claim. Unfortunately, the key worked, and as she turned the truth-seeking metal in the lock, she noticed her station's logo on the cuff of her sleeve.

She wasn't an investigator; she was a reporter. Her job was to listen to people and report the facts with impartiality, not break into a church trying to determine if its patrons were training little boys to kill people.

But it *was* a church, adorned with plush, red satin pews and a pulpit at the front. The light switch, which she had turned on, also triggered six ceiling fans that were ramping up into what seemed to be a dangerous storm as they shook back and forth. She shivered and cut the switch almost immediately.

She then turned on her phone light and looked at the walls. Right away, she recognized Samuel in a picture by himself, surrounded by other headshots of boys, which included Michael Harmon, the other shooter. The caption above them read *Our Proud Sodium Spartans*. She stepped back and took a picture of the display, knowing everything she saw could be evidence or at least noteworthy. The flash created a spotlight in the middle, and the edges were as dark as death.

All the boys were young, ranging from 9 to 13, and their names were written in gold calligraphy. Samuel had attained several gold-star badges that were pinned to his picture, but there was something about his eyes that didn't match his forced smile.

Inscriptions, diagrams, and scribbles were all along the walls, which served as chalkboards for the educational graffiti. Bri stepped up to one of them to take a closer look and realized that most of it was handwritten in pen, right on the white drywall.

There was a small drawing of three different skulls from the side, arranged in a column, and a child's signature at the bottom as if it were part of a research assignment. The top skull was labeled *Caucasian*, the middle *Chimpanzee*, and the bottom *Negroid*. Unfortunately, the bottom two had elongated jaws and nasal bones drawn in an exaggerated and demeaning manner.

The canvas captured scribbles and hundreds of journal entries that scared her:

> *I hate my Mexican teacher and all the Mexican boys that pick on me.*
>
> *I want to stab him.*
>
> *His brains will be kicked out of his head.*
>
> *God will kill her for me.*

Bri continued to examine the different texts on the wall, witnessing the brainwashing of innocent little boys. Their minds had been stripped of everything beautiful in life and let loose to harp on the evil that was entombed there.

A couple of scripture verses were enshrined on a plaque with gold calligraphy:

> *Let every soul be subject unto the higher powers.*
> *For there is no power but of God: the powers that*
> *be are ordained of God. Whosoever, therefore,*
> *resisteth the power, resisteth the ordinance of God:*
> *and they that resist shall receive to themselves*
> *damnation (Romans 13:1-2).*

Bri had read this before, but because she was surrounded by ill intent, she wondered how these inspired words from Paul could be twisted into something so sinister and emboldening. Instead of explaining the authority of God to judge the wicked, she wondered if these boys assumed the power of God to judge others.

How can people read a passage of scripture so differently? she genuinely wondered. Immediately, she remembered a recent news story in which President McKendrick had written something on social media, and lawyers from both parties argued completely different stances on its meaning.

A sentence, after all, is just a group of symbols with changing meanings across time, cultures, and geography. Even the Bible was translated several times, and hundreds of religions argue their unique interpretation. That is why the Holy Ghost is sent to clarify.

She continued reading the passage on the wall:

> *For rulers are not a terror to good works, but to the*
> *evil. Wilt thou then not be afraid of the power? Do*

that which is good, and thou shalt have praise of
the same: For he is the minister of God to thee for
good. But if thou do that which is evil, be afraid; for
he beareth not the sword in vain: for he is the
minister of God, a revenger to execute wrath upon
him that doeth evil (Romans 13:3-4).

"That's interesting," she said aloud, and it echoed off the blaspheming walls. As if she hadn't examined it too closely before, she reasoned, "What if the ruler *is* a terror to good works? What if he's an iniquitous king?"

Bri walked closer to the pulpit and noticed several passages of scripture written in ornate black lettering:

And now art thou cursed from the earth, which hath
opened her mouth to receive thy brother's blood
from thy hand. A fugitive and a vagabond shalt thou
be in the earth. And the Lord set a mark upon Cain
(Genesis 4:11, 12, 15).

Cursed be Canaan; a servant of servants shall he
be unto his brethren (Genesis 9:25).

Can the Ethiopian change his skin, or the leopard
his spots? Then may ye also do good, that are
accustomed to do evil. Therefore, will I scatter them
as the stubble that passeth away by the wind of the
wilderness (Jeremiah 13:23-24).

113

> *Servants, be obedient to them that are your masters*
> *according to the flesh, with fear and trembling*
> *(Ephesians 6:5).*

The church in which she was standing had become a den of evil and racist hatred. Appalled by the gross selectiveness and perversions of holy scripture, she continued to document all the heinous manifestations on the walls with her phone. Alone, covered by a seething shroud of darkness, her little light had uncovered the true horrors of Sodium and the boys that were subject to the filth of the devil's mind.

Toward the front of the chapel, a sizable etching in the wall of the number sequence *14813* was particularly deep, as if made with a knife. It was sharp and eerie—no curves were used. She took a picture, and after staring at the image on her phone for a few seconds, she deduced that the *813* stood for Heil McKendrick, but she didn't know what the *14* meant.

When she came to the pulpit, she noticed a commanding wooden plaque on the front with curious, hand-chiseled artistry. A blood-colored cushion embellished the old tablet with the following inscription in gold lettering:

> *A Spartan from Sodium knows his worth,*
> *Hewn from the curséd dregs at birth.*
> *Our Lord's noble legion with sacred oath:*
> *Slay Cain's mark, his clay and soul both.*
> *—SS*

It was the stylized *SS* that made her gasp as she jumped back, almost dropping her phone. She held her hand over her mouth and cried, trembling.

Chapter 20

Sin of Sodium

Even though she was alone in the truck, Rebah called out for Merlot on her phone with a barely audible whimper. She closed her eyes and focused on his voice as if it were the only comfort in the world. She had been crying for some time now, and the tears had no reason to stop.

"Charlie, I need you," she continued. "Do you know the old chapel outside of town?" She put down the gun and wiped her eyes.

Staring at the white building in front of her, she sobbed, "There's something I've meant to tell you for a long time, and it can't wait."

After listening to his voice for the last time, her heart seemed to rupture from the memory of all the screams that had haunted her for days.

She remembered looking up at the elementary-school roof and trying to focus on the shooter. Now knowing it was her son, she filled in the distant silhouette with his tearful eyes. There was nothing she could do to bring her boy back. "Charlie, bring the reporter."

THE SOUND OF CAR TIRES COMING TO A STOP on the gravel right outside the chapel filled Bri's heart with excruciating fear. Straight away, she turned off her only light and hid behind the pulpit. She had just recorded so much evidence for the existence of hell that she didn't know what to do with her phone, so she quickly slipped it into her sock.

"Someone's been here." It was a man with a bellowing voice, calm and commanding. There was no place to run. The lights were now on, and the helicopter fans that shook above seemed to be in sync with her rapidly beating heart.

The approaching footsteps were like nails being hammered into a coffin, and she knew that she would die in this white pit of agony and hatred. There was nothing for it except to close her eyes and wish that she was being held by Rafe, far away from Sodium, Texas.

"Hello, my darling," charmed the bellowing voice.

Bri opened her eyes and fell back into the pulpit so hard that she felt she might have left a mark. The heap of wood behind her had become an altar. The man's pale, sharp face was only inches away from hers, and he gently stroked her curly, red hair.

"What may I do for you?" His blue eyes seemed to stab her from head to toe, inspecting her, trying to deduce what churned in her mind. After a second, he looked at his companion to show her that he was not alone.

"Nothing. I'm sorry. I'll leave now." She quickly arose and started for the door.

He slithered toward the first pew and insisted, "You don't have to hide, my darling. Come, sit. Let's talk."

Now several pews back, she recognized the deathly-skinny man. Shocked at how the fog was lifting from the mire and still incredulous, she gasped, "Mr. Kerioth?"

"Yes, you may call me Jude. It's a beautiful church, isn't it? There are many more like it."

His companion, who was also very slender and sported a blond goatee, reached for his phone and dialed. Once Kerioth gave him a nod, he proceeded to utter a series of words for the person on the other end of the call. "Rabbit, Jericho the Dead Sea Solomon. Yes, unleavened bread."

As Bri almost cleared the entrance, Kerioth continued, "Go ahead. We know where to find you, Ms. Gilchrist."

She turned to look at the devil in the church and quickly ran away, hoping the falling tears from heaven could hide her. The morning sun had broken through a few clouds, though, and as she flew toward Rebah's faded scarlet truck, she didn't see her companion in the cab.

It wasn't until she reached for the passenger door that she saw the horror within. Rebah was gone. Her bloody body was there, but her soul, which had been slowly dying for days, had now hopefully found peace.

Bri fell backward in traumatic shock. The world was ending all over again, and she ran as desperately as she could out of hell.

RAFE COULD IDENTIFY HIS LOVE'S RED HAIR A MILE AWAY. She was soaked and trembling as she walked along the side of the empty road, and before the patrol car had come to a stop, he jumped from the passenger seat to embrace her.

"Are you okay? Are you hurt?" he asked as he put his jacket around her.

"No, I'm fine!" She wasn't, though, and with what little she had left, she faintly exclaimed, "Let's get out of here!"

"What happened?" He wanted to take on all the evil that had hurt her. Standing in the pouring rain, his hands clenched, and he had to pick a fight, despite being in the presence of the officer.

Merlot opened the back door of the patrol car and commanded, "Let's get out of the rain. Where's Rebah?"

117

Once inside, Bri blurted, "She's dead. She's dead. She killed herself and left me with that lunatic at the church!"

Merlot watched her cry in his rearview mirror as he sped down the road. "Who?"

"Mr. Kerioth, the Secretary of State. He's behind everything," she answered. "That church is a horrible place! I never want to go back there again!" She retrieved the cell phone from her sock and sobbed, "I recorded everything here. We have to tell everybody!"

"Okay, let's get you both to someplace safe," resolved Merlot. "I'm going to call backup."

The patrol car raced down the empty road back to the Stoddard Haus as Rafe and Bri sat in the back like caged angels. The siren wailed, and the red and blue lights shot into the falling rain like a beacon in an earth-shattering storm.

The sin of Sodium had been discovered.

† † †

EARLY THE FOLLOWING MORNING, a newspaper delivery van crawled down a street in a poor neighborhood in Philadelphia. Bagged newspapers were chucked into every other yard, and a few dogs barked.

The house at the end of the small road was the only one with occupants who were awake, and the light from their living room reached their neighbors' house across the street.

As soon as the paper landed near the porch of this last house, a young African American boy emerged to pick it up. He removed the bundle from the bag and read the front-page headline: *Welcome to the Sodium War: More Racist Violence in Sodium, TX as Lawmakers are Torn on how to "Deal" with School Shootings Nationwide.*

He excitedly yelled out, "Mom, mom!" and dashed inside.

Part Two

Chapter 21

Beneath the Surface

(Six Years Later)

Rafe stared at the static fan on the ceiling and ignored the fact that he was sweating. Only the blade tips closest to the window were barely visible in the dark, but he knew the fan was there. Bri, who was beside him in the bed, was fast asleep.

He stood up to gaze out the open window and study the remains of the day before. The wind was still, only a few crickets chirped, and the darkness of the neighborhood below was only a shade brighter than their bedroom. The lamp posts below were dark. No cars drove by. Nothing.

In the far distance, the Gulf of Mexico seemed especially active in the dim moonlight as the waves crashed onto the shore in mighty grandeur. Gone were the days of the soft waves and the shallow water creeping upon the sand.

He reached for Bri's phone on the dresser and quietly left the room. He knew the hallway and the living room perfectly in the dark, so he didn't need to count his steps or waste the phone battery.

There was a covered cake pan on the kitchen counter, and after opening it, he turned on the phone light to cut and eat a slice. The modest, half-eaten cake had chocolate frosting with a yellow icing inscription: *Happy 5th Anniversary!*

On the way toward his chair in the living room, he picked up a well-used Bible on a stand and began to read by phone light. The darkness enveloped him, but the single light pierced the evil, and it could not reach him.

> *The sun was risen upon the earth when Lot entered into Zoar. Then the Lord rained upon Sodom and upon Gomorrah brimstone and fire from the Lord out of heaven; And he overthrew those cities, and all the plain, and all the inhabitants of the cities, and that which grew upon the ground (Genesis 19:23-25).*

Rafe looked at the ceiling again and whispered, "Why would He do that? Surely, there were good people."

Maybe it was the hour, or perhaps it was the countless, imperfect bumps on the textured ceiling, but he soon fell asleep again, pondering.

IN THE MORNING, BRI OPENED THE CURTAINS to let in the diffused, orange sunlight throughout their small apartment and quietly removed the phone and Bible from Rafe's chest, but he awoke anyway.

"Crazy weather we're having," he commented as he stood up to hug her. "It's been raining for I don't know how many months, and this is just absolutely blinding."

Bri went into the kitchen to start breakfast and replied, "Oh, I think it's wonderful! We've been bogged down for so long—we needed a change."

She seemed to dance and hum along to a tune that only she could hear. Her bubbly movements were almost inspiring as she glided about the kitchen in the warm glow of the blocked sunlight.

Rafe returned a sleepless half-smile as he slowly sat down at the kitchen table. The midnight hours now showed under his eyes, and because he worked from home, he sported a lost, scraggly beard.

Once she poured the last of the ingredients into the electric mixer bowl, she flipped the switch to turn it on, but nothing happened.

"Ugh," she groaned.

"Just give it a minute."

Annoyed, Bri went over to the counter to retrieve her battery-powered tablet computer and turned it on, and this was just the right amount of time the mixer needed to power up on its own.

Even though she had started upbeat, she quickly sank down again. She let out an exasperated sound and griped, "It seems like they're starting it later and later each day."

"I wouldn't worry about it. I'm sure it's fine," Rafe asserted. "How did you sleep last night?"

"Well, I haven't thrown up yet, so I'm good."

Suddenly, the tablet automatically played a news video, and the male reporter announced, "Good morning, everyone! With the sunshine out today, let's all get out and enjoy—"

Like clockwork, Bri handed the device to Rafe, and he put it in the top drawer of the counter under some towels. Unfortunately, the video on the computer could still be heard.

The muffled reporter continued, "It's almost been six years since those brave little boys urged those impurities back to their home countries. They stood on top of their school rooftops and declared to everyone below how much their kindred loved them and needed them home. Let's

123

celebrate Sodium Day with loved ones. Hold them close and hug them. God bless you all."

Even though they knew the reporter was delivering *alternative facts*, even down to the time of year it happened, they just ignored the noise. They both continued their morning routines, and once the video was over, Rafe retrieved the device for her.

"I need to go to the store today," she said as she sat down at the table. "Do you need anything?"

"No. Did you need me to come with you?"

Bri scanned the store site on the tablet and answered, "I'll be okay."

LATER THAT MORNING IN THE ENTRYWAY, Bri leaned over in her black dress to put on the last part of her outfit and then felt the urge to throw up, so she quickly ran to the bathroom.

After a few minutes, she returned to the doorway, and Rafe exclaimed from his desk in the living room, "You look very beautiful! Love you!"

She replied with a polite, hurried smile and rushed out the door.

Their apartment building was small yet adequate. As the ocean was only a good mile away, they enjoyed the proximity of an escape from everything. They didn't have much of a yard, but apartments in the ghetto didn't have much of anything. Of course, they were all dirt anyway.

The tops of buildings disappeared into a low, soupy smog, and luckily, their apartment was a few floors below the visibility line, and they paid extra in rent for it. Even though they had a view, they had their windows closed and curtains drawn during most of the day because they were in the *scorching months*, which were now March through October.

As she climbed into their truck, she stated, "June 19th, 2026. Davidson, Gabriella. Going to the store in downtown Gulf Haven, Texas.

Estimated time: one hour." After the recitation, she was able to turn the key, and she drove off.

"YES, MOM, THAT WAS BRI," RAFE CONFIRMED on his phone as he watched his wife leave. "It's good to hear from you. It's been a year maybe—"

Edith turned a page in the magazine she read and continued the inquiry. "How is she doing?" His mother now had long, silver hair and a youthful face due to several plastic surgeries. Her lavish bedroom was in stark contrast to her son's humble abode.

"Fine, fine," he replied.

"Well, she's the reason I called. It looks like the two of you are *finally* pregnant, and I wanted to check up on you."

"How did you—" he started, but he soon realized the connection. "Oh, I see. Yes, the doctor said everything's normal."

Unfortunately, all dissenter biometrics were now available online for anyone to view, complete with update notifications for specific individuals.

"So, who is this Doctor Abrams? Does he practice there in that ghetto?" she probed with undue suspicion.

He had long been exposed to her racist and unsympathetic tone toward everyone. "Yes, he is a doctor here in the area. We went to him because he was highly recommended."

"It doesn't matter. He probably cheated his way to his degree. Is he from Africa?"

"No, I believe his family is originally from the Middle East."

"Why hasn't he left yet? I thought President McKendrick ordered everyone to leave. They all have to go back to their home countries."

"Not everyone has to—"

She then glanced at her TV, which was always on. It was the heartwarming music that drew her attention. "Look, they're showing one

125

of those commercials on TV now," she argued. "It's that one where a young, black boy is holding his mom's hand, and they're both smiling and waving as they board a plane to Africa. It's where they all belong anyway."

"Mom—" He was getting agitated.

"We probably pay for all their plane tickets. I guess it's the least we can do."

By that time, he could no longer stand her blatant racism and calmly interjected, "Okay, Mom. I got to go."

"Alright, my love. Take care of the baby for me."

On the street below, he could hear a rack truck coming. They always had a distinct sound as they approached—like a fire truck siren but more awful and eerie. As Rafe stared down at the horrible display through the window, the middle-aged black man on the rack raised his head defiantly.

The man had a name, but he probably had not heard it for years. Strapped onto a metal rack in the back of the pickup truck, he was stripped down to almost nothing, and his head was shaved. His chest was bare and protruding because his arms were tied behind him, and he bled from countless beatings.

"Okay, Mom. Love you." Rafe hung up the phone just in time for his mother not to hear the gunshot that tore apart the racked man's chest. It was a daily show for those in the ghetto. Because the brain-etching sound echoed between all the apartment buildings along the street, Rafe was never able to pinpoint from which direction the racist blow came.

The driver stopped to cut the straps holding the body, and it fell to the pavement. He then pulled the next victim from the back of his cab and strapped her to the rack. This display was a constant reminder of the new barbaric normal, and there was nothing Rafe could do about it.

126

Chapter 22

The New Normal

B ri never liked shopping anymore; it was a chore. Everything was overpriced and low quality, but she tried not to complain. Complaining never really got anyone anywhere.

There were several dozen women in the checkout lanes, and all Bri could focus on was the scratched elevator music that always seemed to play in a loop in this particular store. Unfortunately, though, she accidentally made eye contact with the guard at the front entrance. He was stockier than the usual one, and he held his rifle against the opposite shoulder.

He was an *SA officer*. There was some debate over the meaning of SA, as it was never explained in any official capacity. Still, depending on the source, it could be *Safety Administrator* or *Security Angel*. Most people just called them the *brownsuits* because of their uniform color, which always included a dark brown bulletproof vest.

They were a form of military police, positioned at each city block corner, on top of buildings, and inside each business to ensure that *peace* was maintained in the ghetto. Each public facility was also required to have a brownsuit to remain open.

Because they were not to engage in friendly conversation and wore special dark glasses, they seemed inhuman, devoid of any emotion. There were theories that they could be AI, but they were probably volunteers; no government could employ that many. They were fixtures with rifles, and it was best not to stare.

Outside the store, the storm clouds had gathered again, and it began to pour. It seemed that everyone in the store noticed, and they were all immediately depressed.

When Bri glanced toward the brownsuit again, she noticed that he was now walking toward her, so she quickly looked down at her basket, but there was nothing she could do.

"Dissenter!" he blasted.

"Yes, sir?"

"Your band has fallen off. Locate it quickly!"

Bri frantically searched for the missing item and found it on the floor, not too far from where she was standing. She tried to stop her hands from shaking as she put the black band on her ankle, but the brownsuit hovered over her with the rifle barrel pointed at her forehead. In her mind, she barely survived.

"There will be no charges, dissenter." He then marched off to his post.

All the women had stopped to watch the spectacle, and afterward, they each glanced down at their ankles to check that they were still in compliance.

From far away, this thick, elastic cloth that dissenter women had to wear on their right ankle in public resembled the clasp of a ball and chain, and it was a mental reminder of their choice.

128

The law also required them to wear high heels and a dress that came down to the knee. It was the only time that Bri stood taller than Rafe, but he didn't mind. Any dress above or below the knee was not allowed in public, and by this point, there was no complaining. It was life.

Bri shuddered with a painful moan when she left the store—as if she had been raped without recourse, and dozens of reluctant spectators just stood by. She reached for her phone to scream at Rafe. He would understand.

"I don't know why they make us wear dresses. It feels like I'm in a sexualized fantasy from the 1950s with segregation and McCarthyism. With all that Catholic schoolboy repression, I feel like I'm on a page of a dirty magazine when those guards look at me!" she exclaimed in one full breath. It seemed rehearsed.

After a few seconds, Rafe finally responded, "But they have to be modest. I think you look nice." There wasn't a greeting, but sometimes they weren't necessary after so many years of marriage. Regardless, she didn't need a rebuttal.

"I'm not a show! I don't want some guy with a gun looking at me because it's the law to dress a certain way!"

"What happened?"

"Oh, nothing. It's just stupid, that's all." She had said her piece, and as she approached the truck, she realized that she had received the concern and comfort from his voice that she needed.

"I'm sorry you feel that way." He sounded defeated and depressed, as if everything that she had gone through was his fault.

"Oh well, I'll be home soon." After she ended the call, she reached down to remove the band and threw it in the back of the cab as hard as she could.

BRI FELT LIGHT-HEADED AND HUNGRY, so she bit into an apple as she finally turned on the windshield wipers to full speed. Unfortunately, it was still hard to see the oncoming traffic with the downpour that beat the glass.

When she reached a stoplight, she looked down at her belly and thought about her baby. *This was no place to raise a child.* No one should ever live in constant fear of being victimized by law enforcement because of social distinction or skin color. She felt so helpless. Everything that had happened was beyond what a single person could change.

Suddenly, from out of the corner of her eye, she noticed a ten-year-old girl running in the rain toward the passenger side of her truck, followed by a brownsuit. And when she collided with the door, it sounded like a small deer falling into a dumpster.

The door flew open, and Bri jumped.

"Help me—" It was all the young girl could utter before the shot was fired and her blood splattered across the truck seat. The pursuing brownsuit yanked the girl's body out of the truck and threw her to the ground.

"Dissenter, leave now!" he screamed at Bri as he aimed his rifle at the young girl's head, which was already soaked in blood on the pavement.

Bri floored the gas pedal and sped through the red light as the open passenger door flailed in the rain. In the mirror, she witnessed him shoot the girl once more, and she could hear the gunshot echo off the walls of nearby apartment buildings as she drove off.

Her mind raced to figure out what the young girl could have possibly done to warrant such a horrible punishment. There was nothing.

BRI RETURNED TO THEIR APARTMENT still shaking and faintly whimpered, "Davidson, Gabriella. Returning home after shopping. Actual time: 98 minutes."

As soon as she entered the front door, Rafe hugged her and inquired, "Are you okay?" She nodded with her head down and went straight into the bedroom, almost running.

"I'm glad you're feeling better," he consoled. Returning to his video-editing project in the living room, he earnestly offered, "Let me know if I can do anything for you."

She couldn't respond. Her hands trembled. Now without the public dollhouse costume tearing at her skin, she covered herself with a blanket and sank onto the floor.

After several minutes, she finally revealed through the closed door, "I don't know if we should do this anymore." Something needed to change, but she couldn't come up with any possible solution. She needed to move on from this complacency—they needed to do more than just survive.

"What do you mean?" He calmly walked over to the door and turned the knob, but it was locked. A wooden veil separated them.

"The baby," she responded. She needed to make it simple.

"What are you talking about?"

"A little girl was shot in the head right in front of me today. I don't know if I could bring a baby into this place—it's so full of senseless hate and murder! It's as if the world has gone mad!" she confided without a drop of hope.

"Don't say that!" he whispered. "You know they can hear you. They'll make us go full-term, and if they know a white baby is unwanted, they'll just take him away!"

Through the door, his voice was muffled and somewhat distant. It was almost as if her only friend in the world was beyond hope and too complacent to listen.

Rafe sat down with his back to the door and continued, "I'm sorry that happened to you today. From now on, I'll go with you. I don't want you to be alone anymore. I love you."

All she could do was hold her unborn baby and silently cry.

Chapter 23

Indoctrination

R afe couldn't sleep that night as he lay on the couch in the living room. The harsh rain beat the windows hypnotically, and the moon had all but disappeared. There seemed to be a certain solace in staring into the dark as he tried to find the ceiling above.

He thought about the phylactery hanging from his neck like a noose. For almost five and a half years, he had been required to wear it—even while bathing. It was an ominous, black orb at the end of a cheap, plastic string, and most dissenters had long disregarded it as just another mindless part of their existence.

Instead of a box carrying parchment scrolls from the Torah to remind the wearer of their devotion to God and the Exodus from Egypt, this modern device continually transmitted the dissenter's speech and precise location coordinates. It required obedience out of fear.

Rafe pulled at the phylactery, and the plastic string dug more into his neck, making the mark he already had even more red. He wanted to yank the *Big Brother* device from his body and run as far away as possible. But of course, if he did, a horde of SA officers would soon be at their front door.

Suddenly, he reached for his phone and turned on the light. He quietly walked toward the hallway closet and opened a few archive boxes while holding his *modern lantern*. After rummaging through several stacks of papers, he happened upon an old, crumpled-up letter. It read as follows:

> *Greetings, Mr. Rafe Davidson,*
>
> *We are pleased to inform you that you and your family have been selected for the privilege of joining the holy brethren at our indoctrination camp, based on your Caucasian status and unmarked dissenter records.*
>
> *If you accept this honor, please report to Fort Caine, Texas. The SA officer posted at the southern entrance of Gulf Haven will give you further instructions.*
>
> *Your Brethren*

A blood-red wax Sodium seal and a dozen pompous signatures took up most of the space on the page, along with several symbols at the bottom that he couldn't read. He searched online for their meaning several times before, but he knew for all the secrecy, they probably didn't have an ethical translation.

IN THE MORNING, RAFE NOTICED that his breakfast was on the table—a lone muffin on a plate and a glass of milk. Bri was not to be found.

The bedroom door was locked again, and he could hear her typing something on the other side. Although he wasn't with her the day before, he reminded himself that what she had gone through was undoubtedly his fault.

AFTER CONGRESS PASSED NEW VOTING STATUTES to regain confidence in elections, a *Secure National Poll* was created as an online voting platform in the upcoming general election. Unfortunately, there was a breach in the platform's database server within a month after the election, called the *Election Hack of 2020*.

A group of loyalists to the president made all the ballot data available online, including every voter's name, address, and specifically how they voted. What was meant to prove ballot validity eventually wreaked havoc and unspeakable violence across the nation.

In this *Last Great Election*, democracy was pitted against an authoritarian, anti-democratic regime, and the overwhelming majority of Americans chose President McKendrick and all of his racist tenets. Guardrails were shattered, and a dictator ruled the land, promising power to his loyalists and revenge to everyone who voted against him.

Those who voted for his challenger, Amos Gorman, and his platform of racial equality and democracy were ostracized and labeled as *Un-Americans* or *Dissenters to American Values*. Through mounting mob-like pressure and corrupt political maneuvers, these *Gormanites* or *Dissenters* were eventually stripped of their civil rights with the ratification of the *Citizen Status Edicts*, which restructured everything, and they became second- and third-class citizens.

A special session in Congress had lawyers prove that Gormanites could not comprehend the ramifications of the votes they had cast and deemed them *mentally incompetent*, giving legislators the machination to revoke their rights to vote, bear arms, and peaceably assemble (for fear of insurrection). Even though Rafe and Bri both voted for Gorman, his vote characterized their new citizenship status.

Dissenters could work whatever job they wanted, sleep as long as needed, and search online for anything they desired, but their freedoms were gone. They could not speak against the president, own a weapon, assemble into a group of more than ten people, or leave the ghetto in which they lived. Their purpose was to work and pay taxes.

RAFE COULD NEVER COME UP WITH THE RIGHT WORDS to say or the right actions to take. He had fumbled through five years of marriage, and he was just grateful that Bri hadn't left him yet. Before he knew it, he had slipped the invitation letter underneath the door, and she stopped typing.

After a few seconds, she opened the door and grilled, "What is this?"

"An indoctrination letter—"

"What does that mean?"

Rafe looked at her as if he hadn't seen her for a week, happy that she was talking again. "I don't know."

She looked at the date. "It's three years old—why are you showing this to me? I'm in no mood to discuss any of this stupid hell we're in." She then threw the letter at his face and slammed the door. It was wrong. Everything he did was always wrong.

"I know. I just had an idea," he tried. "What if we go down south and do this indoctrination thing? I hear that they pay well, and we wouldn't worry about getting shot at any second because of a mistake we may make. We would be safe—"

Bri opened the door, looked him straight in the eyes, and stated with cold disapproval, "I feel like I don't know you anymore. I am not about to trade my life for someone else's—I would rather *die* than be a racist!"

136

"I know," he humbly replied as he picked up the letter again. He wrote on the back of it as he whispered, "But the baby would be safe. Nothing would happen to him, and we could keep him."

He handed her the wrinkled paper, and on the reverse side of the filth, he had written what could not be transmitted by his phylactery: *We could just lie and play along so that we could find out more about everything. We could EXPOSE them.*

Watching her take it in, he didn't know what she would say. Nobody knew what *indoctrination* meant or what they would have to say or do, but he knew that he could awaken her dormant desire to spread the truth. After many years of misinformation and a lack of knowledge about anything outside their neighborhood, the truth seemed like a distant, philosophical idea.

For them, the internet was closed-circuit with curated information coming from a handful of government-controlled servers. International news was non-existent, legal services were unavailable, and beauty products were in abundance.

Bri took Rafe's hand and knelt next to the bed with him. The filth-ridden letter was before them on the bed like at an altar, and she wrote a reply to his suggestion: *Can't we just wait until all this blows over? Won't someone rescue us?*

He picked up the pencil and answered below her line: *No one may ever come because no one knows about us. It may not end.*

She looked up at him through her tears, and he kissed her cheek. They had come to a point where they needed to live a lie for the sake of their family. All this time, they had been in the fiery furnace of not bowing down to what the country had become, and the Lord had been with them.

"Everything will be okay," he whispered, hoping to comfort her.

As they knelt at the bed, they prayed silently together.

Chapter 24

Goliath

(Day One)

They sat in silence as they drove toward the decaying south side of town on July 4th.

Rafe had shaved his lost, scraggly beard that morning so that there would be one less senseless reason to be executed by a brownsuit at the southern entrance. No longer a victim to circumstance, he knew what they needed to do for the sake of their family and the nation.

To his amazement, their part of town wasn't as bad in comparison. Since Rafe worked at home and their only errands were to the store and the maternity clinic, they hadn't seen what had become of their small town by the shore.

Many buildings were torn down and left in shambles. Helicopters flew over, and strong gusts of wind hurled trash in the streets. Cars were stranded on the freeway, so Rafe had to drive around them.

At the edge of town, a checkpoint station had been built on the freeway. There was an impenetrable metal boom barrier that prevented cars from speeding through, and several brownsuits were on duty.

Rafe looked at the Sodium symbol on the side of the checkpoint building, and a rush of indescribable fear surged up. He was there at the Sodium Massacres, before everything had happened.

"Are you okay?" Bri asked.

He looked over at her and confided, "Maybe we shouldn't do this."

Before she could answer, a hard tap on the driver's side window made him jump. He quickly rolled down the window, and as soon as there was a crack, the brownsuit demanded, "Name?"

"Davidson, Rafe and Davidson, Gabriella to report to Fort Caine for indoctrination," Rafe managed.

The brownsuit shined a flashlight right in their faces. "Dissenter numbers?"

Bri rolled up the left sleeve of her dress to display a five-digit number tattooed on her left wrist along with a barcode. She calmly said, "39812."

"Bring it closer," he commanded, and he scanned her barcode with a device that sent the data to his computer tablet. After confirming all of her information, he continued the interrogation.

"What is your dissenter number?" he questioned Rafe after he hadn't spoken quickly enough.

Rafe woke up out of a trance, turned over his left arm for him to scan, and recited, "39813." He then pulled out the letter for the guard to see. "Here is our indoctrination letter."

It was at that point that he wondered whether or not they had erased what they had written on the back of the letter. Rafe looked over at Bri, and he knew that the next thing they would share would be a bullet. *At least we'll be together*, he thought.

The officer took the letter and barked, "Dissenter, step out of the truck and come with me." Rafe left the vehicle, and just before he was forced around a corner, the couple took one last look at each other. The end was near.

"Forward," the brownsuit demanded in a rough, inhuman tone.

Rafe walked several yards past the checkpoint building with a pistol right at his back. The brownsuit stopped, looked around for a second, and ordered, "On one knee, now!"

The officer took off his dark glasses and inspected his prisoner with fierce, sharklike eyes, devoid of life. Rafe wore the required attire as a dissenter: a white T-shirt, white pants, and a black dissenter band around his right upper arm. He had always wondered why men wore white in public.

Rafe awaited his fate with his head down, and the brownsuit pistol-whipped his face so hard that blood dripped down his shirt. Now he knew the reason.

"Repeat after me: Christ is my savior; He is my king!"

Rafe wiped his bloody mouth and closed his eyes. "Christ is my savior." Tears welled up as he tried to make sense of what they were experiencing. He wondered if Bri was receiving the same treatment (or worse) and why God allowed their suffering to occur. "He is my king."

With his eyes still closed, he thought about the Lord. A sudden pain surged from his stomach as he realized that he had been kicked in the gut and slapped again with the pistol.

As Rafe fell to the ground, he focused on the Lord's face. He could see a comforting smile behind an ancient beard and the Lord's arms outstretched toward him. The hands and wrists had been pierced, and the wounds were healed over.

He couldn't see His eyes, but he could feel an overwhelming love that was so indescribable that he felt it throughout his whole body. The Lord's arms were wrapped around him as he closed his eyes. When he finally reached the ground, it didn't hurt as much as he thought it would, and he dreamed.

RAFE OPENED THE DOOR TO THE OFFICE, and he noticed an empty seat by Bri. It seemed like all the managers from the whole station had been able to find room in the cramped space, and they were now all staring at him.

"Sorry. I was editing a last-minute package for the 6 PM news," he admitted.

Mr. Porter, the general manager, sat behind his desk and motioned for him to sit next to Bri. He was a small man with a full head of white hair, pleasant and friendly. "Thank you, everybody, for coming. We have a lot to talk about."

Everyone in the office seemed restless and fidgety. Bri bit her bottom lip as she sometimes did when she knew something was wrong, and Rafe caught himself thinking about the video he had just edited.

"Ms. Gilchrist, the story that you reported on a couple of weeks ago has had a lot of us worried. I know the two of you went through some horrible things over there, and I'm glad that you are both okay," Mr. Porter began.

Bri bit her lip a little harder, and Rafe noticed that she was playing with one of the rings on her hand. "Is there something wrong?" she asked.

"You did a fine job reporting the mass shootings," Mr. Porter continued, "and we were all shaken when you were hit on the side of your head, on-air. We were all so scared for the both of you."

Another manager, Mrs. Collins, decided to chime in. "Yes, we wanted to send you more help, but as you know, our two other reporters were covering the hurricane damage here. It seemed like everything was hitting us at once."

"But you both did well," Mr. Porter praised with a gleam in his eye, "and the national outpouring of support for what you went through and all those who were affected in Sodium is phenomenal. It was a horrible, horrible catastrophe that happened, and we all hope everyone in the town heals from it."

Mr. Porter stood up and walked toward Bri and Rafe, who were sitting next to the open door. He then closed the blinds to the office so that no one from the studio could see through the glass walls and shut the door. "Unfortunately, the video you showed of the chapel has also gained some attention."

Rafe and Bri looked at each other as Mr. Porter continued, "As you know, many people have been hesitant to believe what you showed, and the station has received many different threats. A couple of days ago, we all know that Jared was punched outside while giving a forecast. And the chapel that you shot has not been found, according to the FBI."

Bri opened her mouth as if she were about to debate him but didn't.

"I believe you. I do," the manager sympathized and pointed at his exterior window. "But the people out there are furious." He then sat down as if hope had been sucked out of him.

"This morning," he continued while picking up an envelope from his desk, "we received a letter from the Secretary of State, Mr. Kerioth. I'm not going to read it to you as it's lengthy, but he says that the *'allegations you have asserted are atrociously false.'* He is currently seeking legal retribution against the station."

Bri couldn't contain herself anymore. "But he was there!"

"I know he was. I honestly believe you, but I think we should have broken the story differently. We should have brought in legal counsel before going forward with the story," Mr. Porter said, trying to console her.

Mrs. Collins then commented, "I think that this story is bigger than all of us. If the White House is linked to these mass murders, as you've said Bri, and that there are more training chapels that we don't know about

—this could be our modern Watergate. The problem is that we just don't have enough proof."

Rafe looked at the floor and finally decided to speak. "Captain Merlot said the judge waited a few days before he issued the search warrant. It was enough time to bulldoze the chapel to the ground, and Charlie was forced into early retirement. They also ransacked our apartments. I don't know who it was or what they would have found. The video had already been posted online."

Mr. Porter paced in the middle of the small office and declared, "Bri and Rafe, I need you to take some time off. We're in way over our heads here, and I don't know if the White House will allow our small station to survive. I bet our FCC license is next."

Rafe continued to look at the ground and remarked, "David and Goliath."

"Yes," Mr. Porter responded, "David and Goliath. We're not going to win, though."

RAFE AWOKE TO RAIN SPLASHING ON HIS FACE and the brownsuit shaking him. The side of his head and bloody mouth hurt like a divorce, and the guard jolted him to his feet. Of course, he had never been divorced, but he felt that it was the most painful ache he could fathom.

He inched toward the truck and fell into the cab. Bri couldn't take the horror anymore and sobbed uncontrollably.

Another brownsuit left the checkpoint station building with a wide black marker and drew a massive, black Sodium symbol across the whole front hood of the truck.

Rafe turned on the engine and prayed, "Father, forgive them. They know not what they do." His soaked shirt and pants had blood smears, and Bri took a nearby cloth to dab his mouth.

"Let me drive," Bri offered, shaking, but the metal boom lifted, and a brownsuit slapped the back of the truck for them to leave.

For the first time in several years, they had received permission to leave their small town of Gulf Haven. The Sodium symbol on the hood was upside down to them, and despite the association with death that it had, the lower half looked like a compass pointing south. That was their destination and fate.

Chapter 25
Big Brother

After some time, Rafe looked at his rearview mirror and noticed that they were alone on the freeway to Fort Caine for as far as he could see. He glanced over at Bri, who was sleeping, and gently said, "Bri, wake up. I need you to be awake." It wasn't until he took her hand that she opened her eyes.

"Are you okay?" she asked.

"Yeah. Hold on."

"Why? What's wrong?"

Without a second thought, he jerked at the steering wheel and drove off the freeway and into the adjoining grassy field. There was a small ditch full of rainwater, and as they traversed it, they were both jolted about in the cab.

"What are you doing?" she screamed in a panic. She was definitely awake now.

"Don't worry!" He slowed down and drove the truck into a thicket of brown brush and dying trees as far as he could go. The backend cleared the line of brush, and the truck was no longer visible from the freeway.

They both opened their doors, and she pleaded, "What's going on?"

"We don't have much time. The truck is networked and bugged," he explained as he retrieved two frame backpacks that were hidden in the back of the truck. "We need to get away as fast as we can. I figure we have about 30 minutes before a search party gets here."

With all the force he could muster, he yanked at his phylactery, and the plastic string broke on his neck. He clenched it so hard that it probably would have stopped functioning if he hadn't hurled it into the woods toward the south.

"Don't forget to remove that thing," he advised her, pointing to her phylactery. "We don't want them to know where we are."

BRI OBLIGED, STILL UNSURE ABOUT WHAT WAS HAPPENING, and she placed the Big Brother device and her ankle bracelet in the cab of the truck. It didn't matter where they fell—a swarm of SA officers would soon comb the whole area.

Discarding the last of her shackles was liberating. The necklace had been an unwelcome part of her body for so long, silencing her voice, and now she could finally speak without any restraint.

For the past two weeks, she had mentally prepared herself to investigate and report on the corruption of the new Loyalist Party and the indoctrination process at Fort Caine.

After McKendrick's third inauguration and the stripping away of their citizenship, it was impossible to rip the propaganda curtain. More than anything, she wanted to know the truth about what had happened to the country since the fall of 2020 and how to correct its course if she could. For her, honest journalism was exhilarating again.

"I don't understand. What are we doing?" she asked, her plans now shattered.

Rafe, now several yards away, looked back at her and calmly invited, "Come on. This is the only way."

There was something in how he outstretched his hand and pleaded with her that made him seem like the only other human for miles. Still confused, she took his hand, and they left all their belongings except what they were carrying on their backs. She glanced one last time at the truck, wondering if anything of value was left behind, but she felt a certain peace that everything would be okay.

After quickly walking for a few minutes, he confided, "I'm sorry. I just can't subject you to any more of this that we're going through. We can't go south. The only way that our life will be normal again is if we go north."

"But I thought we were going to infiltrate Fort Caine and expose everything," she immediately returned. "I thought we were going to report on whatever the indoctrination is and try to get someone to help us."

"I know, I know. I wanted to do that too, but I figured since they monitored our computers back home, they probably do the same to everyone—not just the dissenters.

"There have been so many times that my clients' video files have been deleted from my computer remotely by whoever monitors me because they were deemed to be outside of their propaganda code. So, even if we shot some incriminating video, we couldn't get it out to anyone —even if we were in Fort Caine."

Bri followed his lead through the trees and small brush, wondering what was in their backpacks and slowly realizing the logistics of this new path they were taking.

It was getting dark, and there was a little rain. All she could see of him was the backpack he was carrying, and she wanted to know what he was thinking. This had been a significant decision in their lives, and she needed to talk it out. "So, we're just running away?"

He stopped and calmly turned around. "No, I think we should go to Canada. We can show them what we have, and hopefully, they can do something to end all this. I mean—we don't even know how much of the country is affected by this administration. All we get is state-run propaganda."

"Canada? That's 2,000 miles away! You want to hike *all* the way to Canada?" she protested as she sat on a nearby log.

"Yeah. Since every vehicle is required to have dissenter scanners, we'll have to walk, unfortunately," he replied while catching his breath. "Someone once told me that even trains have scanners. I got a letter from Charlie a year ago, and he's a poultry farmer in Ottawa. We could probably live with him for a while as refugees."

"How did you get a letter from him? They open everything."

"I don't know exactly. They probably figured it was harmless, or they weren't paying attention."

They started hiking again, and she took his hand. "Do we have anything to show anybody?" she asked.

"Yeah. I've recorded a few things over the years: people being shot in the street, the electricity going out at curfew, files being deleted by whoever monitors me, propaganda videos that are streamed every morning. It's all on a video card in your backpack, and I never transferred it to a computer."

"I wonder if anyone else has *escaped* America," she commented, finally coming to grips with what was happening.

"I don't know."

The sun lowered, and it was getting harder to see through the trees. She stopped him, gave him a kiss, and whispered, "Thank you."

RIGHT THEN, RAFE'S PHONE RANG, and it automatically answered because they were dissenters. They both looked at each other in horror as a voice

150

could be heard on the other end. Their location had just been compromised.

"Hello? Hello?" Rafe's mother called out from the phone. He put it on speakerphone because he didn't want to be close to her in any way.

"Hey, Mom," he answered at last.

"So, I see that your truck isn't at your apartment," she started.

Not knowing what else to say, Rafe responded, "Yes, we're on a hike."

"They let you do that?" his mother returned with undue scrutiny.

They both looked at the inanimate object in his hand, and all Rafe could do was shake his head—his mother had truly considered them lost. They couldn't submit to a government ruled by racism, so they were branded as outcasts.

"We needed some fresh air," Bri interjected.

Rafe was grateful she said something, as he would've later regretted what was on the tip of his tongue.

"Well, I suppose it's good for the baby," his mother stated coldly. After a few seconds without a response, she continued, "You know, dears, if you don't want your baby, I can look after her. I can give her a good life."

Rafe put the phone to his ear, fuming. He closed his eyes, took a deep breath, and calmly said, "No, Mom. *We're* going to raise our child. We may be dissenters to your racist government, but we know how to teach *love thy neighbor as thyself.*" He pulled the phone away and stared at it. The first love of his life was in his hand, and he didn't know how to help her.

Because she was no longer on speakerphone, his mother's rebuttal could be heard faintly. "But they're not our neighbors. They're from a different country."

Rafe turned off the power and threw the phone as hard as he could into the dark thicket of trees behind them. It was the hardest thing he had ever done. "Goodbye, Mom," he mouthed and started to cry as they hurried away.

Chapter 26

Paths of Redemption

Mr. Kerioth sat behind his ornate cherrywood desk with a wall of unread books behind him. The gold and crimson curtains kept the stormy weather outside, and the only light in the office came from a green desk lamp by his laptop computer.

He opened his politician mouth and spoke, "Mr. Davidson and Ms. Gilchrist, come in. Or should I address you as the future Mr. and Mrs. Davidson? Congratulations are in order. Come, sit down." He motioned Rafe and Bri, standing at the entryway, to the two very ornate chairs in front of his desk, and they obliged. "What may I do for you?"

Bri leaped inside the office in front of Rafe, approaching her nightmare head-on, and said, "Thank you, Mr. Kerioth, for seeing us."

"It is my pleasure," the official returned. "You're not recording me, are you?"

Rafe refused to sit in a chair and blurted, "No, they took our phones and everything else we had. Right now, it's just our word against yours!" He was already picking a fight.

"No need to be salty, Mr. Davidson. We'll just converse like human beings. Why invite the whole nation into our little colloquy?" All three of them sat down, and the court was in session.

"Mr. Kerioth," Bri started, "why have you done this to us? Why did the FCC revoke our station's broadcast license?"

Kerioth jabbed a double-edged smile, both welcoming and evil. He nodded at Rafe and answered her, "Well, as your fiancé so eloquently stated, it is your word against mine. I will be as forthcoming as I can because this present quarrel we're having may end in a wholesome meeting of the minds and with your subservience to the cause."

Rafe couldn't take it any longer and asked him, point-blank, "Can I just punch you now?"

"Mr. Davidson, violence has its place, and I admire that about you." The devil's voice was charming and soothing, like a sweet poison. Rafe tried to look past the salesman antics as if he were being offered fruit from the tree of knowledge of good and evil—he wasn't buying whatever it was.

"Unfortunately, my good sir," Kerioth continued, "*you* were the one who asked your lovely fiancée to proceed with the report at the funeral, even though there was a turbulent protest right outside of the church. *You* delivered her to the mob—"

"How did you know that?" Rafe returned, confused.

Kerioth explained, "Although your hearts bled for those little victims, the exact reason for your persistence was for the story and your selfish greed. You both were making less than a dollar over minimum wage at the time, and you happened upon a little town that we had been grooming. Eventually, you entered our sanctuary—illegally, I might add—and this was your moment to seize."

"If you're so open about it, why did you have it torn down?" Rafe demanded.

Kerioth stood up with a sinister grin. "Do you still think this is about a couple of kids shooting their black and brown classmates? Do you think this is about *racism* exploiting every branch of state and federal government—that we just want to *hurt* people of color? I hoped you could see beyond that. You're both of European origin, educated, and Christian, I believe. Am I mistaken?"

They refused to answer.

"What happened to Sodom and Gomorrah, Jericho, Jerusalem, and countless other cities in the Holy scriptures? They were all destroyed, pillaged, and trampled under the foot of God for their disobedience—for their love of sin," the deathly-skinny man preached behind his grand desk.

Kerioth took to pacing around the office, encircling Rafe and Bri with his doctrine. "Whenever a nation sinned, God would have another nation rise and destroy it. When the world became corrupt, God baptized the earth with a flood and saved only a few. What is preventing another flood? What is preventing God from taking vengeance upon all of us?"

Bri answered, "A rainbow."

"Yes, but there are still wars," he countered. "There are nations destroying nations around the world, and it is all because of sin."

The Secretary of State walked across the McKendrick seal in the middle of his office and stated his proposal. "Mr. Davidson and Ms. Gilchrist, what we are trying to do here is create a whole nation of God-fearing saints. If our nation has its eye single to the glory of God and is obedient to Him, then He will not destroy us."

Rafe stood up in defiance and blasted, "Are you trying to tell me that you want to kill anyone that is not a white Christian and who doesn't believe in whatever twisted gospel you've come up with?"

"Mr. Davidson, my brother," Kerioth coaxed in persuasive subtlety, "this is how the Lord performs His heavenly work. He destroys the wicked, both individually and, at times, whole nations. If we don't root out the wicked, then we will also be engulfed in His anger. Do you want that to happen?"

"No, but He loves all of us. He wouldn't do that!" Rafe declared with simple and immoveable conviction as if he knew the Lord personally.

Bri looked at the physically ill man, who was now on the other side of the office, standing in a shadow. "Why would God destroy someone who doesn't believe in Him when He has given everyone the right to choose how they believe? What if they have never heard of Him?"

"Exodus, Ms. Gilchrist. *Thou shalt have no other gods before me.* Whenever the Israelites prayed to a foreign deity, they were destroyed. Those who never hear of the Lord will be destroyed, and only His chosen will be saved."

"And who are His chosen?" Bri inquired.

"You are, your fiancé is, and I am of the chosen. We need to root out all the atrocities across the country that have angered the Lord, especially dark-skinned people."

As soon as the blaspheming filth left the devil's mouth, Rafe punched him, and he flew several feet into the air as if Sampson had hit him. "I'm done here. It's my word against his," Rafe huffed, and he walked in a rage toward the door.

"Wait!" Bri called out to Rafe. "Why would God want to destroy anyone who has dark skin?" she sincerely asked the Secretary of State.

Kerioth wiped his mouth as blood dripped onto the McKendrick seal, and he exclaimed, "Dark skin is the curse of God for the sins their ancestors committed, and they should all be taken away from this land. All sin, all filth, and anyone who commits crimes against God will be expunged from this country, and we will have a heaven on earth. The streets will be lined with gold, and the lion will lie down with the lamb."

Bri stood up, calmly walked over to Kerioth, and bent over him in much the same way that he hovered over her in the white church eight months before. "That is exactly what Satan wanted when we had our War in Heaven," she informed. "He planned to force everyone to obey all the commandments of God so that no soul was lost, stripping away our right to choose and learn for ourselves. He wanted to take Christ's place as the savior. *Repentance* is the only path to heaven."

Kerioth looked up and curiously asked, "Where did you hear that?"

"Why cast pearls before swine?" she quipped with a smile and walked toward Rafe at the door.

The fallen man on the floor turned around to face his leaving guests and barked like a madman, "There is nothing you can do. No one will believe you. *14813: We must secure the existence of our people and a future for white children—Heil, McKendrick.* The tracks are laid for the Lord's plan, and this nation will be cleansed from all of its filth. Laws are being enacted, judges are being persuaded, and this government is bending to the will of the one true God."

Rafe and Bri left the office, and as the door was about to close, Kerioth gave one more hiss. "And so should you!"

THE SUN BEAMED THROUGH THE THIN PLASTIC TENT, and there was a peaceful calm. Rafe opened his eyes to the sound of movement close by, and he slowly unzipped part of the tent window.

Several yards away, a deer grazed on the grass. There was no wind, and it seemed like the only movement for miles were the deer's light footsteps and its mouth partaking of the goodness of the earth.

The deer paused and turned his head to look right at Rafe, who was now transfixed with the animal. Rafe didn't know how to respond to the inspection. He thought about how they needed more food for their trek, but the only weapon he had that had not been seized was a slingshot. Unfortunately, the weak weapon would be futile against a deer. It would

157

probably just run off and die a couple of miles away without leaving a trace of blood.

And yet, the animal continued to stare at Rafe as if he were trying to communicate with him. The deer's eyes seemed so close that they transcended any division of man and animal, and as soon as Rafe reached over to wake Bri, the magnificent form had fled into the trees. For a moment, he felt inclined to follow him, as if he wanted more of what they had briefly shared.

Chapter 27

Lost Freedoms

(Day Four)

When Bri left their small tent in the morning, she gave Rafe an exhausted smile as he made breakfast on a tiny camp stove; unfortunately, a fire would give away their location. They only had the bare essentials: several sets of clothes, a few pairs of shoes, keepsakes, tools, an old FM radio, and a food supply to last them a couple of weeks.

So far, the plan was to hike about 15 miles a day for four months to reach Canada before winter. It was ambitious, but their situation was dire —they had to leave the dying country.

"How are you feeling?" Rafe asked.

She walked slowly around the campsite and admitted, "Well, it's not the best time for me to be doing this. We should have done it last year or something."

"You're right. I'm sorry I'm having you hike so much every day. There are so many things I wish were different."

Sitting on a log to rest, she could tell that he was blaming himself for everything again. "Me, too," she lamented, and she pulled on her hiking boots—her feet already ached.

"Is there anything else we could have done?" he asked sincerely.

"What do you mean?"

He stopped cooking for a second. "Could we have stopped all this from happening?"

"No," Bri answered as she studied his crestfallen demeanor. She hated to see him this way, and her heart went out toward him. "I think a lot of things were already in motion way before we went to Sodium. McKendrick was already above the law by then. His whole party in Congress feared his voter base, so they were in lockstep to whatever he did. The Department of Justice had already started going after his opponents and whistleblowers. No, the country was already headed this way."

Rafe handed her a bowl of oatmeal and commented, "Yeah, but some of that we didn't know yet. It was so hard to sort through all the misinformation."

"And of course, there was August 13th," she added with a sigh.

"Yeah, it seems like it was yesterday."

A flood of memories came back to her, and she recounted, "I was shopping for a new suit for my job interview, and I looked down at my phone. McKendrick had posted that video of the newspaper building on fire and commented, 'Let it burn! Let them all burn!' I can't believe he said that."

Rafe quickly summarized, "Yep, he didn't like the truth, and he knew his voter base would take the message and run with it."

For whatever reason, a small-town newspaper building accidentally caught fire at night, and it only made national headlines when McKendrick came across it a few days later, on that day of infamy. Over the next few weeks, news-media buildings across the nation were ravaged and set ablaze. One pundit even compared it to Nazi book-burning.

Arsonists all over the country were soon incarcerated, and even though they didn't commit federal crimes, McKendrick pardoned them without any oversight or retribution. The American dictator had been enabled by those unwilling to put the country before job security and wealth. There was no legal recourse. The Republic could no longer be kept.

The other political party, which was in the minority, tried to impeach the president many times, but it was all in vain. He was a bull in a china shop, and his party loved him for it. They loved to see the other party suffer more than anything.

Bri looked down at her bowl and couldn't eat. "Freedom of the press—gone."

Rafe turned on the battery-powered FM radio as he sat next to her on the log. She never liked the morning ritual of listening to it, but they did find value in it from time to time.

"Mornin', y'all," the radio announcer shouted. "This is KKKD Radio, Kicked Country! And let me put it to y'all out there—what are we going to do with all this rain? I keep looking over my fence to see if any of my neighbors are building arks, and the closest I've come is a doghouse for a pit bull.

"Hurricane season is getting longer and longer every year, and my friends up north keep asking me why I don't just leave. Do ya know what I tell 'em? I say I've got Texas in my blood, and there ain't no way that they're gonna make me leave God's country! It's beautiful out there today, folks!"

By then, Rafe and Bri had started to take down their tent and put everything in their packs, which were getting lighter day by day. They were burning through their food at an alarming rate.

After counting the remainder of their supply, Rafe humbly advised, "We should probably ration our food a little better."

"You know I'm eating for two, right?" They both chuckled and continued working as they exchanged a few smiles.

The announcer broke the moment. "Well, I've just received something across my desk that I need to let y'all in on. Apparently, we need to stay vigilant about dissenters flyin' the coop. If you see one of those people, call the authorities at the dissenter hotline. Y'all know the number. It's easy to remember, 666-8130."

He sang, *If you see the devil, McKendrick will wrestle!*"

Rafe and Bri looked at each other, and they were not amused at the jingle; they were more afraid of being found and beaten. They had done something illegal, and there was no telling what would happen.

"Y'all know how to spot them, right? They are the very definition of a wolf in sheep's clothing, or how I like to call them: *WISOs* or *Whites in Skin Only*. They are usually doing drugs, living with Mexicans, and having more Mexican babies. It's disgusting and gross!

"They don't obey any laws, and all they want to do is break into your homes and steal all of your things for drug money. They're all Satan-worshipers—those dissenters. We need to kick them out of God's country! I don't even know why we have dissenter cities. All they do is waste our taxes, live on welfare, and take drugs all day long.

"So, if you see one, if you see the whites of the devil's eyes, call that number! Y'all know what I would do, though, if I saw one. I don't need to call a number! This is Ol' Chicky with KKKD, Kicked Country! Have a wonderful and blessed day, folks!"

Rafe finally walked by the radio, turned it off, and put it in his pack.

"Ol' Chicky has problems," Bri remarked. It was worth it to see her husband chuckle.

Chapter 28

The Red Band

(Day 13)

B efore entering the convenience store, Rafe had written on his hand everything they needed after two weeks of hiking. Unfortunately, because it was a sweltering, humid day, most of it smeared, and he searched the shelves for a notepad first. Of all things, he couldn't believe that he had forgotten paper.

This was also the first time he had entered a non-dissenter establishment in several years, so he didn't know what to expect. For that reason, Bri stayed with the gear in a patch of woods behind the store. He didn't want anything else to happen to her.

He felt out of place wearing his *home clothes*, a pair of jeans and a polo shirt, in public. Without the black dissenter band on his arm, though, he felt naked. He had been conditioned to wear it anytime he was around other people, and that scared him.

Going down each aisle methodically, he grabbed almost everything without thinking twice. The experience was liberating, and he thought of himself as a character in a video game gathering supplies at a market square before departing on a very humid journey. He was almost expecting to run into a wise sage to give him advice before his quest began.

The convenience-store attendant was significantly overweight, smelly, and he used a wheelchair. When Rafe approached the counter with three full baskets, the man looked at him as if he were being robbed and that it would take months to restock the shelves.

The attendant violently dumped out the first basket on the counter, and several items slid off onto the floor, including a few that landed next to his wheelchair.

"Here, I can get it for you." Rafe offered.

"No, I got it!" exclaimed the repulsive man as he reached for the items in vain. He moved his wheelchair and accidentally rolled over a pack of health bars, ruining them. "Stupid wheelchair!"

Rafe walked around the counter and said, "Here, let me help."

"I don't need your help!" the attendant scolded. "Get away from me!"

"Sorry, I don't mean any harm," Rafe assured, backing away with his hands up. He almost thought about returning the items and leaving the store if it would help the attendant in one way or another.

"Look here, you! I've been in this wheelchair for six years! God put me in it, and no one on earth is going to help me out! So, just get yourself back over there, and I'll ring you up."

Rafe thought about asking him what happened all those years ago, but he figured he wasn't much for conversation and that he probably didn't even want his business.

The man scanned each item with a painful grimace and heavy breathing. He wore a white tank top and a curious red band on his right bicep that had long been overstretched. Rafe had never seen a red band before and wondered if it was required just as much as the dissenter bands were.

For a moment, he sympathized with him, watching his every move and the way his long, tangled hair got in the way of his work. *What kind of life does he live?* Rafe pondered. *What are they even called, the people that aren't dissenters? What kind of restrictions do they have?*

"That'll be $208.99," the attendant finally said with a long exhale.

Rafe had been withdrawing cash over the years, a little at a time, so that it wouldn't cause any alarm. Not knowing how much of their lives was monitored, he wanted nothing more than to just be another cog in the machine. He worked, paid his taxes, and followed all the rules, fearing that a brownsuit might storm through his front door and shoot them both for not following a new law just passed the day before.

They had kept their heads low and succumbed to surviving for so long, and this escape into the wild had brought a breath of new life for them. He wondered if they would make it; nothing was certain.

Rafe pulled out the cash, laid it right in front of the attendant, and picked up his several bags of groceries. "Have a good day, sir." A thunderclap roared in the distance.

"Heil McKendrick," the attendant returned.

Rafe was immobile at first, trying to calculate whether he should repeat the phrase, thereby communicating his allegiance to the United States dictator. Bri wasn't there to cry foul if he had given in to the immoral gesture. It would ensure his safety, though. *They're just words, right?*

He then thought about all the slaughtered children, the chapel full of mourners, and the black men who were shot in front of his apartment almost every day. These were all carried out by people that supported McKendrick and his ideals.

Instead of repeating back the filth, Rafe whispered, "Father—"

The attendant quickly rolled his wheelchair to another part of the counter as Rafe backed up, and then he pulled out a rifle. Without much

165

warning, the attendant took aim and uttered, "Christ is my savior and my king. All dissenters are devils!"

Rafe almost fell as he turned around and fled as fast as he could. He thought about running into the woods toward Bri, but he figured it would be too far. He even imagined a gunshot in his lower back if he tried.

Fortunately, a car was pulling away from one of the convenience-store gas pumps just as Rafe exited the building, and he ran around the corner, behind the store. When the attendant finally rolled out into the rain, he shot at the car a few times, causing it to swerve, but it kept driving.

Rafe watched the sick man roll slowly back into the store with excruciating pain from each movement. Even though he was far away, Rafe could hear him cursing the Lord.

Now kneeling by a dumpster under a roof overhang, he put down the bags of groceries to check them over, hoping that they hadn't ripped, and he noticed an old, muddy cloth by one of the wheels. It was a red band, like the one the attendant wore.

Ants curiously surrounded the dirty rag, and he thought about how wearing it might help him the next time he needed to be in public. He didn't have to say anything; he could pretend to be deaf. Somehow, he couldn't bring himself to utter those words. "I just can't say it. *It is that which cometh out of the mouth that defileth a man*," he whispered to himself.

He thought about Rahab, the harlot of Jericho, and how she was justified in hiding the two Israelite spies. She knew that the Lord would eventually destroy her city, and yet she helped them. By telling the guards they had escaped when they were actually on her roof, Rafe felt that deceiving everyone around him by wearing a red cloth was for the greater good. They had to get to Canada.

He quickly snatched the rag and ran into the woods.

Chapter 29

God of This World

(Night 42)

There was a horrible wind outside their dome tent, and as Rafe looked up at the ceiling with his flashlight, he wondered if the poles would break. The rain pelted the nylon walls as if it came from a machine gun, and the trees violently creaked and moaned.

When Bri rolled over onto her side in her sleep, a broken branch brushed the tent with an unsettling swipe, and it startled her. "What was that?"

"Just a little branch. It's okay, don't worry," Rafe consoled.

"When did it start raining?"

Rafe glanced at his watch and responded, "A couple of hours ago. I think it may be Hurricane Dawn."

"They said on the radio that it wouldn't make it this far north. We're too far away," she insisted with fear in her eyes.

Although he had been through many hurricanes in his life, this was the first time he was scared. The thin tent walls offered no protection against the onslaught of such a storm; there was nowhere to hide. They were like deer in an open field.

In an effort to comfort her, he remembered how his mother held him in her closet during that hurricane when he was a boy and how she hummed to him. As the memory came flooding back, he thought about how his mother had shown her love for him throughout his whole life. She had eased his pain in every scrape and heartache, encouraged him when he was depressed, and cheered him on through his challenges.

And yet, she said such horrible things. *How could a loving person also be so offensive?* he thought to himself. *Maybe she doesn't realize the hurt she can cause. Or perhaps, she's caught up in the racist fear and lies that framed her childhood.*

Could she be justified by claiming herself as a product of her culture? In the end, how would the Lord judge her? What would be her eternal fate? The tent shook, and he thought about her soul.

Unfortunately, he couldn't take back what he said to her before violently throwing the phone into the woods. From his youth, he had wanted to say something, but he could never find the courage to do so; he couldn't disrespect her. Even when his friends from school came over, she had to dehumanize them with racial slurs. It was a part of her DNA, and sometimes, he loathingly found traces in himself.

After reprimanding her in such a way, though, he was heartbroken, and she was probably hurting just the same.

Bri continued to watch the tent walls as they shook ferociously, and Rafe tried to remember the tune his mother hummed to him that night. It provided an overwhelming peace and solace, and he wanted to share it, but the song eluded him.

"I'm sorry to put you through this," he lamented, trying to talk over the horrific noise that was picking up. By now, the storm sounded like a jet engine flying over them. "We probably should have stayed at home. Maybe we should have waited until the spring."

"What do we do?" she cried.

He focused on her trembling hands and the tears that were flowing. "Here, come closer." They wrapped the sleeping bags around themselves and held each other as tight as possible while sitting up.

"Father in Heaven," he prayed, "We thank Thee for watching over us, for helping us with what we're going through. If it is Thy will, please see us through this night. In the name of Jesus Christ, Amen."

The tent continued to shake, and Rafe turned out the flashlight. He could still hear her crying in the dark, and as he rocked her to sleep, he thought about his mother and how she might be handling the storm.

WHEN THE MORNING LIGHT FINALLY CAME THROUGH THE TENT WALLS, Rafe looked around the tent for any damage and chuckled to himself that they had both fallen asleep sitting up, huddling each other.

After he laid Bri back down, he left the tent and noticed that they had been marooned. Unknowingly, they had selected the only small hill in the area to put up their tent, and they were now surrounded by stagnant water about a foot deep.

The hurricane had ripped out several weak trees from the ground overnight, and fallen branches were scattered everywhere. The sun was shining bright, and because the days were getting shorter, Rafe knew that they needed to leave soon.

Instead of cooking breakfast, they opted to eat a few health bars, and they quickly packed the tent and their backpacks. The schedule of sleeping, eating, and walking was now routine. Even though their bodies continually ached, they knew they had to keep going.

Unfortunately, Rafe hadn't thought about trudging through a marsh and getting their shoes and clothes wet. "If only we had some waders and boots," he grumbled.

Bri put on her backpack and replied, "Well, we couldn't carry everything for every kind of situation. Who knew we were going to hike right through a hurricane?"

He pulled out his lensatic compass to orient himself. "Yep, she did a real number. Remind me not to do this again."

Off in the far distance to the east, Bri spotted a buck drinking some water. "Hey, there's a deer over there, and it looks like he's standing on land. Do you think we can make it over there?"

"Yeah, I guess so. Hopefully, it's completely dry."

As soon as they stepped into the water, the deer looked up and ran off into the woods. For the first time in his life, Rafe didn't feel any urge to shoot it—he simply enjoyed watching the beautiful creature move beyond his sight.

He thought about how the water would undoubtedly slow them down that morning, and he studied the sky to gauge the amount of hiking time they had left for the day. They probably wouldn't make their goal of 15 miles again, and he realized that there was an increasing coefficient of friction to their hike. With the constant barrage of changing weather, its aftermath, and their growing daily fatigue, they were hiking slower and slower.

It was right then, while he was lost in calculating a mathematical formula for picking up speed, that Bri noticed a snake swimming with its head just above the water, right toward her.

"Rafe! There's a snake—"

Before she could even finish, the sinister beast tried to strike her. And without thinking, she raised her foot and came down hard on its head.

"What happened?" Rafe asked, finally turning around to see the commotion.

She moved quickly away from where she splashed down and exclaimed, "I think I killed it!" She urged Rafe to move with her away from the battlefield. "I don't see it! Do you see it?"

"No, are you okay?" He fumbled over his words in a panic. Their lives were seemingly in nature's crosshairs.

"Let's get out of the water!" she exclaimed. They ran as fast as they could in the marsh toward where the deer was standing before, splashing and making enough noise for all the wildlife in the vicinity to leave them alone.

Chapter 30

Price of Happiness

(Day 68)

It seemed that there were always uncertainties around every corner of their fugitive life. So far, Rafe's red band allowed him to go unnoticed as a dissenter, and he wore long sleeves to hide the tattooed number and barcode on his arm. As the designated shopper between the two of them, he had no idea what he was doing half the time.

Bri wasn't the same after the snake incident. She had been able to deal with so many different human atrocities in the past several years that Rafe marveled at her strength. But now, it seemed like nature was after them as well, as if they were in the middle of an unseen war. Every time she walked around camp, she looked under objects for snakes and other creatures.

Her shoes were her primary concern, though. Before she put them on, she would tap the heel against the ground to see if a snake had curled up inside overnight and was now waiting to strike. But it really boiled down to the fact that they were getting tighter, so Rafe needed to purchase a new pair.

And so, as he approached the women's shoe section of the department store, he reached into his pocket and pulled out a paper cutout of his wife's current shoe sole that he had traced. In the back of his mind, though, he knew he would probably pick out the wrong shoe size, if not the wrong style and color also.

"It really doesn't matter," she told him as he had brought up his concern one evening. "Unfortunately, I'm the one who has to break them in by walking in circles around camp every night."

He smiled as he remembered the joke he had made about breaking in the small shoes for her by putting them on his hands. It was a stupid joke, but she chuckled, and that's what mattered.

A pair of hiking boots seemed to be close to the paper cutout, so he took them and a pair of the next size up to account for her growing feet. *Hopefully, she'll be okay.*

As part of the department store's marketing strategy for selling more products, massive screens were affixed to the ceiling throughout the building. They each played a looping video of an idealized, oversaturated depiction of nature against a backdrop of elevator music.

It was as if the editor couldn't remember how beautiful the grass used to be or how blue the sky was only a handful of years beforehand. The whole experience was nauseating.

Suddenly, a commercial interrupted the video, and because it had been several months since Rafe created one, he found himself curious to find out the current trend.

Unfortunately, it was the same flashy, quick-paced video montage that screamed, *"You need to buy this shirt because I'm sexy, and you're not."* It was an assault on the eyes and devoid of any human connection.

Rafe then shook his head and returned to the impossible task of shopping for his wife.

174

"Hello, my brothers and sisters." The familiar voice of President McKendrick then seeped from the speakers throughout the store like poison. His face filled the screens, and he looked straight ahead as if he were wanting to lock eyes with everyone watching and preach a sermon.

"Salomé Spirit wants you to know that I find a woman who wears their beauty products and fragrances very attractive," the president enchanted with his fake Southern accent. "She speaks to me in a way that goes beyond words. Our eyes meet, and I can see her Salomé Spirit."

In the commercial, McKendrick's morbidly obese face floated above a brown skyline as if he were a god, and he looked down at the ocean beneath him. On the surface of the water, some distance from the shore, all 18 bottles of Salomé Spirit products defied the oncoming waves, and the logo and seductive merchandise names eventually filled the screen.

A woman with long, flowing hair then ambled along the shore only to discover the alluring treasure floating on the surface, and she dove into the water toward it.

Rafe hoped he would never see President McKendrick again and wondered how he would stoop so low as to do cheesy commercials. Then again, the nation and the government were treading in abnormal waters. Anything was possible.

As he looked around the department store, he noticed that everyone had crossed their heart with their right hand. They all habitually took part in this weird allegiance toward him brought on by just hearing his voice. No one looked at the screens, though; they just kept shopping or performing their jobs while complying with this odd Pavlov-dog protocol.

Rafe reluctantly crossed his heart and repackaged the hiking boots in the box as best he could. No one paid attention, though. It was hard to find a smile, an emotion, or any kind of humanity in anyone's face.

One striking oddity he found to be almost unavoidable was that most non-dissenter women wore an excruciating amount of facial makeup. Perhaps, the practice hid everyone's ghostly complexion, but it rendered them to appear like seductive corpses.

"If you're a small-business owner and need a little presidential seal of approval, just holler at me, and we'll make some pigs fly for you," the sellout government official continued. "I've got your back, America, and I'll find you the best deals, the best products, and the *things* that will make you happy!"

As Rafe approached a checkout counter with his basket, he noticed that the young blonde cashier looked eerily pale. He caught a glimpse of her blue eyes, but it seemed as if there was no soul behind them.

"And now on to some big news!" the president continued with another pre-recorded segment. "We've now apprehended our 100,000th druggy and taken him off the streets so you and your family can be safe! With *Pattern Tracker* installation in all motorized vehicles and the *Dissenter and Colored Phylactery Protocol* that we implemented five years ago, our team of investigators has worked tirelessly to analyze and track all these thugs and bring them to justice.

"You know, what's funny is that most of them drove ATVs and motorcycles. All those Mexicans like to drive down alleyways and in places that it's hard to follow. We got 'em, though! I just want to thank you for allowing us to keep tabs on everyone so that we can weed out the bad guys, the Un-Americans!

"And speaking of some really bad hombres, here are tonight's pictures of those we need help finding. Just give us a holler if you spot one."

Rafe watched a screen that was just behind the blonde girl's shoulder as it cycled through pictures and names. His heart raced, and he felt the blood pumping in his ears. He thought the entire store of zombies

176

would suddenly look up and come running after him. Or maybe they would shuffle.

As soon as she finished scanning each of his items, Bri's name and picture appeared on the screen. He gazed into his wife's digital eyes and realized that the racist dystopia in which they lived was beyond comprehension. Humanity had been turned upside down, and there was almost no glimmer of hope.

The nation's future now rested in what they were slowly carrying to Canada, and he wondered if they would even arrive. He thought about the video clips he had captured to prove that the United States was in peril, and he questioned whether or not another country would dare invade.

Before the propaganda filled the airwaves, President McKendrick had befriended many dictators and dissolved relationships with the country's allies. He and his party favored an isolationist tactic to improve the economy, but the outcome was unknown.

His wife's eyes seemed to penetrate his soul. He needed to get her and their unborn baby to safety, to start a new life on foreign soil. It was there, in a cold department store, staring at his wife's face on a television screen, that he resolved that their baby would never have to see what gave him nightmares and what was really driving him out of hell.

As soon as his own picture and name flashed on all the screens for everyone to see, the blonde girl sneezed violently, and a few spots of blood spattered on the counter. Without waiting for the total, he threw down the cash on the counter, picked up his bags, and ran out the door.

"Heil McKendrick," she mumbled as she slowly wiped up her blood off the sales counter with a nearby cloth.

Chapter 31

Cross to Bear

(Day 85)

B ri watched Rafe traverse the thick, decaying Ohio brush in front of her. They always tried to stay off the beaten path as best they could during most of the day. After dusk and before dawn, they made up time by walking on a trail, if there was one, but they never ventured onto the road.

She was always better at maintaining a sense of direction, but she let Rafe lead the way. Every night, she would look at one of the maps and figure out where they needed to go, which roads and highways they could use as guides, and which cities were nearby. They were making good time, but she still worried about winter, which was quickly approaching.

Several weeks before, Rafe put together a cart of sorts that strapped to his waist. He also wore a harness across his chest to help him pull the wagon, as they called it, over the terrain. It held all of the gear and both framed backpacks, but Bri frequently lightened the load by carrying one.

Rafe didn't talk much anymore. He was a stubborn, desperation-forged mule, consigned to be the muscle that would get his small family to Canada. Always charging forward in front of her and crashing hard at the end of the day, he had become a faceless force of nature that was dragging them through the mire to a hopeful haven.

Bri admired his tenacity and focus. The hike across the country had become an obsession for him, and she leaned on it, especially on the days when she wanted to be as far away from her hiking boots as possible, but there was a cost.

From her best guess, she was about 19 weeks pregnant with 740 miles left to hike before winter. Because they were fugitives, they were afraid of walking into an American hospital to deliver the baby or even get a checkup. They knew the baby would be ripped away from them and sold if they were discovered. White babies did well on the black market, even though everything was done in the open. There was no hiding evil anymore.

He pushed them hard, and they had frequent breaks, but sometimes she unwillingly continued walking, even with a surging pain. She wished for her mother, a nurse, or anybody to comfort her and tell her the baby growing inside her was healthy and surviving the journey.

How did Mary do it? she thought to herself. Mary and Joseph had to travel roughly 90 miles from Nazareth to Bethlehem. Only after their excruciating journey and childbirth in a cave was her sorrow replaced with the precious joy of bringing the Savior into the world and holding Him close.

Despite the need to keep going, she finally begged Rafe, "Can we stop? I'm sorry. I need to sit down." There was a throbbing soreness in her feet and what seemed like a hyper-focused pain in the side of her belly that felt like someone had driven an awl right through the skin.

She quickly sank onto the grass next to a tree, and the voice of her mother seemed to comfort her in her mind: *Don't worry, dear. It will soon be over. Have faith.* As she took deep breaths, she closed her eyes tight and reached out into the dark for her husband, hoping to feel his hand, but his touch wasn't coming soon enough.

The side of her head was also throbbing, and she could feel drops of tears flowing down her cheeks. A veil of darkness enshrouded her as she felt pierced against the wood. There was no end—all had been lost!

And then it was gone. She opened her eyes, and Rafe was kneeling next to her with the sun right behind his head. Looking down at her hands, she realized that she had been squeezing his hands so hard that they were red.

As if he had already asked several times, he repeated, "Are you okay?"

"That was weird," she commented. "I'm sorry. Did I hurt you?"

"No, but I was worried. How about we just stop for the day?"

She looked at the dead trees around them and the rot that seemed to infect everywhere they went and resolved, "No, I'm good. I just needed to rest for a second."

He helped her to her feet and questioned, "Are you sure? Maybe we can check that book about pregnancy that we have." Without a nurse or the internet, this was their only source of information as first-time parents.

After a quick search, he opened the cover for the first time and admitted, "I didn't know this was a library book."

"Yeah, I got it the day we found out. Now we're really fugitives." They both chuckled.

Rafe flipped through the pages and asked, "So, what happened?"

She wasn't interested. She knew everything was okay and that whatever the pain was, it was probably necessary, just like pulling a thorn out of the lion's paw. The voice of her mother came to her mind: *A mother's deepest pains blossom into her greatest joys.*

Bri looked at him with a warm smile and softly reassured, "Don't worry. I'm fine."

He went up to her and gently removed the day pack she was wearing. "You know, I wish I could carry you as well."

"Don't be silly. I can make it; it just takes me a while. You're already doing so much."

She watched him strap the wagon to his waist and wrap the harness across his chest. "You'll be a great father," she exclaimed.

He responded with an exhausted smile.

"He'll learn how to love from you," she continued. "I'll be the hotheaded mess that's yelling at him to clean up his toys, and you'll be the one that teaches him to share and love everyone. I'm just apologizing in advance."

"No need to apologize. You're a great teacher, too, you know." He stopped to look back at her and confessed, "I'd probably still be an idiot if it weren't for you."

Chapter 32

The Void

(Night 118)

R afe and Bri came to the edge of a high cliff overlooking a city with millions of lights and gas-guzzling cars that flowed through the metropolis like a continuous stream of electricity. The smog and dust that had settled long ago only weakened the glow, and it was in stark contrast to the heavenly stars above.

"I believe that's Rusty, Ohio," Rafe said, unhooking the wagon from his waist.

"It's very peaceful up here." Bri took in a deep breath of cold air and asked, "Do you think that's a dissenter town or, you know, one of the other ones?"

"I guess it's a regular town. They always move up the lights-out curfew an hour or so during the winter."

She sat down on the dying grass and remarked, "It's hard to think that behind each light is someone with so much hate. Why are people like that? It just doesn't make sense to me."

Rafe sat next to her and took her hand. "Do you think my mom would pick up a gun and shoot somebody because they were black?"

"No! Of course not."

"They're not all bad. My mom says a lot of things, some of which she doesn't even think are offensive. Maybe it's just the culture or the way she was raised, but she's not a horrible person."

"Well, she doesn't help. All that hatred just spreads like cancer—infecting and killing off every part. She may not pull a trigger, but she loads the gun."

"Yeah, you're probably right," he agreed. He exhaled a long and frustrated breath. "I'm sorry if she ever hurt you. I'm sorry."

She responded with a sympathetic smile and looked off into the distant horizon. "Do you think Canada is any different?"

"I hope so. There's not a perfect place anywhere, unfortunately. There will always be crime and people who flat-out hate others. I think America has just—" He shook his head, not knowing how to describe it.

She filled in the blank for him, "Gone too far."

"Yeah," he responded grimly.

"Sometimes, I wonder why we're the ones who have to hike 2,000 miles to deliver some footage and ask for help," she admitted. "Why can't someone else do it?"

He turned to look at her blue eyes and her curly red hair moving in the cool breeze. "Well, God would have someone else lined up if we didn't do it. It's going to be okay." He motioned to her shoes and said, "Here, let me massage your feet again."

Although they had been married for several years, he once told her that he had recently graduated from marriage kindergarten into first grade, putting his lack of knowledge on the subject in perspective. He figured he would be around 90 years old when he would finally graduate and be a good husband. As he put it, marriage was only invented to help a guy learn how to be a decent person. Everything else was incidental.

He took off her hiking shoes and massaged her throbbing feet. They were now only averaging about ten miles a day, and it was still too much. The trek was grueling, and they took turns complaining and leaning on each other for support.

IN THE DISTANCE, A SMALL BLACK VOID MOVED ABOVE THE CITY. Rafe noticed that it carried a few lights, and it seemed to grow in size as it slowly slithered across the night sky. It drew toward them like a faceless predator.

Before he could take another breath, its bright spotlight found them both, and the pulsating blades created violent gusts of wind all around them as if Hurricane Dawn had followed them to that cliff.

"Halt! You are in violation of curfew order 8-2-8!" barked an officer through an exterior speaker. "Do not move, or we will shoot!"

They both stood up, raised their hands, and Rafe asked Bri, "Can you run?"

"No," she said with a whimper.

There was nothing for it. A massive helicopter hovered right in front of them at the edge of a cliff, and the number of rifles aimed at them was unknown. When the machine moved to the side a little and the spotlight didn't blind them, Rafe noticed a Sodium symbol on the front.

As he grappled with a tactical solution to overcome the massive beast in front of them, he thought about the dark figure approaching his hunting tree at night when he was a boy.

Surely, his father had enough faith to leave him alone in the forest with whatever animal that could have come near. He had given his son a shotgun, and now Rafe wondered after all this time if it was for hunting or protection.

"Put your hands behind your head!" demanded the hovering beast.

185

The helicopter moved, and when the spotlight beam allowed him to see again, Rafe noticed a small rock by his foot.

"When I throw this rock, I need for you to run behind that tree over there to your left," he instructed Bri. "It's going to be okay."

"Are you sure?"

"Trust me."

Like a bolt of lightning, he quickly picked up the rock and hurled it at the spotlight. It shattered, and the whole area immediately went pitch-black until their eyes adjusted. The helicopter retaliated by flying up, and several shots were fired.

"Bri!" he shouted in the dark.

"Yeah?"

He raced over to her behind the tree and cried out, "Are you okay?"

"Where's it going?"

"I think they're trying to find a place to land," he explained. "Grab your shoes and get on!" His hands shook as he quickly strapped the wagon to his waist, and she climbed on top of the gear.

"Alright, I'm ready!" she yelled out, trying to find a place to hold on.

Rafe saw her shoes by the edge of the cliff and took off toward them, knowing that they only had seconds to escape. When he retrieved them, another shot fired, but it hit the ground several feet away.

"Just go!" she screamed.

Something took over when he ran. It felt as if several people were helping push the wagon behind him. Although the trees towered overhead, the moonlight was just enough for him to see, and the ground seemed remarkably smooth.

His legs didn't feel like his own, and all he could think about was running to Canada in a single night. He pulled his wife, his baby, and

186

everything they owned with every ounce of life that he had, knowing that at any point, it could all be taken away.

The beast continued to buzz over the treetops, searching for them, but they could not be found.

BRI AWOKE TO SOFT RAIN BOUNCING OFF HER FACE. Now mid-morning, her hands were still clenched to the sides of the wagon. Rafe continued walking in front of her, taking small steps.

"Are you okay?" she asked gently.

No response.

"Are you hurt?" Again, he didn't say anything but kept going forward. "You can stop now. They're gone."

He turned around, and it looked like he had been crying for hours.

She quickly jumped off the wagon and unfastened his waist strap. "You must be exhausted!"

As soon as he was free, he leaned on her as if he were dead weight, and she helped him to a nearby tree, where he plopped down like a pale corpse. She then flew to the wagon to retrieve a dry blanket for him, and when he was completely covered, he leaned over on her shoulder and fell asleep.

She kissed his forehead and lovingly whispered, "Thank you." The light, drizzling rain continued to fall as they both sat on the ground, weathered and beaten.

As she held her husband close, Bri noticed how the raindrops slowly moved down a decaying blade of grass. For all the water, there was no saving the cursed land all around them. Everything in sight was bleak and somber.

Chapter 33

Love of God

(Day 141)

Much of the view was now white. The waves of Lake Ontario had come to a standstill in ice, and many of the trees along the shoreline were trapped in ice cycles. Rafe didn't know how deep the snow was as much of the smaller brush was now absent. Being a southerner, he enjoyed calling his new snowshoes, which he had never worn before, his Peter shoes.

Now, about 27 weeks pregnant, Bri wasn't allowed to carry anything, and when she occasionally snatched a backpack from their sled, he would come back and tickle her until she complied. They were averaging about five miles a day, but more than anything, they enjoyed how the snow had made everything beautiful again.

After strapping the empty sled to his waist, he confessed, "You know, I don't like to leave you alone." He then looked around their little campsite in the woods to check for anything that needed attention.

Inside the tent, she had already gathered all the blankets around her, ready to read a book. "Don't worry," she replied with a comforting smile while holding her stomach, "I've got someone to keep me company. Just come back to me."

He put the harness on across his chest and uttered, "I love you."

"I love you, too."

There was something in how she zipped up the tent that reminded him that it was his decision to make the trek. As her face was slowly taken away from him, he thought about the comforts they left behind and how she suffered every day. She was truly a saint.

As Rafe entered the small town of White Port, New York, the streets were abandoned. It had been a harsh winter, and he figured that perhaps there was a universal unwillingness to go anywhere in the community. All he heard were his sled skis sliding across the snow. If it weren't for the feeling that he was being watched from both sides of the street, the *spit town*, as his mother would say, appeared to be the victim of a plague.

The convenience-store shelves were almost empty, but he could still find most of what they needed. His original goal of arriving in Ottawa within 120 days had long passed, and his cash was almost gone. He thought about selling something or bartering like he was part of a medieval game, but he didn't have anything of value.

Finding a job for a few days had too many unknown variables, and he feared for their safety with such an endeavor. And withdrawing more cash from their bank would only disclose their location.

Staring at the empty shelves made him think of rationing their food again. They had to move faster, but each passing day only brought more discomfort for her.

As he paid for the groceries at the counter, he silently prayed, *Father, please help us.* Before the Sodium Massacres, he hadn't read the Bible or prayed since he was a boy. Now, he was almost always in the middle of a prayer.

"Heil McKendrick," the clerk uttered with a groan.

As he had done many times before when asked to repeat the filth, he put his bags on the floor and performed a series of unintelligible hand gestures. He had no idea how to sign, but for him, the meaning was clear: *Leave me alone—I don't care.* Hopefully, any angels taking notes weren't offended by his misuse and indifference toward signing; it was saving his life.

The clerk went back to watching the newscast on the TV that was mounted by the door, and before Rafe could pick up his bags and leave, he was compelled to watch as well.

"So, as of tonight," Surgeon General August Ripley reported in the newscast, "every person within the United States borders is required to take an ancestry test. Only those who have 98% Western European ancestry will be allowed to retain their American status.

"That means that if all your great-great-grandparents came from England, Scotland, Wales, Germany, the Netherlands, Denmark, Norway, Sweden, Switzerland, or Austria, you can retain your SS 28 Card. President McKendrick has disallowed ancestry from every other European country because of the political uprising in the recent Antermine-Poliney War. All other countries are considered subordinate."

Rafe was awestruck. *What is going on in the world?*

The blond anchor on the other side of the split-screen asked, "So, are the dissenters required to take the test? And how are we funding this *DNA census*, as it's been called?"

Ready for all these prepared questions, the surgeon general responded without missing a beat. "Yes, everyone. Well, all those who are clearly people of color will not need the test and will retain their status as AA 147B, so we will save an estimated 2.4 billion in testing in that regard. Every county health administrator will determine these prescreening measures."

"So," the anchor responded with some kind of self-adulation, "where can I pick up a test, and how much is it?"

"I am so glad you asked," the surgeon general mouthed. There was no audio.

"Wait a minute. Wait a minute. It looks like we're having some technical difficulties. It's probably the Chinese again." The blond anchor chuckled to himself as the official kept blabbing on in silence.

"And that's how it'll all work," the surgeon general finished with a wide grin of complete contentment.

The anchor then begged, "Okay, sorry to do this to you, sir. Can you repeat that, please? We had some technical problems, and heads are rolling as we speak."

Rafe looked around at everyone in the convenience store. They all looked like normal human beings that he would talk to at work or ask to go fly-fishing. A man in the back looked a little sick and was roaming around the medicine aisle. Two other men were thumbing through magazines and laughing at something in one of them.

The official in the broadcast looked down at his notes again and stroked his gray beard. "Yes, certainly. With the recent Servitude Ordinance Act SS24, President McKendrick allows all states to implement Negroid asset confiscation and liquidation to acquire funds for purchasing these tests from the federal government. That's how you and I will get free testing to be slave owners."

"I see, I see. Thank you, sir, for your time! We'll be checking in with you as more news develops on this exciting new front!" The anchor was ecstatic and very comfortable with hissing evil.

"Yes, thank you for having me." The split-screen transitioned into a full screen of the anchor by himself.

"In fact," he continued with the newscast, "even Canada is ramping up on this new program."

The anchor's shot transitioned to a video clip of the Canadian Prime Minister standing in front of a crowd of reporters with the Canadian flag behind him. In response to an unknown question, the Prime Minister answered, "Yes, yes, we're definitely looking into that." The video ended, and it transitioned back to the anchor.

"So, this is where I turn to you, Dr. Scottsman. What is the scientific proof that legitimizes these new ordinances that the McKendrick administration is rolling out?" The close-up transitioned to a wide shot of the anchor and the doctor sitting at a desk with a graphic at the bottom of the screen that read *Scientific Proof for Slavery* in bold letters.

"Well, I'm not only an anthropologist, I'm also a man of faith," the feeble doctor with deep wrinkles answered. "Throughout history, slavery has always been used, especially in biblical times. It is God's way of separating the righteous from those that have truly sinned. The Negroid population exists because of sin, and it has always been the right of the Caucasoid to rule over them as God's purebreds. The Caucasoid are their god—it's only the natural order. I brought a few skeletal remains with me today—"

It was then that Rafe noticed a graphic text crawl that ran at the bottom of the screen:

> *Attention citizens of White Port County: Several dissenters have escaped their detention centers. Please be on the lookout for the following dissenters: R. Tableau, age 38, male, dark brown hair, brown eyes; S. Stephenson, age 24, female, blonde hair, brown eyes; T. Andrews, age 26, male, light brown hair, blue eyes.*

One of the men looking at magazine pictures earlier turned to Rafe as if to give him the third degree. "Hey, man, I've never seen you in here before. What's your name?" The horribly thin man then adjusted his glasses to study the foreigner.

Rafe jumped. He had been in a horrid trance from the newscast, and he accidentally gave the inquisitor a pale, terrified look of hopelessness. With all this evil on unapologetic display, he realized that he was now on the receiving end of a McCarthyism-like scare.

"What's your name, Nigger-Lover?" grilled the thin man's companion, who was morbidly obese.

Rafe didn't know how to respond to this, so he quickly invented new hand gestures and signed, *You are both idiots.*

"What's wrong? Nigger got your tongue?" mocked the obese man as he went up to the counter to pay for an open bag of peanuts.

"Hey, man," taunted the man with glasses, "how can you watch TV if you're deaf, dumb, and stupid?"

By now, Rafe had already picked up his grocery bags and was heading toward the door. They didn't deserve his time.

"You know," the thin man heckled, "I bet God is punishing you with being deaf, dumb, and stupid because you have one of them Injun wives."

Rafe turned around, shocked at his twisted and perverse statement.

In the course of his US presidency, McKendrick had managed to legitimize the satanic disease of racism. No longer suppressed by political correctness and morality, citizens were proud to be racists—the epidemic had become synonymous with being American.

Rafe wondered if he should cast pearls before swine. These men were obviously past feeling, past any hope of returning to a place of having the pure love of Jesus Christ in their hearts.

"In the name of the one true God," the thin man pronounced, "I punish you for mixing your seed."

194

Before Rafe knew it, a surge of indescribable pain welled up in his stomach, causing him to fall to the cold, hard floor and lie in a fetal position. Without end, he was kicked in his stomach and face.

He saw his blood on the tile next to him, and he closed his eyes. Each kick echoed in his mind, bouncing off each boundary, and he tried to find a reason for it. There was none.

The clerk then asked, "Hey, buddy, are you okay?"

Rafe opened his eyes to find out if he was the one being addressed. Unfortunately, the clerk's concern was for the obese man, who was choking on a peanut that had been lodged in his throat.

"Breathe, son! Breathe!" the clerk shouted as he slapped his back.

His frail companion opened a nearby bottle of water for him. "Hey, man, here's something to drink!" But as soon as he shoved the bottle in front of his face, the dying man pushed it away so hard that it fell to the floor.

Rafe watched the water slowly pour out onto the tile and spread toward him. When it eventually touched his skin, it was soothing. As the men continued to address the crisis, Rafe closed his eyes because of the pain and dreamed.

SOMEHOW, HOPE HAD COCOONED RAFE IN HIS SUFFERING, and he found himself in a long-forgotten memory, standing in front of a Sunday-school class of six-year-olds with Bri. After the Sodium Massacres, they were asked to team-teach in a small classroom at their church, and Bri was ecstatic from the get-go.

Four out of the five children held up their hands, full of excitement, but Rafe chose the girl who was looking at the ground.

"Cindy," he asked, "what do you think these people over here in the painting are doing?" He turned the page with the painting toward her so that she could analyze it better.

She then looked up and mumbled, "I dunno."

"Look," he gently described while pointing, "this is Noah, and he's building an ark. Why do you think he was building an ark or a big boat?"

Timmy, a blond boy full of energy, exclaimed, "God told him to do it!"

"That's right, Timmy. But why did He tell him to build a boat?"

Bri, who sat next to Timmy, then asked the whole class, "Do you think God loved Noah's family?"

It was then that Cindy answered with immovable conviction, "He loves everyone!"

"Yes, He definitely loves everyone," Rafe agreed. "Even the ones that were making fun of Noah—even the ones who were being mean to him."

Timmy then smiled and raised his hand while jumping up and down.

"Yes, Timmy?" Rafe asked.

The boy looked at all the other kids as if he had the best comeback ever. "And then he made the rain fall, and they all *died*!"

Cindy mumbled, "My dad says that God baptized the earth because everyone was naughty."

Allison, who was now sitting behind her chair, then elaborated, "They were naughty, and then God watered them all like flowers."

"No! God watered them, and they're all *dead*. Dead, dead, dead!" Timmy put his foot down in the conversation and continued, "Everyone went to the bottom of the sea, and the fish looked at them and went—" Timmy then puckered up his lips and moved his hands like gills on the side of his face.

"Alright," Bri said firmly, "that's enough of that. Timmy, come over here and sit in my lap." He then walked over to her, and she held him close. "Yes, everyone but Noah and his family died, but you know what?

God still loved everyone that drowned. He was so sad that they were all being so mean to each other. Noah told them to repent, and they didn't listen.

"And so, God commanded Noah to build an ark and gather all the animals: a girl and a boy zebra, a girl and a boy giraffe, a girl and a boy dog, a girl and a boy cat. All the animals were on that ark along with Noah and his family."

Rafe leaned back against the wall and enjoyed how well she taught the children. He loved how her curly red hair bounced when she turned to each of them in turn and how her blue eyes lit up when she talked about the animals. He thought about how wonderful of a mother she would be.

"And then God made it rain for 40 days and 40 nights," she continued. "Okay, everybody, sway with me." Bri and the children moved back and forth, imagining they were on a boat. "Can you sway like this for 40 days? It's a long time. Isn't it?"

"Yeah, I'm getting dizzy," Timmy confessed.

"After all that time, a dove with a little olive branch came to Noah. And what do you think that meant?" she asked the attentive class.

"God loves everyone?" Cindy answered, a little unsure of herself.

Bri beamed at the beautiful response and taught, "Yes, God loves us all so much that He gave us His son, Jesus Christ, who sacrificed Himself on a piece of wood to save us all. The dove brought us peace and the knowledge of dry land, where we can work hard to repent when we make mistakes."

It was always in these Sunday-school classes where Rafe learned the most. Either one of the children would say something so simple and profound or Bri would explain a gospel principle so clearly that the Holy Ghost would whisper to his heart that it was true. There was so much that he needed to learn.

RAFE AWOKE TO THE CHOKING MAN WRESTLING ABOUT, still unable to breathe, and he stood up in the puddle of blood and water with troubled resolution. A horrendous ache from each part of his body blasted his brain at the same time, and he knew at any moment that he would probably fall over, but he persisted. They were right—he was a sympathizer of those oppressed for the color of their skin.

Every movement felt like it could be his last, and yet, he felt a resurgence of life with each step toward his dying brother at the counter. The choking man recoiled as soon as Rafe reached out to him, but the bruised and battered angel was determined to help. Rafe quickly turned the obese man around and performed the Heimlich maneuver, saving his life.

"Get off me, you Nigger-Lover," shouted the man with the first breath he could take. The three men then picked up something to continue beating Rafe, but he slowly walked toward his grocery bags at the door. He was leaving, and that's all they wanted.

There was a small trail of blood that followed him in the snow. The sled was somehow a comforting sight, and he fastened it to his waist, knowing that everyone watched him from their warm houses. All he needed to do was focus on one step at a time as they each brought him closer to Bri.

Chapter 34

A Man Named Job

The sound of the front doorknob being jiggled repeatedly caused young Rafe to come out of a deep sleep. His father always performed the unnecessary task when he left for work in the middle of the night. He once told the young boy that it was a debilitating comfort because he had to check the doors, the windows, and the kitchen stove several times before he knew his family was safe.

When Rafe jumped down from the top bunk, he looked at the clock and realized that it was earlier than usual for his father to leave. As he did every evening, he went to the window to watch his father get into the car.

A thick fog surrounded the house, causing only the streetlamps below to be visible. His father soon came into view, and he walked toward the car carrying a small suitcase. *That's not right*, Rafe thought. *He never took any luggage before.*

Something told him that he should say a prayer, and so the 12-year-old boy whispered, "Father in Heaven, please help my dad come back!" But it was all in vain.

Rafe pounded the glass and cried. He watched the scene play out right in front of him, and he couldn't stop it. The fog enveloped his father as he walked across the yard. Seconds later, the unforgettable sounds of the car door squeaking and clanging shut had all but sealed the reality.

He memorized the last of his father through his tears: two brake lights that eventually disappeared at the end of the foggy street. He was gone.

RAFE WOKE UP, AND HIS HEART WAS POUNDING. It was still dark, and all he could hear was the blizzard outside whipping around the trees and blowing the tent in one direction. Every hour, he had to push off the snow that had accumulated on top so that it wouldn't cave in.

He was living with fatigue, but it was for his family.

The morning brought another foot of snow that they had to dig through to get out, and within an hour, they were already trudging along with the sled between them.

"I had a dream about my dad last night," Rafe started, breaking the silence. "I don't know why I keep thinking about him."

Bri didn't say anything at first and finally replied, "I wish I could have met him. What was he like?"

"Well, I guess he was a dreamer who slowly forgot the dream. He never said much, but I read his journal from time to time as a boy. What he really wanted to do was travel to developing countries and treat childhood diseases."

Shocked, she responded, "But, I thought he was a janitor."

"Yeah, he was. And I guess the original plan was for him to work overnight and go to school during the day, but somewhere along the way, it didn't work. He said he was inspired by someone at church who went to different countries and helped children who were born with cleft palates."

Bri took a deep breath and grabbed the sled to lean on it. "Hey, can we stop for a minute? I need to rest." After a few breaths, she continued, "That's awesome that he wanted to do that. I wonder what happened."

Rafe unfastened the sled and leaned on it next to her. "It was probably money. They married before he graduated from high school, and I'm sure medical school was too much for them."

"I wonder what your mom would say."

"Yeah, *if* I ever get to speak to her again. I don't know. He did go to school for a while, and he was always studying."

"I wish he could have made it. He sounds like a nice guy," she determined.

Rafe chuckled to himself and said, "There was one time, when I waited to the very end of the day, after washing the dishes and cleaning up the kitchen, that I finally said to him, 'Happy Father's Day,' and you know what he told me?

"He said, 'I'm always happy with you around. Thank you for being in my life.' I've always thought about that because he was hardly home, and if he was, he was sleeping. My mom once told me that he just saw the good in people and that that was his flaw."

BRI WATCHED HIM MELT DOWN RIGHT IN FRONT OF HER. In all the time that they had been together, he had never really talked about his father. She held him close and added, "I hope you see him again someday. I'm sure he'd love to meet our little girl."

"Yeah, he would," Rafe returned. "You think it's a girl?"

She gently rubbed her belly with all the love a mother could give. "Yeah, I do."

The expecting mother smiled as she looked out over the field of snow in front of them. Close to the tree line on the other side, a buck seemed to be searching for something.

"Hey," she exclaimed, stepping several feet into the field to get closer, "there's a deer over there."

Rafe grinned and commented, "Looks like it might be a ten-pointer. Beautiful, isn't it?"

She glanced back at her husband as he attached the sled to his waist. "I wonder if it's the same one from Louisiana."

"Probably not," he admitted. "It would be awesome if it was, though."

She looked for the magnificent animal again, but it had quietly spirited away. "And there it goes," she lamented. "I wish we could have shot some footage of it. We could have shown it to our baby when we tell her about all of this."

A LOUD CRACK ECHOED IN THE WOODS.

Rafe looked around quickly as he knew exactly what it was.

Bri turned toward him again to figure out what had just happened, but she soon buckled to the ground in horrible pain. The blood in the snow was as red as her hair.

"No, no, no!" Rafe unfastened himself and went toward her, ducking behind the sled.

Another shot was fired. The bullet lodged itself into a tree between them, and he recoiled out of fear back toward the sled. Bri watched him leave and stretched out her hand in agony.

Again, there was another thunderous crack, and the echo seemed to bounce off everything.

"Rafe!" she shrieked. More blood spilled all over the snow.

They were being hunted.

In desperation, he pulled out a stone from his pocket and aimlessly threw it into the woods with all his might, giving out an excruciating, heart-piercing scream. Perhaps, it might hit the shooter. Probably not.

"Where are you hit?" He moved toward her again, and as soon as he cleared the sled, another shot was fired. This one barely missed his arm but tore a hole in his sleeve.

"I don't know! My back—my side!" she barely uttered, gasping for air and crying with bone-chilling sobs.

They were separated by about 20 feet, and he desperately wanted to be with her. More than anything, he had to hold her hand and make the hurt go away. He needed to kiss her forehead and cry with her. He *had* to run to her.

Through her tears, she shook her head, and he stayed. She took a deep breath and painfully whispered the chorus of her favorite song. "A black mare in the middle of the night—"

"No, no!"

She tried to sing more, but it was too difficult for her.

"I love you so much!" It was all he could say as they both locked eyes for the last time.

"I love you, Rafe—" And then she closed them.

THE HOURS PASSED WITH LITTLE MOVEMENT. Rafe covered his wife with a sleeping bag and sat next to her as the snow fell. There was only one thought that kept repeating: if he would've just flown to her side the second that she fell, they would now be together. It would've probably been all in vain, though, and he would've just gone straight to hell. Maybe. Maybe not.

When he finally crawled toward her, he was begging to be shot, but that relief never came. For all he knew, the shooter was gone, and he was left with a wicked torment.

What a thing it is, death—and the power to dole it out. Why would anyone put themselves on par with God and take on that mantle? he silently contemplated. Only one death had ever been essential, and the power to live or die was His own.

That evening, Rafe slowly separated all of their gear and took stock of what he had. Something needed to preoccupy his mind as she slept. At last, he carefully put her body in both sleeping bags and laid her inside the tent.

He thought about their baby girl receiving the last of the nutrients from her mother before she died in the dark. At best guess, Bri was only about 30 weeks pregnant, and there was nothing he could have done—the side of Bri's belly was covered in blood. His family had been ripped from him, and he would never be whole again.

As the night grew on, he did sleep a little. Like a sentinel, he wrapped himself with several blankets and sat outside the plastic mausoleum to keep her safe from approaching animals. It didn't seem that cold, and the night sky was clear.

"Father, in heaven," he prayed with a heavy heart, "I'm sorry I couldn't protect my family like you wanted me to. I failed you again."

The treetops blew a little, and a small animal scurried off.

"I know I shouldn't say that. I tried so hard, and the only reason I was doing this was for her and our baby. We were so close!"

He broke down and cried from the very bottom of his soul, leaving nothing. He sobbed like a trembling, hungry baby, but he knew that he couldn't be comforted.

"Why did you want me to do this if it was all for naught?"

The wind picked up, causing him to shiver. Behind him, the tent walls flapped, and he clutched onto his blankets even tighter.

"What do you want from me?" he wailed loud enough for all the angels in heaven to hear.

It was then that a helicopter flew over with its maddening hum while its deathly searchlight poked through the trees. There was a mechanical hiss that trailed the beast as it blocked the stars above.

A bag containing a flashlight was just within reach, and Rafe stared at it as the helicopter methodically hunted. As the Reaper came closer, he found himself reaching for the poison and turning it on. Something was controlling him.

He held the flashlight with his left hand, and the beam shot out across the ground in front of him. The snow glistened in the light, and for some reason, the flashlight was so terribly heavy.

"*Let your light so shine before men,*" he whispered, shaking at the sudden onset of an immense temperature drop. He looked down at his arm, and he felt like it had some sort of rigor mortis. Maybe, he would join her soon.

He unwillingly continued his Sunday-school recitation, clinging onto something so far removed from him at that moment. "*That they may see your good works—*"

The sound of the flying devil was heart-wrenching, and he felt a cold, unearthly hand gripping his throat. He must push through—he must finish the scripture. Gasping for any last ounce of air, he concluded, "*And glorify your Father, which is in heaven.*"

As he raised his left arm with the beacon of death, his sleeve drew back, and he looked down at his bare wrist. There on his flesh was the coffin lid—a set of numbers that had already set him at naught.

He had already been sentenced and buried for his crime of loving as Christ loved, and Satan had branded him himself.

"*See your good works and glorify your Father,*" he barely mouthed.

He took another breath and slowly repeated, "Good works." The cold fingers from around his neck soon eased away, and a surge of warmth filled his whole body.

"Have I done any good?" he begged his Father in Heaven. In a moment as quick as lightning, hundreds of memories flooded his mind, but one took center stage.

"HON, CAN YOU FETCH A CLOTH and run it under some hot water—as hot as your hands can make it?" Rafe's mother asked as she sat down on the couch in the living room. Sometimes, she would come home during her lunch break and eat a sandwich with him, but that afternoon it would be different.

Young Rafe helped her lie down, and he took off her shoes. He then brought over a blanket and covered her.

"Can you also close the curtains for me, dear? The light just has to go with this headache."

"Okay, Mom," he responded and then dutifully made it dark for her.

It was now just the two of them, and he was the *man of the house*, as his mother used to say. As a 12-year-old boy, he took it upon himself to look after her. That's what his father would have wanted him to do.

As he ran a bathroom cloth under the hot water, the steam rose, and he prayed, "Father in Heaven, please bless my mom. She's not feeling well today." He doused it until his fingers couldn't touch it anymore, wrung it out, and cradled it in his hands so that it wouldn't get exposed.

When he brought it to her, she was almost asleep. "Here you go, Mom."

"Thank you, dear." She put it on her forehead and closed her eyes. "Oh, that feels wonderful. I think it's going away already."

Young Rafe sat down in a chair in the living room and continued to watch his mother sleep. Each breath became shallower as she drifted. Eventually, the small breaths were further apart, and he knew she was no longer in pain.

STARING AT HIS BRANDED WRIST, RAFE PROCLAIMED, "I am a child of God, and I am not done."

He turned off the flashlight, and the helicopter buzzed right over him, missing him completely. Eventually, the sounds of the blades chopping the night air were replaced with a peaceful and calming silence. He had a reason to live—unfortunately, he didn't know what it was.

Chapter 35

Straight Is the Gate

(Night 166)

R afe slept during the day again to cross the frozen St. Lawrence River at night. There had been so many blizzards over the past several weeks that he hoped it would be safe enough to cross. Every time he went to the bank, it looked solid enough, and now he was looking for a section that was shorter than a mile across.

Although he could claim himself as a refugee under international law, he still wanted to avoid any confrontation. With his branded arm, he had no political or human rights in the United States, so the goal was getting to Canada without being shot.

He managed to fit the rest of the supplies into one of the backpacks, and he used the sled to carry her body. Two days had passed since she had been taken away from him.

The moonlight helped as he slowly traversed the deep snow; he knew better than to use his flashlight again. In the clear, bone-chilling stillness of the December midnight hour, his legs could barely move as they were stiff and freezing. If it weren't for his Peter shoes, his feet would have turned black many weeks before.

After looking to his left for hours, trying to find the perfect place to cross the frozen river, he came across the top of an old wooden gate that was just wide enough to walk through with the sled. Low-hanging trees and shriveled vines covered the ancient structure, and had he not been constantly searching, he wouldn't have found it. A decrepit fence as old as New York state stretched for miles in both directions from the gate, but he didn't see a house. Something told him to cross there.

He cleared about three feet of snow to get to the bottom of the gate, and the top hinge creaked as he opened it. Because the wood appeared to be very weathered, he figured that no one had passed that way in a long time. He had to duck to get through, and it reminded him of a camel going through the eye of the needle in Jerusalem. The sled was almost too wide, but he wouldn't leave without his family.

At the bank, he looked around for guards or any other obstacle that would prevent him from crossing the border. He figured there might be a trooper or searchlight of some sort, but the only companion to see him off was a buck further up the bank.

When he stepped onto the ice, the deer looked up at him and ventured out as well, sniffing the ice as it went. At first, Rafe figured he should probably disconnect the sled if something happened but resolved that the fate of his family was intertwined.

Since he had never walked on ice before, he took slow, cautious steps, and every time there was a cracking sound, he would pause for a few seconds before going forward. The deer continued to walk along at the same pace about a hundred yards away as if it were supporting him somehow.

The ice was thinner toward the middle of the massive river, and Rafe stopped as soon as he witnessed a loud crack splitting the ice by his feet. Ripples moved just below the surface, now only a few inches thick.

Motionless and exhausted, he closed his eyes, surrendering to whatever the outcome would be—he had put up a good fight. The opposition was too much, and all he desired now was his wife's warm embrace.

Only a shallow, icy veil separated him from the comfort of being with her again. He imagined her blue eyes, her red hair, and her inspiring smile. Holding his eyes shut, desiring nothing more than being engulfed with the cold, piercing stab of death, he thought about his Peter shoes.

They truly allowed him to walk on snow and ice, but he knew they couldn't keep him afloat. That was just a Bible story. The Apostle Peter had more faith than he did, and he was a man of God with a purpose. That was not him, and he knew a watery burial would soon come.

He opened his eyes to peek at his fate, and to his astonishment, the male deer stood right in front of him, only several inches away. An expert at listening to the faintest noises, especially with hunting and editing audio, he was amazed at how this creature had stealthily approached him.

After recoiling in fright from the sight of the animal, he realized that he would soon drown or be impaled by an antler. Either way, the end was near.

But it wasn't. They locked in their gaze, and the creature was genuinely magnificent, almost heavenly. Rafe had never been this close and exposed to a live deer before. He didn't know if he should fear it or be in awe.

The deer soon broke away and started walking again. Somehow, it knew a safe route upon the ice, and Rafe followed this angelic guide the rest of the way across the river, which at times was meandering, but he never heard another crack.

As soon as the animal ascended the bank, it ran off at full speed in complete silence and disappeared into the Canadian forest, leaving Rafe grateful and indebted once again. He thought about waving at it but instead whispered, "Thank you, Heavenly Father."

Once he pulled the sled a good mile inland, he finally stopped to rest. All the fears and evil from across the river could no longer reach him. Surrounded by forest and a still twilight, he went into his pack and pulled out a small camping shovel.

There, close to the frozen St. Lawrence River, he buried his wife in Canadian soil. He couldn't bear to have her interred and *incarcerated* in the God-forsaken land of the United States of America.

He whispered a prayer that only God and Bri could hear, he wept uncontrollably, he covered the site with snow, and for the first time in many years, he felt at peace.

Off in the distance, across a few-acre field, he saw smoke rising from a small cabin. Exhausted, he packed the sled with the remaining gear and marked the site with a large rock that he had unearthed.

Before he left, he knelt again and whispered, "I love you, Bri. I'll see you again soon. I promise." He brought his fingers to his lips and then placed them on the rock lovingly. "This is for you—"

He stood up, attached the sled, and declared, "And for Him!" With the last of any energy he had left, he headed toward the cabin, knowing that his Father in Heaven was not too far away, watching over him. And he hoped that his wife was interviewing Him, like the reporter she was.

Part Three

Chapter 36

Only Sleeping

(Seven Years Later)

There was a metal chair that Rafe kept behind a bush by Bri's headstone in the cemetery. The grounds were well-maintained, but so far, he had never had any trouble hiding it there. Hopefully, she approved the little streams, the winding paths, and the footbridges; he liked them.

Visiting her was part of his morning routine after work. He would walk up the hill that seemed to be crowned by her headstone and eat a bowl of cereal by her. Sometimes, he would just read a book or a newspaper. Other times he would talk to her for a while. More than anything, though, he missed brushing several strands of her curly red hair from her face to see her beautiful, blue eyes and spending time with her.

Of course, there was a price that he had to pay. Shortly after he was situated in Ottawa, he spent time in the Ottawa Detention Centre for entering the country illegally and for transporting a dead body. Still, he always felt his actions were appropriate, given the circumstances.

He was sure a sniper would have been planted at the border crossing, and if he had revealed himself, everything would have been for naught. Breaking the law had saved his life.

"I'VE BEEN THINKING OF MY MOM RECENTLY," RAFE SHARED, starting his one-way conversation with his wife while sitting in the metal chair. His face had grown long, sporting a blond beard that made him look like a short Civil War general. He called it a Junker George beard.

"I had a dream about her last night, but it wasn't her," he continued. "She was much younger—like in her early twenties and the most heavenly version of herself."

He poured his bowl of cereal, bowed his head for a few seconds, and then added, "I wonder if you get to talk to her at all. I hope she's doing well, and you know—different than how she was."

There was a pause, as he hoped he hadn't just put his foot in his mouth again. He always seemed to do that, and he imagined how Bri would have reprimanded him. "I'm sorry about that. I wish I would have said something to her about it long ago, but I guess I never did."

The overcast sky soon darkened, and it began to rain. Although he tried to shield his cereal bowl with one hand, the raindrops still managed to find a way to plop into his milk.

"I miss her, though. I wish none of this ever happened and that we were both working at a station down in Texas. You would be in front of the camera, reporting the news, and I would, you know—"

The rain fell more intensely, and he cradled the bowl of diluted mush.

"Work was good this morning—pretty boring, but that's how I like it." He looked around at the sudden onset of the storm and quickly finished, "Oh well, Martin's play is today. He says, 'Hello.' It looks like I gotta go. I love you!"

THE WINDSHIELD WIPERS WERE ON ONE OF THE MIDDLE SETTINGS to keep up with the rain. Rafe missed his old truck, especially when he could just look over at Bri sitting in the passenger seat, and they could talk about anything.

This new truck was just different, and even though he had owned it for several years, he was still trying to get used to it. He even put a small picture of Bri on the dashboard in front of the passenger seat, but Martin thought it was weird, so he eventually took it down.

As far as he was concerned, they were still married. There was no need to replace her—he had found his love, his eternal soulmate, and no one else would ever come close. The emptiness was kept at bay by always considering her to be in the other room, at work, or walking around the neighborhood for a few hours.

He figured he probably had another 60 or so years until he would see her again, and each day was just one step closer to her. This is how he managed it.

The routine carried on as Rafe set his alarm next to the couch in the living room. He didn't dare sleep in his bedroom, which had become more of an office with video equipment and a few dressers.

Sleeping on a bed alone just reinforced the loneliness, so he eventually gave away the bed he had. Resting a few hours here and there on the couch, pretending that Bri was mad at him for the next several decades, seemed more bearable. Eventually, they would make up.

No one else needed to know that, though. Every time he was done sleeping, he would fold the blankets and put them away as if he had never been there. It was all temporary anyway.

Chapter 37

Martin

That evening, Rafe stood in the back of the school auditorium to see Martin's play. Unfortunately, something snapped when his wife died—eventually, he no longer trusted others except those closest to him. It was painful to be around people, so the only way he managed such an important event was to walk through the entrance after it began.

Once a short, athletic force that could take on the world, Rafe now carried on without regard for his life or health. He was aloof, without ambition, and overweight—his only purpose was to take care of his son.

Of course, he never allowed Martin to see this indifference and detachment. Every time the eight-year-old boy came running up to him, Rafe would light up as if his son were the only treasure in the world.

"So, parents of Wartburg Elementary," the headmistress announced on the stage, "without further ado, here is the third-grade production of *Martin Luther at the Diet of Worms*, written by the students." She then initiated an ecstatic round of applause that soon took over the whole auditorium, and she stepped out of the spotlight.

The private school was the cheapest Rafe could find in Ottawa, and he hoped that the teachers would fill in the gaps that he couldn't provide, being a single father who worked two jobs. Most importantly, he wanted his son to know about Jesus Christ and develop a lasting relationship with Him.

Like all the parents in the room, Rafe soon started an application on his phone, which allowed him to tap into a network of small cameras around the auditorium and record his own version of the live event.

A third-grade student wearing academic regalia approached the stage podium and declared, "In the Middle Ages, Pope Leo the Tenth saw the old Saint Peter's Basilica and wanted to rebuild it."

Two eight-year-old boys then walked toward the center of the stage and into the spotlight. One was dressed in full papal attire, and the other donned cardinal robes.

"My name is Pope Leo the Tenth," the first boy announced with conviction to the audience. Pointing at a massive backdrop of the cathedral construction on the stage, he turned to his associate and exclaimed, "This new Saint Peter's Basilica will be magnificent! It will be the grandest edifice in the world, and many will come to see it! How much more money do we have in the treasury to keep building?"

His companion then shook his head sheepishly, and the two characters frowned.

The production was childlike in tone and akin to a Christmas pageant; no disrespect or doctrinal dispute was intended, as it was a non-denominational school. More than anything, the play was a historical retelling through the eyes of elementary-school children.

"Meanwhile, the Archbishop of Mainz, Albert of Brandenburg, also needed money," stated the young narrator at the podium.

A second spotlight illuminated an extravagant office on the stage, complete with a stuffed toy lion. Another third-grader, who was dressed as the archbishop, paced and mumbled to himself, "I need to pay off my loan from the Fuggers; they helped me get my job as an archbishop. Where can I find more money?"

Suddenly, the boy playing Albert stopped pacing and stroked his chin. "I wonder if the pope will allow me to sell more indulgences. I can make a lot of money that way!" he bubbled, raising his finger excitedly from the idea.

Rafe watched the production on his phone, and he enjoyed the adorable manner in which the students brought the poignant story to life. After weeks of reciting lines with his son and studying more about Martin Luther's life, he wondered if he could be as brave as his eight-year-old boy in front of such a large gathering of people.

"Soon, Pope Leo the Tenth and the Archbishop of Mainz had an agreement," the narrator explained. "Half of the indulgence money would go toward the rebuilding of St. Peter's Basilica, and the other half toward the archbishop's debt." The two parties then approached each other on the stage and shook hands in an exaggerated manner for the audience to see.

A boy dressed as a German friar then rushed to center stage, which now had a medieval town square backdrop and a few homely props. Boys and girls dressed as townsfolk soon gathered around him, and he preached with fervor, "My name is Johann Tetzel, and I am here to abuse the sale of indulgences. It may not be Catholic doctrine, but I command you to buy these contracts to help your dead loved ones suffer less in purgatory. Feel their pain! Feel how they need you to pay for their deliverance!"

During his stirring oration, the Tetzel character motioned to his entourage of officials to bring forward his locked coffer, a massive, dark box with peculiar engravings on all sides.

"As soon as a coin in the coffer rings," he continued with a sinister smile, "the soul from purgatory springs!" The townspeople soon clamored around the display with coins in hand, and the boys dressed as church officials dispersed the contracts from the box as best as they could. Unfortunately, everyone in the production was soon swimming in a hurricane of paper, and the audience laughed.

ALTHOUGH RAFE CRACKED A SMILE AT THE MISHAP ON STAGE, an excruciating memory soon flashed across his brain like a bolt of lightning. He sank to the floor, feeling sick to his stomach. In a long slow-motion camera shot in his mind, he recalled being pistol-whipped in the face by a brownsuit at the southern entrance to Gulf Haven and falling to the ground.

Echoing across the years was the *un-Christlike* demand to repeat that phrase at gunpoint: *Christ is my savior; He is my king*. Behind the laughing parents, Rafe rubbed the side of his face that bled that day, and he cried.

For more than two thousand years, the name of Jesus Christ had been used by some with authority to accomplish their vile designs. The archbishop preyed on those with the endearing desire to make oneself right before God to satisfy the demands of a personal loan.

People, unfortunately, can defile the true teachings of Christ— thank God for personal prayer and the Holy Ghost.

RAFE FOCUSED ON A CLOSE-UP OF MARTIN ON HIS DEVICE, and the memory slowly faded. The pain from his gut and face receded as he remembered his son. Various cameras around the room followed the actors' movements, and he chose one that zoomed in on Martin, who was dressed in a monk's tunic.

"I am Martin Luther, a professor of theology and a monk," his eight-year-old son announced as he stepped into the spotlight. As an African American boy, he was tall and lanky, and Rafe figured that they would probably share the same height within a few years.

222

Martin pulled a small hammer from his robe pocket and nailed his 95 Thesis of debate ideas to a wooden door in front of a castle-church backdrop. He was alone and declared to the audience, "Any true Christian, whether living or dead, participates in all the blessings of Christ and the church; and this is granted him by God, even without indulgence letters. Because love grows by works of love, man thereby becomes better. Man does not, however, become better by means of indulgences but is merely freed from penalties."

Rafe admired his son and the character he played. The young boy may not have understood the recited lines, but he delivered them in such a way as to show their import. They and the actions surrounding the event changed how God's love and mercy were perceived.

Despite his honest efforts, Rafe felt like a failed father, though. In his mind, Bri would have done a better job at raising him. She would have taught Martin how to be a responsible and ethical person that contributed to society. By the age of eight, she would have had him memorize the United States Constitution and the Sermon on the Mount. They would have delivered meals every evening to people that didn't have anything, volunteered at numerous charities, made petitions for worthy causes, and stood in protest lines to help the disadvantaged.

Rafe didn't do any of that. He had become a teacher that was too afraid to abide by the lesson. Like a permanent divorcee praising marriage or a non-practicing Christian sharing the benefits of the eucharist, he saw the value of helping the community but couldn't take part in it. At times, he felt that he no longer deserved Bri or Martin.

THE PLAY PROGRESSED, and the stage had been dressed to appear like the courtroom at the Diet of Worms. Many students from different grades played the officials of the Diet, including Holy Roman Emperor Charles V and Johann Maier von Eck, the accusing officer.

Martin addressed the entire court humbly and stated, "Unless I am convinced by the testimony of the scriptures or by clear reason, for I do not trust either in the pope or in councils alone, since it is well known that they have often erred and contradicted themselves, I am bound by the scriptures I have quoted, and my conscience is captive to the Word of God. I cannot and will not recant anything since it is neither safe nor right to go against conscience."

The boy appeared as a valiant warrior in God's Army, angelic, defiant, and full of eternal purpose. "Here I stand; I can do no other. May God help me. Amen."

It was at this point that Rafe was in awe. In the three months since his son had received the role, he had thought about Martin Luther extensively, rehearsing in his mind all the events that led up to the Reformation, and he imagined how the monk must have felt at any given point along the way. In the face of excommunication and an execution like Jan Hus, a theologian who also protested indulgences, Martin Luther continued with moral courage and conviction for his beliefs. The obstacles were seemingly insurmountable, but in the end, the cause succeeded.

RAFE WAS REMINDED, THOUGH, OF LUTHER'S WRITINGS that condemned the Jews for their crucifixion of Jesus and unwillingness to align with Christianity. Eventually, his words were utilized by Nazi leaders as justification for the Jewish Holocaust, and Rafe often tried to make sense of the juxtaposition of the two opposing outcomes of his work.

How could a man of God who helped many come closer to Christ also have written such horrid condemnations that called for burning property and the murder of Jews? he often pondered. Indeed, Martin Luther's words may have inspired the Kristallnacht.

Rafe could never find a solution. He trusted in God's final judgment of His imperfect children.

As the curtains closed to signify the end of the second act, Martin continued to stand boldly before the council, and families cheered in the crowd. Rafe quietly clapped for his son in the back of the room, grateful and contemplative.

LATER THAT EVENING, RAFE CARRIED A SLEEPING MARTIN TO HIS BED, kissed him on the forehead, and whispered, "Goodnight. Love you!" The boy moved a little, but he was fast asleep again once he was under his favorite reindeer blanket.

As soon as Rafe turned off the light switch by the door, though, Martin called out, "Dad, did I do a good job tonight?"

"You were wonderful! I'm so proud of you!" the father replied with a smile. "I'll see you tomorrow, okay? Love you!"

"Love you, Dad."

Rafe rubbed his eyes as he stepped into his office and turned on the computer, ready to edit a commercial for a client before going to work. The light was dim, and the computer made a humming sound as it warmed up, lulling him to sleep as he waited.

Chapter 38

New Eden

It was toward the end of his shift at work that things started happening. There was a notification from the television network that a special report would soon be broadcast. Rafe skimmed the email again, mouthing and whispering different parts.

"A special report concerning New Eden is expected in approximately two minutes... live feed within network programming... if in local programming, please take the channel 15 satellite feed... interview in English. What is *New Eden*?"

He quickly scanned several TV screens and multiple monitors to make sure his video sources could be switched appropriately. It was a moderately-sized master control room, but they could still feed a half-dozen television stations across Ontario with unique programming.

His fingers flew across the bypass switchers to make sure they were all unlocked just in case, and by the time he finished checking everything, the opening graphic for the special report had started. He notated the time, 6:17 AM.

The network anchor, Ms. Tallon, opened the segment, "This is a special report. We have just received a communication about an interview coming from the United States, now called *New Eden*. Secretary of State, Mr. Jude Kerioth, joins us live."

The graphic changed to a split-screen that showed both the anchor and a picture of Kerioth. Maybe it was the fact that he was more clean-cut than Rafe remembered, or perhaps it was his grin that seemed to speak volumes, but there was something that wasn't quite right.

"Good morning, sir. It is good to hear from you," the anchor began.

A raspy voice, which clashed with the perfectly composed picture, then spewed, "Good morning, Diane."

"Mr. Kerioth, you sound ill. Are you okay?"

"Yes, my dear. It's just a little cold."

"I'm sorry you don't feel well. I hope you get better soon! Where are you calling from, Mr. Kerioth?"

There was a little forced, breathy chuckle. "I am here at our capital, Sacred Sodium, at the Temple of the Holy See." There was a sense of odd reverence that he bestowed on each word as if they were too sacred for anyone outside New Eden to hear.

Ms. Tallon, taken aback, quickly asked, "So, are you still the Secretary of State?"

"You may call me the Secretary of the Holy See of New Eden."

Within seconds, the graphic for the split-screen changed with updated text for the location and title for Kerioth. For the rest of the world, all this was completely new information. The secrecy of this enigma was bleeding out.

"My apologies, sir. Thank you for contacting our newsroom. What would you like to share with us today?"

There was a long, awkward pause as Ms. Tallon sat attentively behind her desk. She didn't even blink as she waited, and it seemed like the world was waiting for Kerioth's picture to move. The suspense was frightening.

"Mr. Kerioth?"

"Yes, the time has come," he pronounced as if from the grave, "for the citizens of New Eden to petition your country for aid."

Alarmed, she leaned forward and asked, "Aid? What can we do for you?"

"A list will be forthcoming," he barely managed. "Thank you for your time." The call ended abruptly, and the sound of the phone disengagement went over the air.

Awestruck, Ms. Tallon sat up and tried to quickly process the short interview. "That was Mr. Kerioth, now the Secretary of the Holy See of New Eden. His shaken demeanor was one of grief, and although the interview was rushed, he has requested aid from Canada."

Rafe shook his head in disbelief; he had met this man. He had punched him and left him bleeding in his office in Washington because of the things he said. *Whatever it is, it's all an act,* he silently judged.

The anchor continued, "Mr. Kerioth has indicated that a list of the items needed will be 'forthcoming' and—"

She nodded, indicating that she was receiving instructions in her earpiece. "Alright, we are now live with Prime Minister Marceau." The graphic changed so that both the anchor and the Prime Minister were in a split-screen. "Good morning to you, sir."

"Good morning, Ms. Tallon. I apologize for the rather sudden and seemingly impromptu situation with which we are dealing. During your interview with Secretary Kerioth, I received a substantial list that outlined the supplies and materials needed by the New Eden administration. I just want to go on record to say that after the events that transpired six years ago, we have always been willing to work with President McKendrick and his administration."

229

For the next two hours of television programming, Canadian analysts and pundits submitted hypotheticals and discussed the strained financial and political relationship with their neighboring country. The phone call was even compared to the return of the Prodigal Son.

Everyone had an opinion, but no one knew what to expect. The whole situation took on the same excitement and confusion as an asteroid on a deadly collision course with earth.

Luckily, though, Rafe only had to listen to 43 minutes of it.

RAFE COULDN'T SLEEP AFTER COMING HOME FROM THE CEMETERY. All the room-darkening curtains in the living room were closed, but he still tossed and turned on the couch. Even the usual sounds of cars on the street below and the wind blowing through the trees bothered him.

As far as he was concerned, he had done what he could for the United States, and all that had transpired afterward was beyond his control. He wasn't anybody of consequence. He wasn't a politician, military leader, economic strategist, or influencer; he was a nobody.

Right now, his job was to operate the equipment that broadcast the news. It was the equivalent of having the responsibility of closing Martin's window at night so that he wouldn't get cold. The point of his life now was to make sure that his son had a life.

Although he had set his phone to silent mode, the device defied its programming, and a call came through. It was Merlot.

Rafe held the phone and studied the picture of his friend on the screen as it continued to ring. Undoubtedly, he was sure to talk about the interview with Kerioth. It was the topic of every public discussion, and honestly, Rafe just wanted to tune it all out.

"Afternoon, Charlie," he finally greeted him. He said it in the same tone as when his son left his bike out in the rain. It was a part of life, and there's no reason to put negative energy out into the world.

"Did you see the special report with the Secretary of State of the See or something or the other this morning?"

"Yeah, I did."

"That's good," Merlot replied, and he took a few seconds before he continued. "I have to talk to you about something. The two of you have a history, and I wasn't able to apprehend him in Sodium, so I never met him."

"I don't trust him at all. Whatever he wants is of no consequence. They should all just rot," Rafe condemned.

"I see. I was hoping you could do me a favor, though."

Over the past several years, the two men had acquired a certain rapport. Merlot came over to Rafe's apartment a few times a month to have dinner, and he always brought a couple of dozen eggs for them.

He was a lonely man who carried on almost defeated in many ways but still hopeful about whatever was around the bend. The old cop had seen how far humanity had fallen firsthand, and sometimes, he would call Rafe at work just to hear a joke, hoping that it would help him get out of bed.

"Marceau has asked me to be a part of the initial caravan to New Eden," Merlot explained. "They're estimating that a couple of dozen military-grade cargo trucks will be needed. Apparently, there is a *no-fly edict*, as they call it."

"Really? I'm sorry to hear that."

"Well, I was there at ground zero, and they put me on the shortlist. To tell you the truth, I don't want to go; I've seen too much." The phone intensified his gruff voice, which sounded like sandpaper slowly grinding away his life.

Rafe glanced at the clock, and it read 2:45 PM—he had been trying to sleep for five hours. Agitated, he eventually conceded, "Sure, yeah. Whatever you need."

231

"Would you be willing to pray for me? It seems He always listens to you."

"That's not true," protested Rafe. "He loves you as much as He does anyone. I'll pray for you, though." He exhaled, realizing what his friend needed, and assured him, "Don't worry. Everything will be alright."

"Okay, thank you." The grateful smile from the old man could be felt over the phone.

"Look, I need to pick up Martin. I've got to go."

"Alright, thank you again. Goodbye."

"I'll talk to you later, Charlie."

Rafe hurriedly put on his shoes, grabbed his keys, and left.

Chapter 39

Nineveh

From behind the desk, the secretary softly announced, "The deputy minister will see you now."

Rafe was still trying to get used to the courtesy and politeness of Canadians. Instead of worrying about being shot at any second, he wondered if they would all break out into song right in front of him to make him feel better.

Of course, it had just been a few weeks since he had crossed the border, and he was only half a person now. He thought about his wife constantly.

"Mr. Davidson, thank you for visiting with me. Please, come in," said Mrs. Kiernan, the deputy minister of foreign affairs. She was a businesswoman, and Rafe realized from her quick movements around the office that he probably had about six minutes of her time. There was something in how she earnestly shook his hand that indicated her complete engagement in the conversation. He could trust her.

"Thank you, ma'am." Rafe followed her to the desk, and they both sat down. Her government office was decorated with historical artifacts and paintings, and he marveled at how different it appeared in comparison to Kerioth's office. Instead of a den of thieves, it was almost a home.

"I hear that you have recently come from the United States," she started.

He had yet to tell anyone the whole story, at least anyone of an official capacity, and he didn't know where to begin. Everything was so convoluted and far-fetched that he didn't want to believe it, but it was a reality.

The burial site was probably on private property, and he knew that his wife would undoubtedly be found at some point in the future, so it was time to come clean.

"Yes, I recently escaped from the country, and I am declaring myself to be a refugee."

"Escaped?"

"Yes, ma'am. I'm not sure what you may know, but the United States has become so corrupt that people of color are being sold as slaves or shot in the streets. Many would not be associated with the killing spree, and they are called dissenters, like my wife and me. We fled from Texas on foot, and I crossed the border into Canada a few weeks ago."

It was good to get it off his chest, and although he delivered it as calmly as he could, he was still enraged by his wife's murder. He was visibly shaken, but there wasn't anything the official could do to hurt him as the worst had already happened.

As he watched the deputy minister process the information, he wondered if his wife was speaking through him—he felt her presence.

"I am so sorry that all that happened to you and your wife," she lamented. It was the grief and genuine sympathy that helped him through the rest of the interview. Although it was probably not altogether professional, she took his hand, and a few tears streamed down her cheek.

She then informed him, "There have been a few dozen cases like yours that we know about."

"Really? More people left?"

"Yes, other refugees have come, and they are now residing in various locations in Ontario. We have been providing assistance and care for them the best that we can. I am truly sorry for everything that has happened to your family. You mentioned your wife—is she still in the United States?"

"No, she was shot by a sniper several miles from the border, and I carried her across the Saint Lawrence River when it was frozen over. No matter what, I wanted her to be buried in Canadian soil." He knew it was a confession, but he felt peace as the words left his mouth.

"I am so sorry, Mr. Davidson. Truly, I am," the deputy minister managed with as much care as she could render. After a deep breath, she continued, "Well, there are a few people I need you to talk to so we can start your refugee processing. And there's a matter—"

"Actually," he interrupted, "I have something to share with you. And it's the reason I'm here." He pulled out a thumb drive and said, "I was a cameraman for a news station, and I shot a lot of footage over the years of things that I thought were incriminating for the United States."

"Interesting."

"I know that others have probably taken pictures and video with their phones, but those devices were monitored, and any *undesirable* data was deleted remotely by the government before it could be uploaded or shared."

He handed her the drive as if it was more valuable than his own life. "My wife's blood was on the original video card, and I barely extracted the data. It was in her backpack when she was shot, and it took eight tries for the transfer to work."

Standing up, he thought about the gravity of the situation and admitted, "I don't know if you could use it or what showing you all those things could do, but my wife thought it was important. And that's why I'm here." His eyes were now completely wet, and it was hard to stop weeping.

She looked up at him and confessed, "Honestly, we don't have any evidence to corroborate what has been said. We just have everyone's testimony."

"Do you think your country can do something for the people that are still there and suffering?" This last question turned the table as Rafe finally displayed his impatience, and his intentions were made clear.

The deputy minister slowly exhaled and swiveled her chair to look out the window. "You may not know this—the other refugees didn't know either—but several years ago, on January 6th, 2021, legislators on Capitol Hill in Washington, DC were pressured to permanently close the Canadian border to all trade and travel, among other things. Our economy has been crippled, families have been torn in half, and all forms of telecommunication have become non-existent. The United States is off the grid, closed-circuit, and a silent void."

"Really?" Rafe shook his head in disgust and shame.

Finally standing, she turned to him and admitted, "Look, I don't know what we can do, but I want to thank you for this video. I will show it to the minister of foreign affairs—"

THE LONG CAR HONK WAS JOLTING. A few cars in front of Rafe had stopped on the road, and he figured that the only one honking was an American. He would probably be late in picking up Martin from school.

Although it was challenging at times, he had promised himself that he would say a prayer whenever he was stressed or agitated. He shook his head as he couldn't come to terms with what he was going through, so he prayed for Merlot. After all, he had given his word.

"Dear Father in Heaven, I'm sorry I was upset in the conversation with Charlie earlier. He's a good man, and he needs a lot of help right now. Please help him as he goes back down to the States or *Eden* and—"

As he peered around the car in front of him while praying, the cause for the roadway impedance emerged. A deer had wandered across the road and was now slowly meandering toward Rafe's truck on the driver's side.

The eight-point buck sniffed the pavement, and as soon as the antlers came close to Rafe's window, it quickly raised its head and looked right at him. The time that passed was immeasurable. Its eyes were dark and wide as if a whole universe were hidden away behind its gaze.

Rafe didn't know if he would soon be run through with its antlers or if the buck had an entirely different intention. The encounter reminded him of the Bible story of Balaam and the animal he rode as he traveled with the princes of Moab.

Three different times Balaam beat the animal: once for leaving the path for a field, another for crushing Balaam's foot against a wall, and the last was for lying down while still saddled.

At last, the Lord opened the animal's mouth, and it spoke to Balaam.

Rafe wondered if the deer by his truck had a message for him and why all these deer were always guiding him. Suddenly, he thought about a few verses in Isaiah:

> For my thoughts are not your thoughts, neither are your ways my ways, saith the Lord. For as the heavens are higher than the earth, so are my ways higher than your ways, and my thoughts than your thoughts.

For as the rain cometh down, and the snow from heaven, and returneth not thither, but watereth the earth, and maketh it bring forth and bud, that it may give seed to the sower, and bread to the eater. So shall my word be that goeth forth out of my mouth...

He couldn't remember the passage exactly, but he recalled that there were simple things that always helped the Lord accomplish His plans. Knowing the beginning from the end, His ways were forged without our limitations—we couldn't understand them.

"What?" Rafe yelled without a response from the deer. "I've done everything I was supposed to do!"

Although he figured he probably shouldn't have snapped at a defenseless animal whose only trespass was staring him down, he felt that there was something significant to their meeting.

He soon broke the trance and noticed in the rearview mirror that everyone was passing him on the right. A few drivers were in awe, but most just kept going as if the event was a common occurrence.

When he returned to communicate with the animal again, it was gone, and he looked around briefly in vain. It was time to leave his *Mount Sinai.*

MARTIN EXCITEDLY CLIMBED INTO THE TRUCK, and it wasn't until the door had opened that Rafe realized that it was raining again. The early spring breeze followed him into the cab, and Rafe shivered. His son had learned at an early age to take his hooded jacket to school every day, but Rafe never thought about the weather—he was completely oblivious to it until it stared him in the face.

"Dad, did you know that global warming sometimes causes it to get cold? Today in class, we learned that the warm air causes the polar vortexes to move further south." It was a relatively normal kind of greeting for a youth who was anxious to learn all about the world around them.

Rafe turned on the windshield wipers to combat the sudden onset of the storm, and without truly engaging in the conversation, he responded, "Mm-hmm." Unfortunately, his mind was elsewhere.

The amount of water crashing against the glass and the constant back-and-forth of the wipers reminded him of Jonah on the ship to Tarshish. As the Lord sent out a great wind and a mighty tempest, the ship violently tossed so much that every person on the vessel cried to their god for salvation from the impending doom at sea.

When the shipmaster found Jonah, the prophet was sleeping through the storm, so he woke him up and begged him to pray as well. After they all cast lots to know who brought the evil upon them, it fell upon Jonah, and he confessed to disobeying the Lord. He had been commanded to preach repentance in the town of Nineveh and was fleeing to Tarshish instead.

"Dad?"

Martin looked at his father, but he did not respond. The slow-moving traffic in the school zone seemed to occupy all of Rafe's concentration. Although the wipers were flying across the glass at full speed, only the brake lights from the car in front of them were visible.

The boy continued, "We also talked about our spring projects, and I was hoping that you could help me with my presentation board. It's due in a couple of weeks."

"Sure, yeah," Rafe returned without allowing the request to sink in.

The raindrops pounded on the roof like a machine gun, and the unsettled father blasted, "Why is it raining so much? What's with all this infernal rain? Let's move it along, folks! Let's go!" He then honked his horn like an American: long and as loud as possible.

Martin answered earnestly, "Mr. Thompson said that they predict there will be more Atlantic storms this year." He then giggled to himself as he relayed, "Instead of repeating the Greek alphabet just twice after the normal names, we could have a *Tropical Storm Delta Three*! He says that it's funny because it sounds like a movie title!"

Rafe didn't pick up on Martin's efforts to make light of the situation and continued to consume himself with Eden's aid, the deer staring him down, and now the constant rain. Everything seemed to agitate him, but he knew better than to take it out on his son. None of this was his fault.

He honked the horn again—and then again. The more upset he was, the slower the traffic moved.

"Dad, we're all in this together. Honking isn't going to change anything."

The rain seemed louder and more intense. The water pounded the truck windshield so hard that Rafe couldn't see anything, much like a ship losing a sense of bearing when waves crash from every direction.

After Jonah told the crew that he was running from the Lord, they tried to take him to the shore, but the tempest was too violent. At last, he begged them to throw him overboard to save the crew. Rafe jerked slightly on the steering wheel as he imagined Jonah splashing into the water below.

Finally, he had managed to follow the line of cars to a stop sign, and he put on his blinker to make a right turn onto the main road. All he could see out his window were the unclear blotches of light dancing across the glass from oncoming cars.

"Here, Dad, let me roll it down for you," Martin said, pushing down the driver's window button in the middle console. The father was soon pelted with God's blow, but he could see.

240

He imagined Jonah sinking toward the bottom of the sea—alone, cold, and motionless. Far above the prophet, the sun had come out because the ship's crew had all prayed and cast him away as refuse. The sunlight shimmered on the surface, revealing his lifeless silhouette falling further and further below.

By now, all the traffic had driven past them, and it was clear for Rafe to make the turn. Unfortunately, he continued to peer down the road as the rain pummeled his face, and he didn't move.

As Jonah's body fell deeper into the depths of the sea, a massive form blocked out all the light from above and swallowed the prophet whole. There, in the belly of that whale, he pondered for three days in the dark, begging to be saved, hoping he could still be of use.

Rafe opened his eyes to the onslaught of the storm and noticed the line of cars behind them in the rearview mirror.

"Dad, what's wrong?" Martin asked with a shiver.

Chapter 40

Revelations

Merlot couldn't figure out what was bothering his friend. They had talked about the weather and many of their favorite topics for a couple of hours, but now Rafe just seemed agitated as he meandered around the covered front porch. Far outside Ottawa, Merlot's humble farm was peaceful, with only the sounds of chickens and a few dogs for a pleasant distraction.

"Can I get you another glass of water?" Merlot asked, sitting in his favorite rocking chair.

Rafe looked down at the cup he was holding. The ice had long since melted and was probably on its way to evaporating. "No, I'm okay. Thank you, though."

After a few minutes of silence, Merlot decided to change the subject and informed him, "They tell me that we should be leaving in a couple of weeks. They're getting everything all together, and there's an orientation meeting in a few days."

"That quick, huh?" Rafe was still visibly anxious, with beads of sweat appearing on his forehead. He fiddled with various trinkets and oddities hanging from the railing, including several handmade wind chimes that slowly moved in the cool breeze.

Merlot then glanced at one of his nearby chicken coops and confided, "Unfortunately, I don't know what I'm going to do about my farm. They said we could be there for a couple of months, and I was wondering if you would like to look over it while I'm gone."

"ACTUALLY," RAFE QUIETLY RETURNED while slowly putting down his empty cup, "I think that I need to come with you."

Astonished, Merlot replied, "Really? Why would you do that?"

The reluctant visionary took to pacing again and admitted, "I don't know exactly. Something tells me I should go. After I lost Bri in that nightmare of a country with people sporting guns at every turn, I never wanted to go back. I've seen so much hatred, so much bloodshed, that I just couldn't go back to that literal *hell on earth*."

Rafe felt himself ramping up again like he was ready to pick a fight. He shook his head a few times in utter disgust with everything, and then he slowly sat down in a nearby chair, defeated. There was no need to get fired up about something over which he had no control.

"You know how sometimes God speaks to you?" Rafe asked, trying to confirm that he wasn't crazy.

Merlot smiled anciently. "Yes. I wouldn't say I've ever heard Him, but I occasionally feel that He's guiding me—turn left, speak to that person—that kind of thing. As a police officer, I relied on Him to show me how to proceed in different circumstances. And I guess after all these years, I think we've figured out a system so that He can communicate with this hard-headed old boy."

Rafe looked at him squarely in the eye in an almost confessional kind of way. "When I was about 12, I stopped praying and reading the Bible. I was lost and unhappy for many years, and I didn't know why. It finally took the Sodium Massacres for me to pick up the Bible again—I needed something to help me feel better. Now, I study it constantly.

"Of course, I read many different books with Martin, but I just can't put the scriptures down. Call me crazy, but when all that was happening to us in the ghetto, the words of Jesus Christ helped me feel at peace. I would read, '*Love your enemies, bless them that curse you, do good to them that hate you, and pray for them that despitefully use you and persecute you,*' and not two seconds later, I would hear gunshots from the street below. Death surrounded us at all times, like a skeleton hand reaching for your shoulder from behind."

Almost frightened that he had introduced such a terrifying image, he stood up and tried to shake off the death that permeated the air around him. He didn't want to be still, just in case.

Merlot drew a heavy sigh. "I wonder if it's the End of Days with all that's going on. I wonder if, at any moment, Christ will come down from heaven with a white robe and scarlet sash, ushering in the last millennia. We both know that all of the horrible signs have happened."

He unfolded his arms, dismantling his wise sage posture, and looked at his wrinkled hands. As if he imagined the dust used to make them, he confided, "Honestly, though, I don't know if I could handle the dead rising. If I could see the Lord without that happening, I would be fine."

Rafe smiled at the frail man in front of him and realized that this was a moment in which they were both building each other up, knowing that they would soon need to pay the ferryman for the River Styx together.

"I don't think we'll see zombies if that's what's worrying you," Rafe assured. "That is just 2,000 years of stories trying to pollute the beauty of the resurrection. Every hair, bone, and muscle will be restored to its perfect frame, joined with the soul forever. Even those who were afflicted in life with various ailments will have a perfect body. This time that we have here is just a test with a temporary body. There is no need to fear the resurrection."

Merlot then responded, "I'm not scared. I guess I just don't know what to expect when we go down there. That guy said they needed help, and I'm trying to wrap my head around what that might be."

Rafe walked over to an ornate wind chime with the Eastern and Western Hemispheres painted on opposite sides and slowly spun it on its axis. "You know, I think one of the last things that will happen before the Second Coming is that two prophets will be killed at Jerusalem. Everyone will be too scared to bury them, so their bodies will lie in the street for three and a half days, and then they'll resurrect at the astonishment of all those around them.

"John even said that Jerusalem is like a spiritual Sodom, as they were so willing to kill Jesus that they would also kill His prophets." Rafe then looked at his friend and deduced, "So, until that happens, we don't need to worry."

The small wind chime slowly stopped with the American continents facing them, and it reflected the sunlight. "Whatever they need," Rafe pronounced, "I'm sure that they have been humbled enough to ask, and that's a good thing."

"So, what were you going to say about God telling you something?"

Rafe, taken aback, as if out of a trance, recoiled and sat down again. Somehow, just discussing the scriptures helped him feel safe. "Oh, it's nothing. Sometimes, certain Bible stories come to mind, and I think God is trying to teach me something with them. A few days ago, when it was raining horribly—"

The farmer looked over his acreage and added, "Yeah, that was some storm. It came and went like a flash."

246

"Well, I was watching my windshield wipers move back and forth while driving," Rafe continued, "and it reminded me of Jonah on a ship trying to escape his call to preach repentance. The men threw him overboard because the storm wreaked havoc on the ship, and the whale swallowed him whole. He was in the belly for three days before he was spewed out, and I'm trying to figure out what it all means."

Merlot chuckled a little. "That's one of those stories that makes me wonder. Can a man fit inside a whale? Wouldn't he be digested instead of just being held there? You look at how Jonah, Pinocchio, and Ahab all had their bouts with the fish at a crucial point in their stories. Maybe the whale is some sort of incubator, like an environment to push a character through to something different."

The old man rocked in his chair a little and offered some sage advice. "Jonah prayed in the whale so that the Lord would forgive him for not going to Nineveh. I guess we all go through something that takes us to the depths of despair, and in the end, we become better for it."

Rafe enjoyed analyzing the scriptures with his friend, but he was uncomfortable with the prospect of what the conversation meant. Still, he continued recounting what he knew of the prophet. "Jesus declared that as Jonah was in the whale for three days, so would He, the Son of Man, be in the heart of the earth for three days. And Peter taught that after the crucifixion, Jesus preached to the spirits in prison. Or maybe, since there were so many, He organized angels to preach." He then let out a fatigued sigh and genuinely asked, "I don't know. What should I do?"

Suddenly, Merlot jumped, and the excitement of a biblical correlation was evident in the sparkle in his eyes. "Earlier, you said that it was hell down there in Eden. Maybe you *are* supposed to go."

"That's what I'm afraid of," Rafe said as he pushed off the porch railing, depressed and downtrodden.

Merlot then quickly jabbed, "Just don't forget to bring your harpoon."

In response to the joke, Rafe smiled politely, but he desperately needed to pull away. The thought of returning to the country just made him sick in his heart. "Alright, well, I need to get going. Martin said he was going to cook dinner at our neighbor's house tonight, and I've left him alone long enough as it is."

"Fine. Fine. I'll be here." Merlot continued to rock in his chair as Rafe walked toward his truck. "Actually," the old man suddenly called out, "I have something for you."

ONCE INSIDE HIS LIVING ROOM, Rafe saw how upended Merlot's residence had become. Boxes and a lifetime of keepsakes and trinkets adorned every available nook and cranny. The mess almost seemed illegal.

"I've been going through some old things, trying to sort it all out," Merlot explained. "You know, just in case—"

Rafe couldn't take his eyes off the odd assortment of possessions that were stacked everywhere. It was contrary to the way Merlot maintained every other facet of his life. Although he had seen his friend during some difficult times, this assignment was causing so much anxiety that he wondered if he was crying for help.

"Sorry, it's a mess," he confessed.

Rafe looked up, wanting to make eye contact. "Don't worry. They probably just need more capital for weapons. Nothing is going to happen to you."

"I know," he returned. "A lot of this is just garbage anyway."

Merlot guided him into the kitchen, where he pulled out an old comic book from a box. "I was thinking about Martin and how he likes comic books. I guess if you're coming with me, he may need the extra company. This one inspired me to be a cop and help people."

248

The comic's flashy cover had several figures with wings fighting each other in a cataclysmic war for dozens of worlds. Rafe thumbed through a few pages and imagined how Martin would thoroughly devour it. "This is wonderful! Thank you very much!"

"Well, I hope he enjoys it."

"I'm sure he will. Thank you!"

As Rafe left for the door, he happened upon an old, framed picture on the counter. Most of it was covered with a stack of papers, but something drew his attention.

"What did you find there?"

Rafe couldn't believe his eyes as he slowly removed the papers and brought it closer. "This is my dad!"

The world stopped.

Rafe meticulously analyzed every portion of the picture as quickly as he could. From the grain, he could tell it was over a decade old, and of the ten people in the group, he only recognized his father and Merlot.

"Oh yeah, Davidson. He was a really good guy."

"When was this?"

Merlot took a few seconds to recall the details and replied, "It was before I moved to Sodium. We were in the church choir together, and that was right before we all went to a competition."

"My dad was in a choir? He can't even sing!"

Merlot looked down at the picture with him and chuckled. "Yep, he was good. I miss him, though."

Rafe teared up. "I haven't seen him since I was 12. What happened to him?"

They both took a seat at the kitchen table amidst all the trinkets from Merlot's life, and he recounted, "Well, I only knew him for a handful of years. He mentioned several times that he had a family and felt terrible

249

that he wasn't with them anymore. I remember he did cry several times about it.

"He worked nights on several jobs and went to school during the day, pulling more classes than regular, I think, and he graduated with a doctor's degree in dentistry."

Rafe was beaming. "He did it! He actually did it!"

"Yeah, he left for Africa about six months before I came to Sodium, and he wrote to me several times. He said he enjoyed working on children with cleft palates and how it changed their lives. He had truly found his calling in life."

Rafe was ecstatic about his father's achievements and upset that he had to leave both him and his mother to do it. There wasn't anything for it now. It was in the past, and it couldn't be undone.

He finally separated his eyes from the picture and asked Merlot, "So, how long has it been since you've heard from him?"

Every wrinkle was pronounced with Merlot's ancient frown. "Well, I'm not sure. I haven't seen anything from him since those Sodium shootings. I'm sorry." There was nothing more his friend uttered.

"I SAW MY DAD RECENTLY."

Rafe stared at his wife's tombstone, hoping that she would say something back. It was almost as useless as staring at a picture. There wasn't a conversation, just confessions.

"He became a dentist. It was exactly what he set out to do, and I'm happy for him. I don't know if he's still alive or—" This is the part where he couldn't take it anymore and just let the tears stream down. But of course, it was raining a little, and the tears and water mixed.

"Mrs. Holland is going to take care of Martin while I'm away. She's good to him, as you know. She helps him with his schoolwork, and they talk a lot—probably more than I do with him. I'm just not good at that. I wish you were here."

He reached into a bag with a few raindrops on it and pulled out a daisy. "This is for you." Once he kissed one of the petals and laid it on top of the tombstone, it started to rain heavily, and somehow, only a few drops found the flower.

"Please tell me not to go."

There, on a metal chair in the pouring rain, among a green field of tombstones, a man cried all alone.

Chapter 41

The Sodium War

That night at work, Rafe sat in the TV master control room by himself, surrounded by computers and screens. The overnight newscasts had pundit interviews about only one subject, Eden's aid. Merlot even had an interview with a reporter.

There were segments about what was in the caravan trucks, how many containers of food and supplies they could hold, how many people were assigned to each vehicle, and countless roundtable discussions about what Eden truly wanted.

Rafe's video that he shot many years before seemed to surface occasionally without any graphic violence. He had seen so much of his footage over the years that it was like a singer continually having to revisit the same old emotions in their songs. Every frame was chiseled into his brain, and there was no way of eradicating the memories.

He had only been interviewed once, and it was shortly after his jail release. In an hour-long cable show, the interviewer elicited every horrible facet of their predicament in the United States in such a way that he never wanted to go through the experience again.

Since Kerioth's petition, his phone constantly rang with interview requests, but he never answered. Many online channels had dozens of conspiracy theory videos explaining everything an imagination could create. Of course, there were the other survivors, but they kept mostly quiet. There was no need to sensationalize any of it or make a profit; that was left for the outsiders to do.

This new constant barrage of all things Eden had created so much anxiety that everywhere Rafe went, people discussed it to no end. At one point, after hearing a few people talk about it in front of him at the grocery checkout line, he put down his little cart at the end of the aisle and left the store. There was no escaping the nightmare.

"DAD, WHAT WAS THE SODIUM WAR?"

The words caught Rafe by surprise as he passed Martin's room, and he didn't know how to respond, so he stood in the doorway and thought carefully about his answer.

"That's a good question. It means different things to different people, and it's changed over time. I guess I've never really talked to you about it. What do you know already?"

Rafe wondered what Bri would say. She would find the right balance of insight and concern. After all, Martin was eight years old, and he didn't need to be exposed to everything. He didn't need to have the same nightmares that he had or distrust everyone around him.

"I don't know anything, really," Martin said under his breath as he fidgeted with his comic book. "A few guys at school say that you started it all. But I don't believe that."

Rafe sat down on his bed next to him and confirmed, "You're right, I didn't start it, but I was there at the beginning. I was a cameraperson for a news station in Texas, and I went to a place called Sodium, where a lot of people were killed—"

"Why were they killed?"

"Why? I don't know why." He was trying to be as honest as possible. He could hear his mom telling him that she always talked to children like they were adults because she felt a person's spirit could be millions of years old.

The father continued, "Some people were so full of hate, or rather, they couldn't relate to them or understand them, so they just killed them." Rafe wanted to take it slow so that he wouldn't get lost in all the complexities. The Sodium War, after all, was something that had severely impacted his little family.

At first, Martin was silent, and he looked down at the comic's colorful pages as a place of safety. "Why didn't they understand them? Why didn't they just talk about it?" he managed at last.

Rafe studied his son's face and his arms. He watched his fingers move across the pages, and he smiled at the way he suddenly scratched his nose. He couldn't come to terms with the idea of anyone hurting his little boy because of his skin color. His blood seemed to boil at the mere thought of it. Martin didn't see it, but Rafe clenched his fist as if the whole world were in that room with them, and he needed to fight for his son's life.

"Well, you remember how we've talked about Martin Luther King, Junior, right?"

"I guess so."

"A lot of people were beaten and killed because of the color of their skin, and he wanted the government to change the laws to protect them. He helped them pass the Civil Rights Act and the Voting Rights Act, which outlawed discrimination against someone because of their race, color, or religion.

"Unfortunately, even though there are laws, there will always be racist people. There will always be people that hate others because of their skin color. And sometimes, they talk bad about them, or they beat them. Sometimes they kill them."

Martin looked up at his dad as if his innocence had just been robbed and asked, "Will you ever kill me?"

Rafe couldn't believe the words he'd just heard. It was utterly inhuman even to consider such an action, and then he realized how upset he had suddenly become and how he must appear to the young boy.

"No, Martin, I would *never* do that." He had crossed a line. He had let his emotions get the better of him, and this dark, loathsome path that he was describing had unleashed someone that his boy didn't recognize.

Martin quietly returned to the comic, seemingly unaffected, but Rafe knew better.

"Come here. I'm sorry," he tried to console with his arms outstretched for a hug. They embraced, but it seemed hollow. Rafe wanted nothing more than to place a band-aid on his heart, but he knew that his impulsive, monstrous disdain for everything that the United States had become had separated the two of them a little bit that evening. He stood up, a failed father, and said, "I'm sorry."

"But what was the *war* part?"

"The *war* part?" Rafe stopped right before the door.

"Yeah. Wasn't there a war?"

He glanced at Martin's comic book, full of colorful heroes and villains fighting each other. Each panel had a character delivering a witty line and a punch at the same time. Fighting was the exciting part. It was what he understood, not the politics or racism but the good versus evil.

"Is that the comic book that Mr. Merlot gave you?"

"Yeah."

"What's it about?"

"There's something called the War in Heaven, and all the angels and demons are fighting each other. Raphael and Gabriel are the two main angels that beat up most of the demons, and now that the Human Realm has been created, they have taken the fight there."

"Who's that guy?" Rafe asked, pointing to a character with grotesque features.

"That's the Son of the Morning Light."

Rafe chuckled at the biblical references. "Oh, I see." He waited a few seconds as he admired his son a little bit more. "Did you know that the War in Heaven was a real thing?"

"Really? Did they have swords or guns?"

"I don't think they had either."

"Then how did the good angels win?"

"Well, someday we'll know exactly, but I believe it was a war of words. They bore their testimonies to one another."

"Oh, that's boring!"

To an eight-year-old boy, the idea of arguing was probably less than thrilling. And who could blame him? Anything worthwhile had to have some kind of action.

"You're right; it is kind of boring."

He thought about how to answer his original question and just continued the story, "After those people were killed in Sodium, the government didn't do anything about it, and more people across the country were killed. They let it happen. They had become so corrupt that they encouraged the racism."

"So, the government was the bad guy?"

"Well, the racism had always been there, and the president exploited it to get elected." Martin then nodded as if he knew what exploited meant.

Rafe continued, "Eventually, the president couldn't be stopped because he had become very popular with half of the country. They enjoyed his personality and his policies, but he was like a bull in a china

257

shop. They loved his antics and how he said mean things against anyone who had different ideas about government policies.

"He once ripped up the United States' original Constitution on live TV because he said it was outdated and that we needed a more modern document. It was at a ceremony to honor America's founding fathers, and he just went over to the case holding the Constitution and ripped it up. All the guards standing by didn't move as they didn't know what to do. Everyone gasped. Reporters took pictures. They all just stood still like they were frozen."

"Why was that?" the inquisitive boy asked.

Rafe figured that he needed to explain. "He had just destroyed the most important document in American history, and they couldn't believe he did that. They were shocked."

"Why did so many people like him then?"

"I don't know," the father admitted. "He just said and did things that divided the country. Many people in the government didn't like what he did, but they were too afraid of losing their jobs to stand up to him. They had put him above the law. He was constantly trying to see what else he could break or do wrong, and they allowed him to do it. A few senators like Mack and Ramón did oppose a lot of the things he did, and they were labeled as national heroes, but the party ousted them."

"Didn't you escape the country?"

"Yes, I did. My wife and I were about to have a baby, and we didn't want her to be around so much hate, so we left. We no longer wanted to be Americans, and we hoped that the government of Canada could help everyone that was suffering in the United States."

Martin was finally excited about the story and asked, "So, that's when the Sodium War started?"

That was the tipping point, the part of the story where *good guys* assembled to make a plan of attack, and Rafe could see it in his eyes.

There was always a core need to right the wrong, to balance out whatever evil had prevailed for so long with wholesome goodness.

It was the conditioning of thousands of years of stories, the seventh note leading to the eighth in a key, the resolution, the karma, the restitution of all things to a state of peace. It was the innate notion that, in the end, virtue had to vanquish all the insurmountable obstacles, leading to greater understanding.

If it wasn't for the faith in a being that was in charge of everything, there could never be a feeling of a perfect resolution to anything. All this could not be just chemicals and happenstance.

"Shortly after I arrived with some footage that showed how civil laws were broken and that innocent people were being slaughtered, the government of Canada tried to reprimand the country and hold certain individuals accountable, but it didn't work. Eventually, a task force was mobilized, and within a year, all people of color and sympathizers were escorted to the Canadian border to be free of the tyranny."

"Was there any fighting?" Martin asked.

"I don't know exactly. I wasn't there, but Mr. Merlot volunteered for it, and he said that there were times where he had to fire his weapon. He doesn't like to talk about it."

"Did they shoot the president?"

Rafe wondered why there was a keen attention toward violence. Maybe it was from the idea of a tooth for a tooth, wanting to punish those who wronged someone—a punishment for a crime. Everything was black and white for the child.

"I doubt it. Besides, shooting someone is not always the best way to handle a situation. Even though he did many horrible things, we have no right to end his life. The right thing to do is to have a trial for him, and if he is guilty, he goes to jail. God is the one who will judge his heart."

Rafe looked at the comic again and asked, "Hey, can I see that for a second?" Martin obliged and handed it to him. After thumbing through a few pages, Rafe turned the book around so that Martin could see it, and he pointed to a few characters who were just conversing with one another.

"The Sodium War is still happening," Rafe declared. "We're both a part of it, and right now, we're talking about what we can do to stop all these bad things from happening, just like these two guys. By telling people not to say racist things or by trying to understand how someone else may feel in any kind of situation, we're fighting the war."

Rafe paused for a moment after he said that and realized that maybe he was a good father. He was trying, and that's all that mattered.

"But you know what the best part about the Sodium War was?" he added.

"I don't know. What?"

Rafe put his hand admiringly on his boy's face and said, "You were on one of the first escorts out of the country, and I am so thankful that you are a part of my life. You are everything to me, and I just want you to be happy."

After a loving embrace and giving him the kind of smile he wished his own father had shared with him, he turned off the bedroom light and closed the door.

As he walked down the hall to his room, he faintly remembered a time when his father wished him goodnight as he pretended to be asleep. There was a long pause before his father closed the bedroom door, and Rafe imagined that he probably smiled at him. His father did love him.

Later that evening, Rafe tried to get a little more sleep on the couch before going into work, and as his mind drifted, he recalled the first time he saw Martin.

"THANK YOU FOR DOING THIS," THE ADMINISTRATIVE NURSE STATED as she guided Rafe to the nursery window. She was exhausted and overwhelmed, but somehow, a glimpse of hope made its way across her faint smile and droopy eyes.

"Anything to help," Rafe returned. Still unsure of what he was getting himself into, he thought it was something Bri would have done if their roles were reversed.

The crowded hospital hallway was noisy, with several patients on gurneys and nurses multitasking. Although it was busy, no one complained. They were all running on fumes, and everyone somehow found a little more energy to continue moving forward.

"With all the facilities in town, there are over 500 refugee children, ranging from infant to young adult. Martin, over there, is three," she explained as she pointed through a pane of glass to a malnourished African American boy among a dozen children in the small room. His limbs were thin, and anyone's heart would burst just to look at him, but he happily played with a few toys on the floor by himself.

"All these children here have a family member in critical condition," she continued teary-eyed but as professionally as she could.

Rafe glanced at her and solemnly added, "Yes, the agency mentioned his father. How is he?"

"Well, I can't say much, but he was badly beaten over time. I'm not sure how many weeks or *days* he has left. And he's just one of many cases—hence, the need for many emergency foster care placements. Desperate times call for desperate measures."

Rafe watched the toddler play behind the glass, and he was reminded of the elementary school child he helped during the Sodium shooting. He couldn't stand idly by and watch so many people in need—he had to help in whatever way he could.

When they arrived at the father's medical partition, the nurse gently called out to him through the privacy curtain, "Mr. Bailey, may we come in?"

A soft, beaten voice replied, "Yes, Jessica, you may."

The man on the hospital bed was almost godlike in his composure, hiding many ailments behind his wise, dark eyes. He was skinnier than his boy, and yet, he sat up boldly, defying each broken piece inside of him. If he did smile, it was because he and Martin were free. Any glistening tears below his eyes and on his cheeks were several years old.

"I don't know how you remember all of us," the nurse lovingly teased, "Mr. Bailey, this is Rafe Davidson, the man who will look after Martin for a while." She then finished the introduction, "Rafe, this is Augustus Bailey."

The young father looked over Rafe as if he could see things beyond the veil and declared with difficulty, "Mr. Davidson, you are a good man. I know you don't think so, but you are."

Embarrassed, Rafe replied, "Thank you, sir. I'm so sorry that your family has endured so much." They both locked eyes in silence for a long time, as if they didn't need to say words; they both knew the pain and suffering of inequality.

"But we endured," Augustus acknowledged with a heavy smile. "When I was younger, I wore glasses so that I wouldn't be lynched—so that I would appear more intelligent and less of a threat. Now, I am blind in one eye, but I can still see out of the other—and I'm very grateful!" He exhaled deeply as if he knew better than to dwell on it. "Have you met Martin?"

Rafe shook his head and answered with a stammer, "Not yet, sir. I wanted to meet with you first and ask for your blessing." For some reason, he had trouble articulating what he was trying to say. Although he desired to use the word *permission*, the conversation had become awkwardly religious and formal by the time the request left his mouth.

Augustus chuckled in a heartfelt manner and said, "Yes, you'll do fine; don't worry." He took another long pause and added, "We named him after the Reverend King. With the way the world moves as it does, we all need another fighter for the good in life, and I know that you'll both do just fine."

"Thank you, sir," Rafe replied humbly.

THE DAY THAT THE FIRST CARAVAN OF REFUGEES arrived in Canada was called the *Day of Brotherhood*. Each subsequent arrival had a unique name: *Day of Brotherhood: Freedom, Day of Brotherhood: Selflessness, Day of Brotherhood: Charity, Day of Brotherhood: Compassion.* It was as if each commemoration was a reminder of why we were given this life.

It was quickly dubbed the modern-day Exodus, and moving trucks were provided to families without any means of transporting their belongings. City streets were lined with armed Canadian officials to keep back the brownsuits and maintain a peaceful escort.

Eventually, the task force discovered which cities were ghetto detainment centers, and these became the main focal points for the occupation. Some were for dissenters, and others were holding locations for those who had lost their citizenship because of their skin color. In all, the Canadian occupation of the United States freed over 18 million people.

The Egyptians were forced to let the children of Israel go, but the Americans didn't see it like that. When it came down to it, the United States government agreed to the *expulsion*, as they called it, because they were dead set on a racial purification of the country.

Only those that were deemed *pure Caucasian* by the DNA census could remain in the United States, although there were many exceptions. Most of these were because of the incorporated *Black and Brown Slave*

Trade, which had considered the poor souls as property, and they were hidden from the Canadian task force.

Yet others didn't even know that they were freed from the tyranny because of all the misinformation provided by the only circulated news outlet in the United States, *The New Eden Truth*. It was also impossible for the officials to find everyone, especially in the smaller towns, but slowly, all these things changed.

Canada became a beacon to which many felt the need to migrate without knowing the reason. More than a lighthouse, the country had become a home and sanctuary where the light of God could finally be felt after years of living in what was once the *United States of America.*

Chapter 42

Jericho

W ithin a few days, Rafe had finally accepted his fate. It was the
will of God for him to go, but Rafe begged Him to reconsider.
There was nothing of any consequence that he could add to the outfit, so
many people wondered why he was there. Some considered it a public
relations call.

He kept quiet in the preparation meetings and refused to comment
on or provide any tactical information. The hours at those meetings
seemed like days as there was an endless back-and-forth over conjectures
and hyperboles. No one knew what to expect, but the consensus was to be
prepared for the worst.

A 300-page field manual for the convoy was quickly penned and
distributed to all the personnel involved. Rafe found it to be only valuable
as a place to sketch out his frustrations and fears in the margins.
Everything could be summed up with a frequent comment in his copy:
This is a stupid mission.

On the morning of the deployment, Rafe shaved for the first time in several years, feeling that he was doing the will of the Lord, and that was a comforting thought. He held his son as tight as he could and whispered, "I love you, Martin," not knowing if he would have the chance to repeat those same words.

He watched Martin and Mrs. Holland wave back at him near her apartment front door, and it felt as if he were attending his funeral. More than anything, he wanted to stay in the comfort of his family, but a force pulled him away.

"Rafe, we need to get going," Merlot finally said from inside the cab of his rusty farm truck. "He'll be okay, don't worry." His tone was that of a second father, comforting and heartfelt, so Rafe unwillingly rose to the passenger seat.

Without any particular prompt, Rafe then recalled a conversation he had with Bri in Sodium many years before. As the hordes of demonstrators chanted around the chapel at the joint funeral, there was a moment when they realized they could just stay in the van and do nothing. They could disregard their reporting assignment and justify their inaction by declaring the situation and environment too violent to follow through.

But Rafe handed Bri the microphone and urged her to tell the story. He was the one that put her in harm's way for the sake of waking the nation to the stranglehold of white supremacy on that little town.

As Mrs. Holland escorted Martin back inside her apartment, Rafe memorized how the boy was slowly taken away from his view, and the Sodium memory continued to flood his mind while they drove away.

He remembered admiring Bri through the camera eyepiece as she reported on the funeral, concentrating on her red curls moving with the breeze and her beautiful eyes that radiated her inspiring fortitude. He would follow her anywhere.

Once the stone hit her temple, though, she fell out of frame and out of view. She had commanded the nation's attention with a rallying war cry to end American racial injustice, and now the frame was filled with carnage, confusion, and hatred. Adding to the chaos, Rafe flew to the stone thrower and knocked him out. The frame was unmanned, and the attention was lost.

A PANG OF IMMENSE GUILT SOON CRASHED DOWN ON RAFE as he sat beside the retired officer in his rusty old truck. He was the one who slipped the indoctrination letter under the door and drove off the freeway to escape hell. He was the one that pushed them to Canada, and now she was gone, separated by a slab of cement and a few feet of dirt. For him, everything was his fault.

"He's going to be okay. God will take care of him," Merlot offered.

Rafe wondered how his father might have felt standing in the fog outside his childhood home that one night before he drove away. He had tried to understand his father's actions many times, but at last, the thought came to him that he might have left because of his mother's suffocating racism.

It was a haunting accusation, and it made him cry. He wished a mountain would fall on him and bury him. So indescribable was his guilt that he couldn't climb or pierce it. Rafe could have taught his mother many times how to be more Christian, and his father would have never left.

Merlot then shared, "He takes care of everyone unconditionally. He loves unconditionally. Let Heavenly Father teach him for a while. I've seen the way Martin listens to you, how he adores you. You're a wonderful father."

In the depths of hell, Rafe refuted, "I'm a failure. I've been a failure since the day I was born."

His friend then said in a calm voice, "You know that's not right. Life is a classroom, not a test; you *cannot* fail. Just let go of all of the pain and guilt you may be feeling. Just let it go; Jesus Christ has already experienced it all for you. Let Him help you."

Rafe covered his face so that his friend wouldn't see him cry. It hurt, and the back of his throat ached. "Thanks. I appreciate that," he finally returned after a few sniffles.

UNDER THE RATHER HASTY DEPLOYMENT SCHEDULE of three and a half weeks, the government could only assemble enough food and supplies for 38 military-style supply trucks and other operative military and medical vehicles, along with 17 commercial diesel trucks for most of the food.

This would be the initial and more exploratory convoy as they didn't know what kind of aid was needed. It was Merlot who suggested that there should only be enough weapons for the military personnel. There was no need to make a firearms transaction with the distressed country.

MSE Op Private Charron was assigned to escort Rafe and Merlot in their supply truck, and as soon as she found out that they would accompany her for the 1,000-mile trip, she came at them with all she had.

"I don't believe any of it, and you both are liars," she ripped as she climbed into the driver's side of *her* truck.

Already in the cab, they both looked at her as if she had come from a different solar system. Her sudden rebuke and entrance to the vehicle were both startling and concerning.

"I beg your pardon, dear." It was all that Merlot could manage with all the politeness in the world. After all these years, he had replaced the horror that he had experienced as a cop with the gentleness of a farmer caring for his land. There was no reason to dispute anything as time was short for the old man.

"I've read both of your profiles, and there is no way that any of it is true. Slavery, public executions, total disregard for the law—that is not the United States. I was there when I was a girl," she contested as she started the engine and joined in the line of vehicles.

Disengaged from all of it, Rafe looked out the window and wondered if Bri was close. Sometimes he could feel her presence. She would probably be in the back of a truck, ready to hand-deliver food and clothing to anybody that came up to her. He thought about how people from the community would inform others by saying, "Just go up to the redhead lady. She'll help you." He smiled at the idea that her hair color would make her a beacon to the world.

"Well," Merlot said in a way to disarm the bomb, "I don't want to ruffle your feathers more than they already are. We're just here because someone asked for help."

Undeterred, she continued in full-on rage, "You Americans use racism for all your problems; it's your go-to reason for everything that happens. If a band released a black album, you'd call it racism. If a white guy wore a black shirt and did something stupid, you'd call it racism. All you people just look at everything with racism in mind; you can't see anything else."

Rafe drew out a heavy sigh. This was going to be a long drive, 16 hours over two days. It was already drizzling as they left the base, and while making a turn, he started counting the long train-like caravan of trucks and vehicles behind them.

"Yes, racism is rampant all over the world," Merlot acknowledged. "The United States doesn't own the rights to it. Take a look at World War Two—"

269

Without hesitation, she stabbed, "All that is hogwash too. World War Two never happened, and all that Nazi stuff is made up so that you can all dominate the world with your fear-mongering."

"But what about all the footage and all the stories? Surely you can't negate all of that proof—" Merlot was on the defensive. After all, his family had been involved.

Charron shot back at them like a cannon. "Yes, I can! It's all doctored, just like the Lee Harvey Oswald picture. The government is out to keep us in the dark. No one can be trusted."

"Okay," Merlot returned with a slight chuckle as if to cement the conversation closed. There was no way of arguing with her. A completely bulletproof case couldn't sway someone who has made up their mind. It's like trying to convince a chicken that it has lost its head while it continues to run away.

She abruptly stepped on the brake. The little maneuver was probably not in the doodled manual that Rafe happened to have in his lap, but she performed it just as well.

"You know what this is?" she barked. "Canada has needed the US for economic stability for decades, and one of the two governments has ended the relationship, yours or mine, and I'm not sure which. But this mission isn't going to prove anything. It's not."

The two men sat in silence as if a principal were scolding them in a detention hall. Although it was probably against his better judgment, Merlot reengaged. "So, what are we carrying in the back, dear?" His good-natured tendencies couldn't let the friction endure. She was on their side, and they didn't need any more enemies. She resumed course.

"It is mostly clothing, blankets, and hygienic items. This is the women's truck number two if any female civilians need supplies," she reported.

Yes, Bri would probably be in the back of this truck, Rafe silently resolved.

"I see," Merlot said. "And who distributes that? Do you want us to do it? We'd be glad to help."

"No, the quartermaster will take care of all disbursements and the coordination of those efforts once a situation presents itself. You both are here to talk to Secretary Kerioth. That is all."

Rafe thought about the assignment to be Merlot's assistant for the mission and realized that he found himself finally understanding Jonah's plight. Right then, he didn't want to be surrounded by so much hate and ridicule.

The parable of the master with two sons soon came to mind. The first son said he wouldn't do the father's will by working in the vineyard but eventually did, and the second said he would but didn't. And the Lord told his listeners, the chief priests, that just like the first son in his eventual obedience, the publicans and harlots would go into the Kingdom of God before them. Hopefully, the Lord would see him more like the first son.

Rafe knew that there was a reason for everything. Although he could just step out of that truck and leave the mission at any time, God had prepared all things, and every single atom headed for New Eden was for an eventual good.

AFTER NEARLY SEVEN HOURS OF TORRENTIAL DOWNPOUR with an almost opaque overcast, they had come to their first obstacle. There, in the middle of a field in what was once Pennsylvania, the clouds lifted just a little, and they all witnessed it.

"Isn't that a sight to behold?" Merlot was dumbfounded beyond belief.

Charron stopped the truck just as all the others had done in front of her and admitted, "The satellite imagery depicted the structure to be huge, but this is surreal."

All three of them stepped out of the truck just as many others did in the single-file caravan. The freeway pavement showed eerie signs of neglect as noxious weeds grew from cracks and the paint had long since faded. After hours of driving through the brown, desolate countryside, they had barely seen the place for what it was, *a tomb*. They had not seen a soul since they had crossed the border.

The massive concrete wall before them stood 120 feet high, a story for each of the tribes of Israel. The only way they could see the very top was with the grace of an occasional lightning bolt as it was nearly night at noonday. Looking to both sides of the monster proved fruitless as there seemed to be no end, stretching across the open field like the parted Red Sea. It only begged the question: *Why would anyone want to build something so godly massive?*

In fact, this was just a minuscule portion of a circular wall that spanned a 700-mile radius, all the same height, with a three-foot thickness toward the top and a 24-foot thickness at the bottom. Massive metal fortifications scaled up the inside of the wall, and they had a footprint of 50 feet leading away from it.

Fortunately, the freeway led straight to the open metal gate, which was three feet thick, 36 feet high, and 24 feet wide. Most of the hinges were broken, and the bent gate was weather-worn. The unhinged bottom corner sank several feet into the middle of the pavement, leaving the passage into the mouth of hell wide enough for only one military truck at a time. This door was just 1 of 12 that were all equally placed around the 4,398-mile New Eden perimeter.

AFTER MANY HAD DOCUMENTED THE WALL with their phones and cameras, the caravan started again. Rafe noticed as they drove near the entrance that a jarring 12-foot Sodium symbol had been carved into the wall. He knew what it was. Others probably didn't notice.

All of this, even the crest, was a commemoration toward those little boys who took to killing in the name of racism, the hatred of others, the lack of compassion, and the utter refusal to be human.

Rafe looked out the window and quoted from memory, "*Many will say to me in that day, Lord, Lord, have we not prophesied in thy name and in thy name have cast out devils and in thy name done many wonderful works? And then will I profess unto them, I never knew you: depart from me, ye that work iniquity.*"

Merlot questioned him, "Have you seen this wall before?"

"No," he responded. "We didn't see anything like this. Of course, they could have been building it elsewhere. There was so much misinformation. We probably wouldn't have made it if this were here."

Rafe wondered how long it must have taken to build it. Of course, he didn't know how far it stretched, and with all the lack of information, it could have been started before McKendrick gave his first campaign speech. Whatever weird obsession drove the people of New Eden to build it, they had the unlimited resources of people and money to make it happen.

All he really knew, though, was that the further they went, the more lies and hatred they would uncover.

Chapter 43

Babel

The company had not counted on every town being deserted once they had crossed the border. There was not even a sign of animal life—the land was indeed cursed.

Throughout the excursion, a couple of refueling stops had been required for most of the vehicles as they maintained their course, and at times, they were desperate to find operational gas pumps that had fuel. Many were worried about setting off an explosion because of the lack of maintenance.

The day wore on in continuing darkness and unending rain. Because it was so cold and muddy, once it was agreed that the caravan needed to stop and sleep, everyone somehow made do in their cabs. Stepping outside seemed mysteriously wrong.

The night was almost indistinguishable from the darkness of the day, and once the sun was supposed to come up again, it was nowhere to be found. It was there, though; it just had to compete with the thickness of the air and the onslaught of rain.

WITHIN SEVERAL MORE HOURS OF DRIVING through the Appalachian Mountains, they approached their destination. The Commander in the lead vehicle notified everyone over the radio that the Secretary's call had been traced to the city in front of them. Tactical operations required that most of the company remain 20 miles outside the city. Only a couple of vehicles, including the one with Rafe and Merlot, were to proceed forward.

Their truck was the last of three that continued, and after several miles of traveling through the barren wasteland, the lead truck stopped by a small outpost with a barrier gate. Rafe tried to see around the truck in front of him, but he couldn't. He rolled down the window, allowing the full assault of the rain in, and watched a guard come around the front of the lead truck and climb in peacefully.

"Hey, I think the guard just got in the Commander's truck," he informed them.

Merlot replied, "At least there's somebody here. I was starting to think that we got all dressed up for nothing."

As they continued on the small road toward the city, what demanded their attention was a massive white obelisk with a 300-foot-wide base in the exact center of the civilization. Since the top disappeared into the thick clouds, it appeared to be like a modern-day Tower of Babel. All the other buildings paled in comparison. In fact, the *Sal Sanctorum Obeliscus* (or Holy Salt Obelisk), as it was called, stood at the very center of the 4,398-mile concrete wall that encircled it.

"YOU'RE AWFULLY QUIET," MERLOT SAID as he turned to Charron. The sincere statement was made in the way that a father would ask his daughter how she was feeling right before they sauntered down the aisle.

Out of all the things racing through everyone's mind, Merlot chose to focus on how someone else felt about the situation. Call it a defense mechanism for an elderly gentleman, or the need to protect a passenger as an imminent crash unfolds, or maybe even an act of chivalry, but Merlot cared for her as another human being and wanted her to be at ease.

The silence unfortunately continued, and he said, "I have no idea what's going to happen, but I'm glad that you are both here with me. Do you mind if I say a prayer?"

Rafe looked at his friend with a half-hearted smile and nodded.

After looking at the somewhat stonewalling expression from the driver, Merlot bowed his head and stated, "I'll just say it to myself." He closed his eyes both out of reverence and fear of the unknown. The old man then mouthed his prayer, ending it with a peaceful smile.

The small caravan drove through the deserted civilization, making turns and going straight through intersections. There was no life or light. It was like driving through a forgotten cave, deep in the earth. The flooded streets were paved with gold, and many architectural endeavors referenced symbolism from The Tabernacle and the Holy of Holies.

At long last, the three trucks stopped in the parking lot for a gargantuan indoor stadium, and everyone ran through the downpour to the front entry. Once they were under the entrance overhang, the guard removed his helmet, revealing the face of a young, bruised soldier. His caped, armored suit was entirely white, and there was a sword at his side.

The Asian bowed and said, "I am Dan, a sentry for Sacred Sodium, and I am so thankful you are here! Dr. Xiāo will soon greet you." He then hastily scurried off into the cold, wet void away from the trucks.

Puzzled with each new development, the six men stood there without knowing what would be next. The Commander holstered his weapon to radio back to the base outside of the city, and although Rafe and Merlot were given pistols, they both refused to hold them. They had already seen too much. The three other military officers kept in formation, as they should.

"I wonder what that tower thing is?" Merlot ventured.

Rafe looked at it, as it could be seen from anywhere in the city, and said, "I don't know. These guys sure like to go big in whatever they build. It kind of reminds me of the Egyptians using the slaves to build the pyramids."

"True. Do you think anybody's in there?" Merlot asked.

Before Rafe could come up with any kind of answer, Dr. Xiāo had opened the door and provided the first of many explanations. "No," he said. "Come inside quickly."

A GUST OF WIND CLOSED THE DOOR BEHIND THEM, and Dr. Xiāo led them through the ticketing area with a LED lantern. "I'm Dr. Xiāo. Sorry, it's dark. We try to conserve as much electricity as possible."

Suddenly, he turned around and said, "I want to thank each one of you for coming. We are all very grateful!"

"No problem, Doc," the Commander returned as he looked around, trying to assess the situation. "What can we do for you?"

Finally, after almost four weeks of anticipation, they would all receive some sense of closure, something that would fill in the variables in all the calculations everyone had been running through their minds.

Dr. Xiāo seemed to have no way of explaining the predicament as he just looked at each one of them for several seconds. Perhaps, he was just happy to see someone from the outside. "It is easier just to show you. Follow me."

It didn't take long for them to go through the dark hallway and stop before one of the arena doors. It was mysteriously painted entirely white with a tiny smear of what looked like blood just a few feet from the bottom.

Rafe was the first to see it as he had pointed his flashlight right at it. "What's that?"

"Don't worry. Everything's okay; just don't be afraid," Dr. Xiāo replied. But despite any kind of consolation attempt, the four soldiers held their weapons at the ready.

He opened the door and allowed each of the foreigners into the massive arena. The bleachers were entirely in the dark, and it looked like many rows had been removed to allow for as much room as possible on the field. There were only about 30 feet of bleachers before they reached a handrail that prevented the 50-foot drop to the field below.

They were all beyond stunned. Not only was the arena more massive than any they had ever seen, but they also realized the need for their aid. The soldiers lowered their weapons, and they each looked at the field from the perch in utter disbelief.

"This used to be a gladiator arena. That is why it is so big. And what you see on the floor is the last of everyone from the whole country," explained Dr. Xiāo. "From what we can tell, there isn't anyone else. It has been months since someone new has come."

The field was covered with bunk beds and triple bunk beds, each supporting a dying Edenite. A couple of dozen nurses walked between the beds, which were all spaced a foot apart. It was a sea of white linens holding together an innumerable host of rotting bodies.

"Are they wounded?" the Commander asked.

Dr. Xiāo turned to them and said, "Gentlemen, please sit down."

As soon as they were all seated in the bleachers, the doctor continued, "They are not wounded. Well, maybe their pride is—maybe. They are suffering from what we call the *Curse of God*."

One of the men scoffed, "Seriously?"

"God has cursed them?" Merlot asked as he looked over the hand railing.

Once Rafe had come through the entrance, he immediately took a seat in one of the first rows. He felt queasy, and the idea of going forward

279

was almost unbearable. Although the field of bodies was utterly repulsive and there was the stench of death, what consumed him was the fact that he had lost his wife trying to flee from them.

He watched the men below talk to the doctor and imagined that Bri would've already been on the field feeding the poor souls a half-spoonful of soup at a time. He couldn't do that. She was much better at life than he was.

"THEY ALL SUFFER IT DIFFERENTLY," THE DOCTOR EXPLAINED, "but most of them have severe ocular hemorrhaging, so you will see many with head bandaging. Blood coming from the nostrils is common, along with alopecia or hair loss. What will be most striking is that 100 percent of the patients have had cachexia or severe weight loss. Anorexia and aphasia are very common, so most won't allow you to feed them. They are mostly skin and bones. Boils, severe skin fissure, and many other skin disorders are also present."

At this, the Commander stepped aside to radio the base with an update and ordered most of the soldiers and all the medical officers to join them in the arena.

"How many of them are there?" Merlot asked.

"Honestly, I don't know. Last night, the number of living souls had reached just under 145,000. Those on the field are the most ill. We have over 60 conference rooms around the arena with those that are in different stages of the disorder."

One of the soldiers asked, "Are we going to get this too?"

Merlot continued to look out at the field, and he observed the nurses moving between the patients. None of them were wearing masks or gloves. He watched one patient throw up all over a female nurse, and she wiped it off as if it were a frequent occurrence.

280

"No," Merlot resolved, heartbroken, just above a whisper. "They're cursed. God has done this." The reality of the situation was becoming apparent.

The doctor concurred, "Correct. It doesn't matter which of their body fluids may touch you—they do not have any effect. You will not contract the disease. It has been reserved for them. We have been treating them for over a year now, and our only demise is exhaustion."

After a few seconds of silence, the Commander joined them and relayed to the doctor, "Sir, we have 65 men and women who are on their way right now to assist. Is there a place where we can coordinate what needs to be done?"

"Yes. Follow me."

Chapter 44

Soul of a Man

Rafe thought about Martin as he moved his small chair close to the next patient. Her skin was purplish, and the spider veins caused massive ridges. The muscles had deteriorated so severely that the whiteness of the bone could almost be seen through the skin on her arm. Her lips were very cracked, and the little blood that she had left made a small stream down her sunken cheek and onto the pillow. And yet she lived.

"Ma'am, I'm here for you. Can I give you some soup?"

She mouthed something slowly, barely moving.

"Water perhaps?" he asked.

He then dabbed a cloth into a water container and put it to her lips. Her chin moved ever so slightly. It helped not being able to see her eyes. He then noticed that she had something on her forehead. He stood up to get a better look, and he realized that it was a small tattoo of the stylized McKendrick *M*. The two peaks were pointed, and the lines in the middle crossed at the bottom.

It had been years since he had seen that symbol, and he hoped that it had been purged from his mind. He wore it countless times on his arm to lie about who he was and how he felt about the people around him. He shook his head, knowing that she had espoused such horrid ideals.

On the chart hanging at the head of her bed were her name and a few stats. As he input the data into a medical app on his phone, he stated, "Savannah Lucas, 35 years old." He then went down a list of actions and conditions. He had given her a few drops of water, check. She seemed unresponsive, check. Skin purple, check. Labored breathing, check.

"Do you need anything else, Ms. Lucas?" He didn't receive a response, so he stood up to attend to the person above her.

The skin on the next patient appeared charred as if he had been pulled from a fire, but after glancing at his chart, Rafe found out that it was his version of the curse. By looking at the white sheet covering him, he could tell that the man had no limbs.

"How are you today, sir?" Rafe started.

"Well, I'm better than yesterday," the man said with some strained breathing.

"What happened yesterday?"

"Oh, nothing. Same thing as the day before. I'm just lying here, waiting to die. You don't happen to have any venison on you, do you?"

Taken aback by the odd request, Rafe didn't respond for several seconds. The man on the bed struggled to turn his head toward Rafe, and the effort caused more blood to seep through charred cracks in his neck, making his pillow even wetter.

"Are you still there?" the man asked.

"Yes, I am." Almost frightened of the living corpse, he continued, "Is there anything that you need?" He imagined the man's bloody eyes gazing at him through the bandaging, and he wondered why he should help all these people. God was punishing them for a reason, and maybe he should just let them rot.

"No. It is good just to hear your voice, son. Please, don't end up like me."

Still upset and frightened by the whole ordeal, Rafe walked away slowly, leaving the little stool he was sitting on, and he looked at the decaying bodies that surrounded him. In a sense, he felt like he was buried along with them in a cemetery of linen.

"Goodbye, son," the man faintly said.

By doing this, subjecting himself to his wife's killers, he was hopefully earning the right to have a life of peace for his small family. His service in New Eden was his indulgence.

THAT NIGHT, RAFE SAT DOWN IN HIS ASSIGNED BED in the hallway. The lights were off, and he could hear birds in the rafters flap their wings, looking for anything to eat. Only the imagination could figure out what other animals were seeking shelter from the rain.

He was wide awake but very exhausted. After talking to more than a hundred people and hearing their stories, he tried to process it all. Five of them died while speaking to him, and he had to call an orderly to take them away. The next day, he was to take one of their shifts for several hours, and he wondered what that might entail.

At that moment, Rafe thought of Jesus Christ walking toward Bethany with His Apostles to meet Martha, the sister of Lazarus, who had died.

FOR SHE HAD BEEN IN MOURNING FOR FOUR DAYS since his passing, and many Jews came to comfort her and her sister, Mary. Their home was full of concerned friends and townspeople, and in their time of crisis, they found solace in many of the ancient customs for grieving.

One of the younger cousins approached Martha as she sat in a room, listening to her guests, and she whispered into her ear. Without delay, she excused herself and ran into the yard to meet Jesus and the Apostles.

As soon as she saw Him, she began to cry again, and He embraced her as she wept. The Apostles looked on, including Zebedee's son, John, who stood idly by in the garden, and Thomas, who glanced over his shoulder in fear of being in Judea once again.

Through her tears, she managed, "Lord, if Thou hadst been here, my brother would not have died."

Jesus then pulled away to study her soul and feel her agony. He had plain Middle Eastern features with brilliant eyes that captured the depth of the heavens at night and a smile that radiated a love beyond anything known.

"But I know," she continued humbly, "that even now, whatsoever Thou wilt ask of God, God will give it Thee."

He knew Martha. As the Son of Man of Holiness, he had conversed with her before time began. The veil was still over her eyes, so she could not see what He could, but she had the faith of a child, and this allowed her to know more than most.

Miracles had been performed by His hand, and she had witnessed them. The blind had been given sight, the lame could walk, and those with diverse diseases were made whole. He knew the Father's will and His role to help others believe. "Thy brother shall rise again," He pronounced.

Martha quickly confirmed her knowledge on the matter. "I know that he shall rise again in the resurrection at the last day." She had heard the rabbis preach it to the men her whole life, and she knew it. But beyond just reciting the doctrine, she knew it in her heart.

Jesus gave Martha a brotherly smile and then turned to address the Twelve Apostles. "I am the resurrection and the life. He that believeth in me, though he were dead, yet shall he live. And whosoever liveth and believeth in me shall never die." He returned to Martha and asked, "Believest thou this?"

THE LORD KNELT IN FRONT OF THE CAVE where Lazarus had been entombed. A massive crowd had already encircled round about Him, and Martha and Mary both stood by with their heads covered. Those in league with the chief priests and Pharisees also anxiously watched the famed healer.

"Father, I thank Thee that Thou hast heard me," Jesus prayed just loud enough for everyone to hear. "And I knew that Thou hearest me always, but because the people which stand by, I said it, that they might believe that Thou hast sent me."

The stone had already been cleared from the cave, and the darkness and smell of the flesh had seeped out. Both believers and non-believers had gathered, and some of them had witnessed His miracles. Others had only heard of them.

Many had been taught the words of Job: *And though after my skin worms destroy this body, yet in my flesh shall I see God.* They had heard of the Judgment, the resurrection, and the events of the End, and they wondered what this healer could do to a man four-days-dead.

Jesus perceived all of their thoughts, though. This miracle would not be a resurrection as the time had not come, but the event was meant to draw more believers unto Him.

Rising from His knees, The Lord held His right arm to the square and commanded in a loud voice, "Lazarus, come forth."

To the astonishment of all, Lazarus's once-dead body, dressed in burial clothes and a cloth covering his face, approached the entrance of the cave. Martha and Mary were overjoyed to see their brother again. Everyone there, including the Twelve Apostles, buried the miracle in their hearts, coming to it over and over again throughout their lives.

This was a part of the mystery, the undiscovered country, and they had all witnessed a traveler return. Many millennia had passed away with the old and young questioning this veiled life after the separation, and now they knew. The power of God could not only heal infirmities, but it could bring a soul back from the dead.

RAFE THOUGHT ABOUT THE CHARRED MAN with a cloth holding his bloody eyes shut. Not seeing those windows into his soul had scared him, as if the man had reached into the deepest part of Rafe's imagination and pulled out a devil of a nightmare.

The man couldn't harm him, though. His body was only dust, a tool with which to roam the earth and learn how to be a god. He didn't even have arms or legs to reach him. All he had was the remains of a savage heart and the desire to inflict pain on anyone whose dust was different from his.

Rafe wondered if the Lord would stand by the charred man's bed and heal him. He could imagine His nail-pierced hand covering the man's bandaged eyes and his skin returning to normal. The man's eyes were clear-blue, and he was smiling. Although Rafe tried, it was hard to find compassion for a blackened man who murdered those with black skin.

Lazarus received life once again because of his righteous faith and that of those around him. The purpose of his death was to bless all those present when he arose and everyone who has read his story since.

But that charred man—he's a monster, Rafe thought. He was also a child of God, and he was charred for a reason.

"You need to get some sleep," advised a woman lying nearby in the dark.

A little defensive, Rafe replied, "How did you know I was still awake?"

288

She exhaled and chuckled in a way that expressed the harsh reality. "We're all a little restless after the first day. It isn't normal to see so many people dying like this. I couldn't breathe, and I passed out on my first day. A few hours later, someone found me, and I was bleeding all over the floor." She stopped as if it were her second day at the facility and painfully continued, "I've never been the same since."

Rafe thought about the blackness and the loneliness of the void that surrounded them and asked, "If this is the *Curse of God*, why doesn't He just take them?" It was a sound question. They were all convicted felons, whether or not they had acted on their racist thoughts. The Book of Life had recorded them. "Why are we even here? Can't we just inject them with poison and drive away?"

"You're upset, aren't you? Whatever you do, don't take it out on them. There have been hundreds of patients that have asked for a lethal injection, and once they got it, they have all continued to live. If there is a god, He or She wants them to be around a little longer. I don't know why, but it doesn't matter. They're still people, and they need help. They need someone to listen to them, to hold their hand. Don't be as heartless as they are."

It was as if the heavens were about to shut him out as well. This disembodied voice could have been an angel steering him from his disgruntled feelings toward the whole mission. She was schooling him just like Bri did, and in a way, he had missed that. As much as he studied the Bible and prayed, there was much he still needed to learn.

"Thank you," he humbly whispered.

Chapter 45

Raising Nehushtan

The *pit*, as they called it, was three times the size of the arena. After discovering how much room was needed, they broke up the golden streets by the makeshift hospital to access the sewage tunnels underneath. It was a massive hole in the earth for burying the dead, complete with a few lines to drain all the fluids and water that had been building up.

Sacred Sodium was their Zion, the last stand for their cause, and all the dying traveled to this Mecca to seek refuge and a cure. It was indeed a scene from medieval times, as they also suffered from something they couldn't pray away. Bodies trampled each other, and money lined the golden streets as it no longer held value. Doctors who were once slaves were revered as gods because their doorways had been miraculously painted with the blood of the Lamb and were passed over by God's wrath.

Thousands of families arrived daily for over a year, finding no room to lay their heads at night. The proud fought for a small sidewalk panel. They made sure to continue reading their Bibles with fine leather covers and white lace bookmarks before they closed their eyes for the last time. And now, because of their black hearts, they rotted in the sewage below their golden Zion.

RAFE COULD CARRY FOUR BODIES AT A TIME in a wheelbarrow because they had been mostly reduced to skin and bones when they passed. They did take up a lot of room, though, so he had to bend their limbs and position them in such a way so that they wouldn't fall out.

It was also imperative to move them before the rigor mortis set in, but the body would eventually go limp again if they missed someone. That was the time when the orderlies usually passed out because of the horrid smell of bacteria eating away at its host. The whole ordeal was a test of their mental fortitude.

As soon as the information was entered into the medical app on his phone, Rafe simply had to lift the corpse onto the wheelbarrow. Sometimes though, this was the step during which a body part would fall off, and he had to look under the beds to locate it. The head orderly said that if there was a resurrection, then all the parts needed to stay close together. Rafe didn't want to argue. He mainly kept to himself on those days.

He wore a thick black apron, and when he looked at himself in the bathroom mirror, covered in blood and other bodily fluids, he didn't know if he was an overworked butcher or a harbinger and executioner of death. Every smudge was the remnant of a racist person's hatred.

The orderly hallway lights remained on 24/7, and there were numerous paintings on the walls. Most of them were pleasant landscapes and other representations of various cheerful moments that helped the orderlies keep sane. There were a lot of quotes about life and jokes. Few laughed, though; it was a somber rotation.

Rafe liked a painting of Jesus carrying one of his lost sheep back to the fold. Every time he passed it, he wondered if he should interpret the poor animal as the set of bodies he carried in his wheelbarrow or himself.

Toward the end of the hallway, there was a painting of Jesus overlooking Jerusalem with a caption that read:

> *O Jerusalem, Jerusalem, thou that killest the prophets, and stonest them which are sent unto thee, how often would I have gathered thy children together, even as a hen gathereth her chickens under her wings, and ye would not!*
>
> *Behold, your house is left unto you desolate. For I say unto you, Ye shall not see me henceforth, till ye shall say, Blessed is he that cometh in the name of the Lord (Matthew 23:37-39).*

There was no end to the onslaught of tears from heaven. Each wheelbarrow had holes punched through the bottom so that it could drain easily. A lot of other fluids and drainage would stop them up sometimes.

The section of the pit that was closest to the arena was full to the brim, so orderlies had to push the bodies several additional blocks to dump them.

Lifting the wheelbarrow handles and watching the bodies disappear into the blackness below was the most challenging part of the whole process. It wasn't the weight that made it difficult but how grave the task was.

On that day, he hauled 368 bodies.

MERLOT HAD BEEN ASSIGNED TO A SMALL SOUP STATION on the edge of the field because he couldn't bend down well. After standing for several days, he eventually snagged a stool from a broom closet, which helped tremendously.

He made it his mission to put a smile on everyone's face, or at least something better than the grimace that the dire situation inflicted. Eventually, all the doctors, nurses, and orderlies knew him as Grandpa, and it was probably because he always shared specific little insights or stories to help people feel better.

He did worry about Charron, though. She had been stationed in the arena broadcast booth as a clerical assistant. Hour after hour, she would update medical data at her computer and print out death certificates. A record needed to be kept for everything.

From his soup table, he could see her from the side, and she would often bury her face in her hands and then walk around the room. One day, she did give Merlot a faint smile, but it was fleeting as another assignment called her away.

She kind of reminded him of Rebah and how utterly hopeless she had become. Whenever Rebah would call him in the middle of the night, her trembling voice always shook his heart like a car that had just been T-boned.

Almost every night for two years, he tried to comfort her as best he could over the phone. She talked about how Jim's hatred for everyone just ate him up from the inside out and how she didn't know how to raise Sam in such a racist environment.

She admitted to feeling like a failed mother and teacher constantly. At the end of every call, they prayed together, and she would describe a feeling of peace that came over her.

And yet, in the end, she killed herself. No matter what advice Merlot shared in all that time or what solace the Lord gave her, it always came back to that fact. She was gone. *She and Sam were both gone. What comfort could I possibly provide anyone else?* he silently asked himself.

Whenever that thought came to mind, he would just force a smile, especially if someone approached him with a bowl.

† † †

OVER THE NEXT SEVERAL WEEKS, RAFE SPENT MORE TIME with each person on his patient route. At one point, a woman with boils on her skin took his hand and held it tight. Bloody tears seeped from under her eye covering, and she said, "Thank you for talking with me."

A man with one arm asked Rafe if he would read a letter to him.

"Sure, I can do that. Where is the letter, sir?"

The man raised his arm, which began to shake from the lack of muscle tissue, and with one finger, he pointed to his shirt pocket. "I always keep it close to me."

Rafe unfolded the letter, which was smeared with blood in several places, and read it.

"Dear Ronald, I hope you make it to Sacred Sodium and that you feel better soon! This morning, I realized that I'm already too weak to move, so you will have to go without me. Know that I love you very much and that you have been my very best friend for all these years. May the Lord keep you safe. May He bless you. I'll see you again after all this is over! I'm already looking forward to seeing your smile again! Love, Marianne."

As soon as Rafe finished, he looked up at Ronald, and he had passed. Underneath the lesions on his face, he could tell that the very last motion he made was a faint smile.

"I'm sorry, Ronald."

He didn't want to notify an orderly right away. Reverently, he folded the letter and gently returned it to his pocket. He didn't know the man, but he was the last person to talk with him, and he tried to understand what he must have been feeling.

Sarah asked him to brush her hair, and a few strands came out with every stroke. Jacob mentioned his pet goldfish and how he loved to watch it swim around because he had been in a wheelchair all of his life. Anita sang *Amazing Grace* for him, and her strained rendition was the most beautiful he had ever heard.

It was heart-wrenching to continually share the last few minutes with someone. The more Rafe listened to their stories, the more a piece of him died along with them.

On his orderly days, he would pray for the people that he was carrying in his wheelbarrow. He memorized every name and every detail from their charts so that his small funeral procession for them was as meaningful as possible.

AT THE END OF RAFE'S SHIFT AT 2 PM, it was dark, as it always was, and he went inside to see Merlot. "I can't take this anymore," he whispered to his friend at the soup station.

"I know how you feel. This is hard for everyone," Merlot admitted with a heavy heart.

Rafe grieved over the dying patients surrounding them and moaned, "All I want to do is lie down in one of these beds and somehow take the pain away from them. It's terrible what they're going through."

Merlot sighed. It hurt that impenetrable part of the heart to witness humanity in such agony. The humble old man opened his mouth and taught, "One thing that helps me is that not only did Christ suffer for our sins in Gethsemane, but He also took on every little pain, every infirmity, and every heartache that all of God's children have suffered throughout all time so that He could heal us. If we lean on Him, if we ask for His help, He will soon be there to carry us through."

Exhausted, Rafe cleaned off his rubber apron full of blood. "Yes, I'm very grateful for *Our Older Brother*. Pride gets in the way, though. One of the nurses told me that they had put up paintings of Christ throughout his ministry all over the arena for everyone to gain some sense of faith and inspiration. Unfortunately, the majority of them only wanted pictures of McKendrick on the walls."

Merlot took a quick peek to see what currently adorned the arena interior, as he hadn't paid any attention. Only a few McKendrick wall hangings were left.

Rafe continued, "And the reason they finally changed them is that she told arena staff about a young boy who was receiving lifesaving treatment a few decades ago."

A FIVE-YEAR-OLD BOY LAY ON A HOSPITAL BED, connected to several machines at his side. Tears streamed down his face as he begged, "Mommy, I want some water."

"I know, sweetie, but the doctor says that we can't give you any right now. It's so that you'll get better," his mother returned as she stroked his head and wiped his cheek. She was crying along with him.

"But, Mommy, I want water." His frown quivered, and he couldn't hold back all the anguish he was feeling.

His father held his hand, and the boy shook ferociously. "Son, it's going to be okay."

"I need water! I need water! Mommy, please!"

RAFE FOCUSED ON A PATIENT TO HIS SIDE as he finished sharing the story with Merlot. "Day after day, he cried, pleading with everything he had for one glass of water. His parents had to sit in the other room as they couldn't bear to hear the torturous screams, and one day he died in their arms.

"They kept telling themselves that the temporary pain was necessary for him to pull through, but after the horrific experience, they wished he could have just died comfortably and at peace."

Merlot then made the connection. "So, they needed to look at McKendrick to make them truly happy."

"I guess so," Rafe said solemnly.

The old scriptorian added, "It kind of reminds me of how Moses raised a serpent on a staff. All the children of Israel had to do was look at the serpent to be healed from the sickness they were experiencing in the wilderness, but they were too proud to do it. They said that it was too easy for it to work."

"Yeah, they raised a serpent alright, and that's all they wanted to worship, even while they were here dying," Rafe declared. "And most of them have the *M* tattooed on their forehead to prove it."

Rafe gazed at one of the pictures of McKendrick, studying his eyes and his awful smirk. He continued the story to its tragic end, "Once these pictures went up, the nurse said that everyone started bleeding from their eyes."

The two men continued to sit on an empty, bloody bed, resting from their shifts in hell. There was nothing more they could say but to witness the end of all things.

Chapter 46

Flaxen Cord

The converted broadcast booth was encased in glass because the rising heat made the horrid smell from the field even worse. Managing the living and the dead seemed easier with a higher vantage point, but in reality, the computers needed to be kept away from all the fluids that were always on the arena floor.

Charron placed a couple of cardboard flaps against the glass in front of her on her first day so that she didn't have to view the sea of bodies below. As with every other job in the hospital-morgue, it was grueling work.

The months in New Eden seemed like a refiner's fire, but she dutifully continued to update the records of the dying in the database. It became harder not to read some of the details as they came across her desk, as those affected by the *Curse of God* were not the only ones who were under their care.

Because every patient suffering from the curse had eye coverings, once there was enough room in the hospital, former slaves were admitted.

Of course, they seemed to pass away and be at peace sooner than those who God was slowly killing.

"CAN PEOPLE REALLY BE THAT VIOLENT?" SHE ASKED.

Dr. Xiāo looked up from his computer at a desk behind Charron in the booth. He had been studying medical data to prepare for an upcoming surgery and praying for help. "What do you mean?"

"People say things that can be hurtful, but they don't follow through with it. You look at social media, and it's full of some horrible threats, but that's all they are," she responded.

"I see."

She continued, "And most people are good. They're not going to hurt someone because of how they feel. I'm not going to shoot someone because I don't like their hair."

Dr. Xiāo sat down next to her in the front of the booth. He wanted to look at her eyes and see what kind of soul rested inside of her. "I am glad that you are a good person who won't shoot me because of my hair. We need more people like you," he said with a disarming chuckle.

Charron pointed to her screen and explained, "I look at these profiles, and I occasionally read about how people were treated; I just don't believe it! I drove Charlie Merlot and Rafe Davidson here, and despite what everyone says, I don't think people can become these mindless animals that everyone is describing." She folded her arms defensively and looked at the doctor as if she were asking him to try and break her.

He sat back in his chair and rubbed his forehead. "Can I tell you a story?"

"Yeah, sure."

"Do you know about Secretary of State Kerioth?"

"Yeah, he's the guy who asked Canada for help on TV."

Dr. Xiāo stood up and walked to another part of the booth with a desk and a landline phone. "Well, he made the call from this phone right here. Of course, he looked terrible. We used a gurney to carry him here, and he insisted on a half-dozen lights for his video feed. One of the nurses applied makeup for over three hours, but in the end, he decided just to use a regular phone."

"Sounds like a pretty messed-up guy."

"Yes, he looked like he had hung himself from a tree and had survived to tell us about it. There was discoloration of the skin and a lot of swelling. As we carried him back to his bed, the gurney split open, and when he hit the floor, body parts covered in various fluids slid in every direction. Only a couple of coins that I guess he had in his pocket were left intact."

That was the easy part of the story, and he began to tear up. He then shook his head as if he wasn't going to go through it again and started to walk off without an explanation.

"What's wrong?" she asked.

There was something in her voice that was genuine, and it helped him return. For whatever reason, he felt that she needed to hear the entire account. "He wrote a post on social media that almost got me killed."

"What did it say?"

A FEW DOZEN GOVERNMENT OFFICIALS, including a much younger Kerioth, viciously argued with one another in a White House conference room. Several flat-screen TVs on the walls blasted different newscasts depicting Chinese street riots.

The lower-third graphic of the network broadcasts contained variations of the text *American/Chinese Trade War Takes a Wrong Turn.* Each network cut to a shot of a chaotic floor of the stock exchange, followed by a graphic showing plummeting losses in the stock market.

301

Kerioth suddenly shouted, "Everyone shut up! I need some heads to roll right now!" He then stormed out of the room.

Once he reached a long hallway, his phone rang, and he answered while almost sprinting. In response to the shouting on the other end, he replied, "Yes, sir. Yes, sir. We'll do that. Don't worry; I can handle it."

As soon as the call ended, Kerioth turned around and threw the phone at a wall, leaving a mark before it slid across the floor. After an excruciating exhale, he went to retrieve it and continued storming down the hallway toward a particular door.

But right as he was about to knock on it, he stopped. He just couldn't do it, and so he retreated into a nearby bathroom, punching a couple of stall partitions as soon as he entered. He paced. He grunted. He kicked.

At last, Kerioth shuttled into a stall, and without stopping, he thumbed an egregious text on his phone that cannot be repeated. As soon as he published the filth, he tried to flush the device down the toilet, but it kept getting stuck. In response, he kicked the bottom of the toilet over and over again.

Exhausted, he finally exclaimed, "Stupid Chinese."

LATER THAT NIGHT, XIĀO WALKED ALONE on a busy street with cars driving at least ten miles over the speed limit. He carried a couple of bags of groceries, and although it wasn't raining, he was frequently splashed by the slow-draining puddles on the side of the road.

As he neared a bridge, the mist from the river below just added to his soaked clothes. He even had to tie the grocery bag handles together so they wouldn't take on more water.

Suddenly, a car skidded to a halt on the wet pavement, right in front of him, and five teenage boys rushed out toward him. Without any hesitation, they surrounded him and beat him with baseball bats. His forehead and jaw soon bled.

"Why are you doing this?" he yelled out in anguish as he tried to protect his face, but it was useless.

They pushed him to the ground and kicked him on his side repeatedly. Once he was on his stomach, one of the boys put his knee onto the back of Xiāo's neck, and another boy ripped open one of the grocery bags.

"I can't— I can't—"

The assault seemed to last for an eternity, and eventually, Xiāo passed out. When a car honked, the boys ran back to their car and took off, allowing a line of cars behind them to finally leave.

CHARRON VIEWED HIM IN A DIFFERENT LIGHT. Dr. Xiāo was no longer just an outsider commenting on things but someone who had lived through a horrific tragedy. She pulled back with her chair a little as if she wasn't ready for this new view on humanity. We could be animals.

He sadly whispered, "They had to put metal plates on my skull, my jaw was wired shut for a very long time, and I had several cracked ribs."

The doctor slowly stood up and continued, "But that's not all." He lifted his shirt at the back to reveal a series of horrible laceration scar lines that started right below his armpit and ended just on the other side of his spine. Charron gasped and jumped up in horror.

It was enough just to show them for a second. The point was made.

"I don't know what they used. I woke up in the hospital, but I remember glass breaking. I had bought several jars of baby food that night. A few nurses said it looked like an *M*, but I don't see it."

Charron turned around and slowly began typing again. Dr. Xiāo returned to his preparation for the upcoming surgery. Nothing more was said. There was no way to fake the moment they shared.

† † †

THE ONLY WAY TO TELL THE TIME WAS TO LOOK AT A WATCH, especially one that had an AM/PM designation. Rafe knew too well the life of a pandemic nurse, racing to serve those who were reaching the end of their cut thread. As inevitable as death was for everyone, he earnestly tried to comfort them, even the ones who rejected it.

When he went to sleep at night, he tried to imagine what they looked like without all the scars of sin. His dreams of them were based on the stories they shared. And as much as he kept to his route, which never repeated, he frequently surprised the friends that hadn't passed with a quick follow-up visit.

He wondered, though, if it was wrong for him to feel that way. They had collectively murdered his wife. They had hunted and ravaged many people of color, and their cries could be heard from the ground if one were to listen. And even if a person hadn't committed a crime outwardly, inside, their hearts rotted with racism.

"IS THERE ANYTHING I CAN DO FOR YOU TODAY, LISA?" Rafe asked while holding the woman's bony hand. It was a question he had repeated thousands of times with Christlike love, but he could no longer do it. Even though the long fingers clutched him like she never wanted to let go, all he wanted to do was go home. He was done.

"Would you sing to me?" she asked.

"What would you like?"

"Do you know *Black Mare*?"

At this, Rafe bit his lip and cried without making a sound. The torture was just not fair, and he wondered if she knew what the lyrics meant. He silently asked God why He required this of him.

304

After a considerable amount of time, he took a deep breath and obliged, singing the first few lines with a shaky voice until he realized that she had passed.

Now, he had to let go of her hand and move on. With a few entries on the app, he updated her status and requested an orderly to take her away. It usually took only ten minutes for someone to come.

He then stood up to look at the next patient's clipboard, which was hanging on the second bunk. It was completely blank, and he drew a heavy sigh as it meant that the patient was new and that someone had hastily admitted him without heeding protocols.

"That was very kind of you to sing to her," the patient said.

"Well, she needed it, and hopefully, she's okay now. Can I get your name, please, so that I can write it on your clipboard?"

For the first time, Rafe looked at the man. He didn't appear to have any skin issues, and he still had all of his hair. There was no bandage on his eyes, and the blanket covering him was spotless and tucked around him perfectly as if it had just been ironed. Not a single irksome dilemma was visible.

"I've got it. I've got it. You were that cameraman in Sodium," the patient asserted as he stared at the bottom of the third bunk, completely motionless.

"What?"

With a slight curl of his lip, the patient stated, "I make it a point to know every critic personally."

"McKendrick?" Rafe jumped back in chaotic fear.

"President Korihor McKendrick, if you please. You can address me as *Your Highness and Glory* if you like. I go by several names, so whatever your heart desires, my son."

He didn't look the same. His morbid obesity had all been shelled, leaving an ironically beautiful man with blond wavy hair instead of the stringy mess he had before. Maybe he used all the products he had been selling over the years.

Rafe dutifully wrote down his name on the clipboard, followed by a frowny face. He remembered the mandatory national celebrations of the president's birthday, so he put that on the clipboard as well. No wife, no kids. It was easier for him that way. In the field for the wife's name, he wrote *Many Mistresses*, but then he scratched it out and replaced it with *NA*.

"Well, sir," Rafe started, not being comfortable with the titles given, "is there anything I can do for you? How long have you been here?" He wondered if someone might have a silver spoon that he could use to shove some soup into his mouth.

Still, without any movement, McKendrick uttered, "I have been here for a while, actually—long enough to memorize the perfume of all 47 nurses. I will try to forget what you are wearing, though."

As Rafe rolled his eyes, he noticed that McKendrick's board had been mysteriously erased again. The Lord had blotted out his name.

The patient continued, "You were the one who exposed our little church back when it was just a fledgling. It had been prophesied for all six millennia, and now it is the whore that is filling the earth."

Rafe wondered if he should call for Merlot, as he would probably enjoy the scripture-laden conversation, so he looked around for him.

"Don't worry about your friend," McKendrick said sinisterly. "This conversation is just for the two of us, and then I must go."

Rafe didn't know how to respond to that. "Okay. Are you hungry?"

"No. You don't need to waste anything on me."

He then checked the database for any special instructions or medical flags that needed his attention, but the query returned the patient as not being admitted yet.

306

"Do you know the story about the devils entering the swine before they went off a cliff?" the patient inquired.

Not paying attention, Rafe stated, "Alright, I'm going to re-enter you into the database. Are you feeling okay today?" It was almost as if he had reset the conversation and started at the beginning. Perhaps it was a knee-jerk reaction from using the app for so long. He needed to be in the database; it was crucial.

"I know Lucifer personally," said the coffined man.

Rafe was too busy re-entering McKendrick's data into his phone. It was the one thing that he could retreat to in this moment of conflict: *Should I be Christlike and listen to a dying man rattle off biblical whimsy, or should I let the devil bring out my rage for destroying a nation and passing laws to murder millions?*

"He came to me while I prayed in a church," McKendrick continued, "I lit a candle, knelt at a pew, and asked God to help me. And then there was this beautiful angel that appeared before me."

AS A MUCH YOUNGER MAN IN HIS TWENTIES, MCKENDRICK looked up at the glowing angel and sat back in the pew in amazement. He wiped away the tears from his prayer and slowly put down a Bible that he had been reading.

"*Why are ye fearful, O ye of little faith?*" asked the spirit. The light around him was blinding, and he moved freely around the pews toward the front, and yet, he was transparent.

The being continued, "*Then he arose and rebuked the winds and the sea, and there was a great calm.*" As the angel spoke, he moved right in front of a painting of Jesus Christ at the front of the Church and stopped.

307

"But the men marveled, saying, 'What manner of man is this, that even the winds and the sea obey him!'" he uttered as he leaned forward toward McKendrick.

The young man glanced at his Bible on the bench and inquired with some hesitation, "You're quoting scripture?"

"Yes," the spirit acknowledged as he began to lift himself into the air in majestic form. "I know all the words that the prophets have written from the beginning, for I was there for every single stroke."

"Are you the Lord?"

"I am the Lord of this earth. I am the Son of the Morning. I am Lucifer, your lord and servant. You may call me Scratch, for, in the end, your teeth will gnash, you will weep, and you will claw," the spirit proclaimed as he raised his arms like a god.

Shocked and mortified, McKendrick asked, "You are the devil? How can you be in a church?"

At this, Lucifer smiled and boasted with a bow of both indentureship and gratitude, "As your servant, you brought me here in your heart. My grace suffers no bounds but few of which you cannot know. This bond you may not sever."

McKendrick stood in the glow of the devil in the church, and so began the blessing and the curse.

RAFE WEPT AS HE BELIEVED THE BEAUTIFUL LIVING CORPSE on the second bunk. Among thousands of his lost souls, McKendrick continued to whisper his confession.

"He told me that he was unjustly cast out of heaven along with his host of angels, and they have ever since had a horrid obsession with the human body, for it was the one gift from God that they couldn't have. Hence their craving for even a pig's body that would eventually drown."

Rafe studied the dying bodies around him and wondered how it could be a gift with all its faults and imperfections. He could smell another one pass.

"You were young once," McKendrick continued as if he were laying out a case. "I was a struggling artist, and I blasphemed the Lord because of my circumstances. Once the devil entered my church, I felt that I could never be forgiven."

Rafe refused to let that slip by and rebutted, "You can always be forgiven."

The devil's proxy smiled and uttered as a trapped soul, "No, not me."

For the first time in the conversation, a single tear left McKendrick's eye, and it slowly fell down his beautiful cheek and onto his white coffin pillow.

"After years of successful business and servitude, he required me to run for president. I submitted my name, and he taught me what to say and how to act. He showed me how to hold the Bible, which scriptures to quote, and how to interpret them. He whispered the secret, despiteful feelings of others so that I could lead them all down paths that were dark and full of hate. If I told them what they were feeling and legitimized it, they would follow me to the end, even here."

Rafe put down his phone and held the man's hand. It was cold, lifeless, and beyond any repair or warmth. "Why are you telling me this?"

Suddenly, Rafe heard a bird flap its wings in the rafters. It came down and flew right over them, landing on some machinery to the side of the arena. Even though it was a common occurrence, the bird had startled him a little.

"They were all deceived. I was the United States president, and I divided, I hated, I spewed filth from my pulpit every day at the bidding of my anointed one, and they believed me. Bishops and priests laid their

309

hands on me and prayed for me as if I were their savior. If I told them the sun rose in the West, they would believe me. So blind and impassioned were my disciples that they took away that most precious gift from others, and he led them all down with his flaxen cord."

Rafe thought about Bri and how she always wanted to record what people said. He had videotaped the violence, shared it with another country, and now he wasn't recording the final part of the story. He wondered if anyone would believe him.

The penitent man continued as if he knew Rafe's thoughts. "I am sorry about Bri. Unfortunately, she had to be a pawn in all of this. Our war is almost over, and the board is on the verge of being wiped clean. Follow the Lord, Jesus Christ. He is full of light and truth. I go to my master now and will be shackled with my reward. Adieu, my brother."

The only thing the paralyzed man could do was close his eyes and his mouth, relinquishing the power that controlled him. The man was dead.

Had it not happened, no one would have ventured to know how one man could do so much wrong. History had just given another example of how a madman could deceive the human race.

Rafe located a nearby empty wheelbarrow and proceeded to start the next part of his shift as an orderly. As he pushed McKendrick down the middle aisle, many of the undead turned their bandaged heads toward the body and raised their arms to cross what was left of their chests. It was frightening to see the blind allegiance.

Chapter 47

The Leper

The rain was the heaviest Rafe had ever seen, and the drops pummeled McKendrick's body in the wheelbarrow so severely that they left marks on the flesh. Luckily, there were holes in the bottom. He was also grateful that the pit before him was massive enough for the dirty work he had to do in hell all this time.

The funeral procession was long, not because of whom he was pushing but because of what the man divulged. The whole story echoed in his mind over and over. Words rattled his heart, and the poor man's plight moved him.

At long last, the soaked pallbearer came to the section where he had been dumping bodies on recent shifts. Wrangled body parts could be seen with flashes of lightning. He would usually close his eyes for the last part of the ceremony, the send-off below, but this time he had to witness McKendrick's fall.

Because the flashes were quick and fleeting, the bodies appeared to move and welcome him home. Rafe stared at the scene in amazement and shock. So many arms—so many legs. Flesh was all mingled together: rotting, soaking, being eaten.

After a deep breath, he sat down on a nearby golden sidewalk panel, and the force of the water gushed by him so forcefully that he almost fell into the street. But he wasn't thinking about being swept away into a storm drain; he needed to rest and run the whole story through his mind again.

He wondered if he would've been able to resist the devil's persuasions upon seeing him in a church—if he was any different from the vile creature he just lowered into the pit of tortured souls.

Rafe closed his eyes.

WITH ALL THE WATER RUSHING AROUND HIM, it felt like he was sitting in shallow water, not too far from a beach. The sound of crashing waves and his soaked back almost brought a smile to his face.

When Rafe opened his eyes, he saw waves receding from the sand only several yards from him, and the ocean came up to his chest. The warmth of the sun filled his whole body like he had been encased in ice for years and was now set free.

The trees blew calmly in the distance, and the beach went on forever in both directions. He could smell the salt in the air and see the small fish swimming in the clear water.

In the far distance, beyond the trees, the salty pillar of Sacred Sodium disappeared into the white clouds above it. He knew it wasn't a dream.

"Father in Heaven," Rafe prayed with open eyes, "I don't know why I'm here. I'm so lost." He didn't want to miss anything as every inch of it was a welcome sight to behold.

"I feel sorry for them—all of them. If the devil came to me, would I have been able to resist him? I'm just as flawed as the next guy."

312

He soon recalled the faces of all those he had helped for several months, and he started to cry. He pleaded their case. "And all those people. They were all deceived; it wasn't their fault. Without thinking, they gave into the lies because everyone around them did. It became a culture; it became an identity. They had crossed Thee, and they couldn't change."

Before he realized it, he implored with all his heart, "Lord, please forgive them. Look past the hate and look at the good. Look at how they cared for their children, how they loved their spouses, and how they tried to be like Thee."

It was then that he gazed at the tree line again, and a deer emerged with extraordinary grandeur, standing resolutely. He wondered what it all meant and what he was supposed to do.

"I know they did unspeakable things, but please forgive them," he uttered from a depth that he had never touched before.

Far away from him, a woman walked along the shore with excruciating difficulty, and she resembled one of his patients who had mangled and rotting skin. He watched her struggle and limp along just a few feet from the water, and the thought came to him that she might have leprosy.

At long last, without enough strength to hold up her frame, she crashed to her knees on the sand, and a little water finally touched her. The ocean seemed to beckon her, and she crawled toward it like a baby, one painful movement at a time.

Rafe stood up and sprinted toward her, kicking up the muddied sand beneath his feet. He wasn't going to let another one pass—she was a lost child of God, just like everyone else. She had made mistakes, but she could be forgiven.

Within seconds, she disappeared below the surface, and the waves crashed down, so Rafe flew toward her even faster. His footprints in the

313

sand were very far apart, but it wasn't enough. Despite every effort, he could not reach her, and he cried out, "Father!"

In a flash as blinding as the sun, the woman suddenly emerged from this Pool of Bethesda, healed and radiant. Her faith had made her whole. Gone were her head coverings and the ripped rags that hung from her, almost weighing her down, and they were replaced with a clean garment of indescribable beauty.

Rafe fell to the ground with amazement and watched her return in the direction from which she came—changed, healed, a different being altogether.

He then noticed his changing surroundings. The sky grew dark, the ocean crept further inland, and the freezing hand of death took hold.

MERLOT FOUND RAFE STILL SITTING on the golden sidewalk in a trance. The onslaught of rain attacked both of them from every direction, and the smell of the pit was unbearable.

"What are you doing out here?" Merlot shouted above the rain.

"What?"

The old man helped him to his feet and answered, "You've been out here for hours! You need to come inside."

As they left toward the arena, Merlot glanced back and asked him, "What about your wheelbarrow?" After all, there was more work to do and more dead bodies to haul.

"Don't worry about it. I need you to do something for me," Rafe replied, shivering.

Chapter 48

Eustace

Drenched even beneath the skin, Rafe and Merlot entered the broadcast booth, and a few nurses, Dr. Xiāo, and Charron all turned back to look at them. It was not uncommon for anyone to walk into the makeshift office as it was not a regular hospital. Rules and regulations were not as stringent as in other settings because the whole operation ran on a volunteer basis.

"Good evening, gentlemen," the doctor greeted. "What can I do for you?"

Merlot turned to his friend as a visual cue to everyone in the room that he had something to say. This was Rafe's moment to speak after many years of anguish, to make sense of all of it and move on from the pain.

"I just put McKendrick in the pit. He died on a bed out there, and I think something's going to happen," Rafe said reverently.

Dr. Xiāo then returned, "I didn't know he was here. He's not in the database."

"I've talked with him a few times," one of the male nurses reported. "Whenever you enter his name in, it just disappears."

The doctor then analyzed the database on a nearby computer, trying to troubleshoot the anomaly, and he uttered, "That's kind of weird."

"Look, I'm not good at this kind of thing," Rafe stated, "You say they have the *Curse of God* and that none of us can get it, right? Something's happening out there that is beyond any medical explanation."

"That's right," Dr. Xião agreed. "What are you getting at?"

Rafe stepped toward the glass, unafraid, unwavering, and declared, "I think God wants us to leave. I believe he's going to change them." He studied the massive amount of people awaiting their doom on the arena floor as if he were Moses about to lead them all to safety on dry land.

The scene reminded him of the children dying on the school grounds and that he recorded them behind a pane of glass. After all these years, he was no longer afraid to be with them and truly rescue them.

"It's like the story of Naaman, who was cleansed of leprosy in the Bible," Merlot added with a nod to Rafe.

"Who?" asked Charron.

Merlot smiled at her inquisitiveness and explained, "Naaman was a captain in Syria who had leprosy. One of his wife's servants was a Jew, and she told him that the prophet in Israel could heal him. So, when he finally went, he was instructed to wash in the River Jordan seven times, and he was healed."

"So, we need to leave so that God can heal them from this *leprosy*?" the doctor asked.

Merlot took the analogy forward even more and shared, "I think God is grateful for what we've all done here—for what you have been doing here for almost two years, and now this is something that is between Him and the people that are dying down there. Just as Naaman had to wash himself to be cleaned, they need to do this themselves."

316

A sense of relief seemed to wash over Dr. Xiāo's face, as if the responsibility for the hospital, however odd and perplexing it might have been, were ending. "Okay, gentlemen, we can make that happen."

The doctor flipped on the microphone switch at one of the consoles and spoke to the whole arena. "May I have everyone's attention, please. We will have a meeting for all staff who are awake in about 20 minutes in the main conference room. Thank you."

Merlot looked at Rafe and asked, "Is that quick enough?"

"I think so. Whatever it is, Heavenly Father is looking out for us," he responded.

Everyone but Rafe went toward the door, and Merlot thanked the doctor for his help. This change from so much monotonous death gave them life.

"Are you coming, Rafe?" Merlot inquired.

"No, I think I need to do something here."

The old man rebutted, "It's your vision, though. You're the one who saw it, not me."

"I know. Can you talk to them? You're better at that kind of stuff anyway," he humbly argued. "You know how to talk to all those military types."

Merlot responded with a smile, "Alright, sir. I'll be your Aaron." They both chuckled, and Merlot left the reluctant prophet there in the broadcast booth alone.

Rafe stood right by the glass, not worried about being shot, yelled at, or hurt in any way, and he looked at the sea of his brothers and sisters for a very long while. Although he had only spoken to a small percentage of them, he felt that he knew them all. A lot of them had died in his arms, and others he only took down the *golden mile*.

317

Wondering what he should do next, he thought about the quick exchange with the doctor. He marveled at how Dr. Xiāo would be willing to end such a massive project by following a spiritual notion.

Bri would probably say something, he thought. *She would know the right words to deliver to everyone listening—something moving, something stirring. She would have written it the night before and rehearsed it over and over—not me. That's not me.*

Suddenly, he turned on the microphone without knowing what he would say and opened his mouth. "Everyone who is suffering from the *Curse of God*, today President McKendrick was laid to rest—he died. I know that he meant a lot to you, but I want to tell you that you are now free from him."

His voice echoed from speakers around the building. Military personnel and nurses stopped what they were doing to listen. Others, who were on their way to the conference room, walked a little slower to let whatever was about to be announced seep in.

Rafe continued boldly, sounding like Martin Luther, "And some of you had something inside you before he even came into your lives. This hatred, this disdain for everyone who isn't like you, this desire to be cruel to your neighbor, to say hurtful things in a text or a post, to not say anything or do anything when you witness someone else doing it, is wrong. It's a golden rule for a reason: *Do unto others as you would have them do unto you.* Love others as yourselves. You don't pick and choose who your neighbors are. Love everyone—forgive everyone."

Merlot and many of the staff had already gathered into the conference room. They each sat in silence to listen to Rafe speak, and some were already in tears. The hatred went both ways. No one was immune from rebuke.

"Repent," he commanded. "Repent from the millions upon millions of your neighbors that you have slain. This nation was cut in half from your words. You have slaughtered your brothers and sisters like ferocious animals. We have dug your pit, and thousands now rot there with room for you to soon be with them.

"You may say that it is too late for you, that you have gone too far down this path, but you have not. Please, don't rob Jesus Christ of His power to heal you. *Ask, and it shall be given* unto you. *Seek, and ye shall find. Knock, and it shall be opened unto you.*"

Just like Saint Eustace, he had come close to the Lord through his own trials and suffering, and now he desired others to turn their hearts honestly to Him.

Rafe looked over the white linen sea, and there was neither movement nor sound. He wondered if he had just cast pearls before swine and if everything had fallen on deaf ears. He was saddened at the prospect that they were so proud and past feeling that they rejected the words of Jesus Christ.

Then suddenly, in an area he hadn't served yet, someone fell off their bed. If he hadn't been studying all of them, he probably would have missed the incident. He then went up to the glass and counted the aisles and beds leading to the patient.

Chapter 49

The Cleansing

The sermon had moved many in the conference room to awkward tears and a place where they didn't want to be emotionally. Merlot stood at the front of the room and observed the nurses, doctors, military officers, and volunteers he now had to address.

It was almost as if they had forgotten who they were serving. Many considered the patients as just names and numbers, but those who put their heart into the assignment looked past the skin and helped them with all they could. But as they were just reminded, the host of dying bodies they attended were murderers and full of hate.

"Ditto," Merlot started. "That was Rafe Davidson, a friend of mine from Ottawa. He experienced a lot of trauma while escaping a dissenter ghetto several years ago."

Merlot looked around the room, and he could feel the anticipation from the unexpected meeting and the awkwardness from Rafe's religious exhortation. "He and I like to talk about the Bible a lot. Hence the stirring speech." A few chuckled.

"But I would like to point out that this is not a normal hospital," he continued. "Most of the people that are dying out there don't have enough muscle on their bones to be alive. Many are missing vital organs, and I don't even know if the soup I make gets absorbed at all." That one received a few laughs.

Merlot then summarized unabashedly, "God's in charge of this place. Whatever that means to you. To some, He grants life; to others, He takes it. There is a reason for all things, and He knows the beginning from the end."

All this was the unspoken notion that everyone accepted in their own way—that this was a magical place. It was an enchanted morgue; the rules of physics and biology did not apply.

"Rafe has received a vision from God that said that we need to leave town so that God can change everyone on the arena floor."

One of the original nurses asked, "So, we're just supposed to leave all this and go home? I don't have anywhere else to go. Everything has been destroyed by looters and whatever else is out there."

"Why now?" asked one of the military men. "If God was going to do this now, why did we have to come?"

The Commander asked, "How long do we need to be away? Is this temporary or permanent?"

Merlot then said, "Look, my friends, I don't have all the answers. I don't know why God does the things He does. All I know is that we just need to leave."

At this, the Commander, who was sitting toward the front of the room, stood up and decided to comply. "Alright, under these unusual circumstances, it appears that we need to organize and relocate quickly." He then turned to Merlot, the current *magician* at hand, and said, "We can be ready to move everyone in three hours. Is that okay?"

With a nod from Merlot, the Commander assigned teams to coordinate the various tasks at hand and sent the room into a flurry.

† † †

THE ARENA FLOOR WAS QUIET AND SOMBER. Rafe had never stepped into the crowd of the dying without at least 20 other nurses present, and he wondered if he had indeed done the will of God.

As he neared the section where he saw the patient fall, he noticed that everyone was completely still. Not a soul moved on their dying beds. He wanted to stop and check to see if they were living, but he continued to the person he knew needed help.

At last, he found her and scooped her up, still enshrouded in bedsheets on the floor. When he tried to lay her back on the bed, she begged, "Please, don't let me go." She only weighed about 45 pounds, and the thin layer of skin that covered her bones had many boils and abrasions.

"Are you hurt?" he asked while gently cradling her. He quickly examined her to see if she was missing anything, as that was a common mishap when someone fell; everything was so brittle. Since he was now sitting down on her bed, he couldn't see the chart to read her medical data.

"My heart aches," she groaned.

"Are you having a heart attack? Do you feel a constriction or pain in your chest or arm?"

"No, my heart hurts," she repeated calmly.

There was something about her that he couldn't place. "Have I met with you before?" he questioned. "Your voice sounds familiar."

Of course, it was raspy as a lot of tissue had worn away, and the eye bandage disallowed any type of recognition. For some reason, it bugged him; he had to know. "What's your name, ma'am?" he finally petitioned her. It was hard for her to talk, and Rafe felt terrible for interviewing her.

"Edith. Edith Davidson."

"Mom?" Everything seemed to crash down on him at that moment. He never expected to see her again.

"Yes, it's me."

He embraced her even more, making sure he didn't hurt her frail body. For the first time, he truly took into account what had become of her. Gone were the cheeks full of life and the muscles in her arms that lifted him millions of times. Everyone he had served over the months at the arena were just acquaintances; they weren't family. They weren't his first love.

"I hurt millions of people. I hurt—"

At this, Rafe realized the heartache was not for him or herself but for the people affected by what she might have done. She had listened to what he said and was now sinking into the depths of despair.

He wondered if he would have rebuked everyone if he knew she was there. His whole life, he was bound by the notion that he couldn't correct her because she was his mother. Throughout his childhood, it was drilled into him: *respect your elders*. Even if an adult was making a mistake, it wasn't his place to say something—unless they were in danger. It was a core Southern value that he couldn't cross.

And yet, he had implored them all to repent, but it wasn't meant to consign them to misery or for them to drown in the horrors of guilt; he wanted to help them resolve to do better. As much as the curse had scourged them all, he knew that it could only be taken away by the same power, but they needed to repent.

She barely whispered, "I hurt your father—"

Confused, he watched the bandaged woman struggle to open her mouth for the lack of muscle in her face. He shook his head with a deep exhale and sobbed. "Ma, save your strength."

"He left because I was so full of hate—"

He wondered how long she had been in Sacred Sodium. After months of lying there, trapped in the confines of memories and introspection, she might have slowly realized her offenses and spent every waking minute praying for forgiveness. He thought about her anguish, and he wanted to take it upon himself so that her soul wouldn't be in pain.

Remembering the last time he saw his father, he imagined what might have sparked his decision to leave. He closed his eyes to concentrate on that evening, but nothing came. Whatever might have happened, he had erased it.

With the very last of any strength she had left, she repented, "I told him black kids didn't need saving. He turned to me, crying, and said, 'Jesus will always love you. Remember that.'"

Suddenly, her head fell back, and if it weren't for her very shallow breathing, he would have consigned her to be dead.

"Mom?" He had just broken her heart, and it killed him. Only God could heal them both.

BY THEN, MANY OF THE VEHICLES WERE BEING LOADED with equipment and supplies. People ran in every direction with their assignments, getting ready for whatever the mobilization was supposed to be.

A few people slipped and fell in the mud, but they got back up; there was no need to wallow. Tarps covered everything, and the sound of water splashing was as commonplace as a ticking clock.

The remaining ten patients who didn't have the *Curse of God* disease were prepared for transport in medical vehicles. Only the self-proclaimed unrighteous would be left in Sacred Sodium.

Depleted semi-trailers were loaded with hospital provisions, computers, records, and lab work from patients with various forms of the disease. It was decided early on that the move was to be treated as a permanent effort. Merlot even told them that they weren't abandoning the patients; they were getting out of the way.

Many were anxious to witness a miracle on a grand scale. Because it needed to affect so many thousands of people at the same time, it had to be a massive spectacle. Despite the outpouring of otherworldly phenomena at the Sacred Sodium hospital or the number of inexplicable events that everyone had witnessed, some felt that this *miracle* would finally convince them of the existence of God.

Still, others just wanted to go home. The move was a welcome resolution, especially for those who had dedicated the past year or more to the cause.

RAFE EMERGED FROM THE BUILDING carrying his mother in a blanket and a plastic covering to keep her from getting wet. He was thoroughly soaked, but he didn't mind.

As the storm surged around them, he instinctively cast his mind back to search for something from his childhood, something that could help the two of them. As the memories came, he finally settled on the time that his mother held him close during the hurricane, and he tried to recall the tune that she hummed.

It helped to focus on that instead of whether or not she would last through the night. Instead of thinking about her sunken face or how the *Curse of God* had ravaged her, he reflected on how warm and inviting she had been. Then, in beautiful clarity as if it had always been a small memory away, the song came to him. It was powerful and soothing.

As he hummed the song, all the pain he felt for her subsided, and it was replaced with an indescribable heaven-sent feeling.

"Who's this?" Merlot questioned Rafe once he reached their truck.

He answered reverently, "This is my mom."

Charron looked down at the tragedy from her driver's seat window and asked, "Is she dead?" It was more of a logistics question than anything else.

"No, she's just sleeping. She'll be okay." He wasn't sure, but he wanted it to be so.

Merlot opened the passenger side of the truck and asked, "Don't you want God to change her? Shouldn't you leave her behind?"

"No," he stated calmly. He didn't know the reason; he just couldn't let her go.

Merlot helped the two of them into the back of the military truck, and as soon as all the doors were closed, the rain came down so violently that they couldn't hear the command over the radio to pull out. Charron took off anyway, following the other drivers in the caravan.

It was dark, as it had been for months, and the downpour seemed like its own curtain of uncertainty. High beams and brake lights were crucial for the journey out of Sacred Sodium.

After the city was behind them, the line of vehicles drove steadily toward the nearby Appalachians, and Merlot asked, "Is it me, or do they seem higher now?" Everything looked like an unclear impediment until a flash of lightning lit up the sky.

"So, what do you think will happen?" Charron asked her passengers. Merlot looked at Rafe in the back seat, but he was silent.

The rain fell harder, and the sound inside the vehicle of hail and water splashing against the metal and glass was frightening. Tires slipped in the mud, and downed trees blocked the road. Gusts of wind howled past them so forcefully that at times trucks were momentarily lifted off the ground. The pavement cracked, and massive chunks were hurled in every direction. Some fragments even became lodged in the windshield like Rafe's nightmare as a child.

In the back seat, Rafe held his mother's head close to him so that nothing would happen to her. The drive out of hell was utterly horrific, as if all things natural were against them. Charron's windshield now had multiple cracks, and water collected on the floorboards. Trees and debris flew at them from nowhere.

All were alarmed; all were worried that they might not make it. Merlot peered out the window as the lightning illuminated the field, and he witnessed eight military vehicles and two semi-trailers off-roading beside them, all driving at full speed toward the mountain pass.

Suddenly, Charron's truck came off the ground on two wheels, so Rafe closed his eyes and mouthed a silent prayer. Without a shadow of a doubt, he knew that this is what needed to happen. Despite all the destruction being hurled at them from every direction, he felt at peace. A surge of warmth surrounded him as if God were right there in the back seat with him, allowing their little caravan to make this one last effort.

Once the lightning became more intense and almost incessant, the trucks resumed formation, and they all flew out of the area at speeds of more than 120 mph. Some would say that fear drove them. Rafe knew what was really happening, though—angels were pushing them to safety.

As soon as the entire company reached the pass, they could finally see the sun above the thick layer of darkness, and it was a beautiful autumn day. One by one, each of the trucks pulled over on the side of the road, not from a given order but from an overwhelming peace they all felt.

Every soldier, nurse, and volunteer stepped out of their broken vehicles to look over the valley of Sacred Sodium. Eventually, the storm's clouds disappeared to reveal many of the buildings that were crushed and destroyed. Every tree was down, and the field was ravaged by the worst that nature could do.

THEN, WITH A HORRIBLE SOUND THAT CAUSED EVERY PERSON to shudder and hold their ears, Heavenly Father's final rebuke came upon the city in the form of a tidal wave so high that the entire valley was flooded in one fell swoop.

Water reached as far as the caravan on the mountain highway, but it did not overtake the truck tires. The massive flow of water caused even the salt tower to crash down, and great was the fall thereof.

Everyone but Rafe and Merlot ran up as far as they could on the mountainside, fearing for their lives. The two men stood firmly, though, in the middle of the road, watching the miracle unfold up to their ankles. Despite the sheer terror that permeated the entire company, Rafe held his mother in his arms, standing in the aftermath of God's blow, at peace.

Looking at the massive body of water and the sun shimmering beautifully upon it, Merlot proclaimed, "'*Vengeance is mine,' saith the Lord*." A few onlookers made the sign of the cross, knelt in the water, and prayed. Many took pictures and videos with their phones. It was a modern-day miracle on the scale of the Red Sea splitting, and everyone was in awe.

"Rafe, can you remove my bandage?" His mother's arms still only consisted of bones being held together by a few strands of tissue.

"Charlie, can you help me?" Rafe asked his friend. "She wants to see what happened." Merlot quickly came to their aid and took away her bloody eye bandage to reveal her sunken eye sockets. Already, her eyelids had healed over, and a few eyelashes were restored.

Rafe had studied cataloged pictures of the curse's various facial manifestations, so he had an idea of what to expect upon the removal of her bandage. The archived images brought him closer to understanding their pain and what their souls were going through.

Already, there was flesh on her cheekbones and nose. Even a few of the freckles below her eyes had returned. Rafe was curious how that happened because she had been in the dark for so long. Although she struggled at first, she opened her eyes slowly and cautiously to adjust to the life-giving sun.

Rafe held her in such a way so that she could look over the vast body of water. Sacred Sodium had held her bound, and she was now free. The wind blew through a few of her remaining strands of hair, and although she labored terribly, a faint smile appeared with the little lips she had left.

"Is it done?" she asked.

Rafe looked over at his friend and calmly answered her, "Yes, it is finished."

He then recalled the story of his wife meeting Kerioth at the Stoddard Haus. After almost 14 years of pondering the meaning of the phrase, it suddenly became clear as he beheld the remains of the mighty destruction. "The Dead Sea Solomon has now been Jerichoed," he humbly whispered. The salt temple was gone.

Upon entering their damaged vehicle, Charron turned to Merlot and gave him a silent nod with a quick, grateful grin before she joined the caravan. They had all changed. Each person there would describe the miracle to their families for decades in a way that they understood.

Chapter 50

An Ancient Battle

Once the entire caravan arrived back in Ottawa, the survivors' collection of stories and archives scared every living soul. It was not from the mysterious diseases or massive flood they witnessed but from realizing how far humanity could go down such a dark and horrible path.

In the end, over 138 million American citizens were slaughtered to build New Eden, but it was just the tip of the iceberg for all the racial injustices committed since God had started counting. Every non-white was beaten. The lucky ones soon rushed home to God and were quickly embraced. Slaves were made, and backs were broken.

Any revolts were swiftly dealt with by the president's *SS Militia*, which was 12 million-strong in force across the country. They had complete authority in all situations and were explicitly given execution orders for any unrest. The volunteer *SA Officers* reported to them, but they, in turn, answered to no one.

At the SS Militia Inaugural Ceremony, McKendrick proclaimed, "I now give them orders to be the law, the judge, and the Reaper. They are my beloved SS Militia; they are the arm of God."

A small fraction of those slain were the *dissenters*. They raised their protest signs to end centuries of systematic injustice and promote the equality of life, but they were all trampled down and burned in mounds of mutilated bodies. Hatred had elected hate, laws were enacted to decimate those who were hated, and none could oppose.

The DNA census allowed the blackest of hearts to set up execution houses in many cities, where those without *pure white heritage* were burned. The sometimes-failing technology to determine ancestry frequently produced differing results between fathers and their children, but only one test was allowed. The decree was: *All tainted blood must be rooted out, no matter who it may be!*

So, the fathers would stand by and watch their children die, believing however that *undesirable* DNA had entered their offspring, it was better that they perished. It was a small sacrifice for the cause of white supremacy for these men. They had crawled so far down the path of hatred that all decency, all respect, all that God had given them to treat others with love, was beyond comprehension. This was Cain-savagery, and it has been a part of humanity from the beginning.

Analysts studied McKendrick's followers for years, and they described them as having several key attributes, including authoritarian personality syndrome and social dominance orientation. They needed an authority to obey blindly and to live by a societal hierarchy.

The Devil knew that many individuals already primed to live by such tenets were in certain churches across America. The history of American Christian organizations had been tainted with racism and injustice for hundreds of years, and McKendrick was taught how to ensnare them like sheep with flaxen cords.

YOU MAY WONDER why the *racism descent*, the spiraling out of control from non-violence to active aggression toward people of color, was so prevalent in that time period. We may never know. Before the *Edicts*, the United States was deeply divided and in a dark place.

A person may argue that they could never even harm a fly, but Satan's plan starts simple enough for anyone to try. It begins with small hints of disdain, even little racial slurs. The person reasons that these little expressions are harmless, that they're just words; no one would get hurt. The phrases are then repeated until they are believed. They eventually become undeniable facts for the person and a part of their psyche and character. Racism eventually becomes a part of their identity.

And once their identity is attacked, they defend it. Over time, these defense mechanisms slowly become more and more violent until there is no virtue left at all. Killing a black man means nothing for a racist that has gone down this path.

Chapter 51

The Mind of God

I t was in his white quarantine room that Rafe learned the extent of the damage. The first day back in Ottawa was full of medical tests and debriefing interviews conducted behind glass. Authorities were aware of the noninfectious nature of the *Curse of God* diseases, but they still needed to take precautions.

After months of treating others, Rafe was assigned a room where he could finally rest. Unfortunately, there wasn't a window, and he was only afforded a bed, a white nightstand, and a TV. For most, it would drive a person mad, like it was part of a psychoanalysis study, but for him, it meant he was one day closer to seeing his son.

When he awoke from a much-needed nap, he turned on the TV, and for some reason, no audio came from the speakers. He adjusted the volume on the remote, but to no avail. The closed captioning function didn't work either, so he was left to reading lips and graphics.

The news anchors and contributors were sad about something. They cried on-air, and although he tried to figure out what was going on, he couldn't. The graphic at the bottom of the screen gave a vague caption: *Surviving the Destruction.*

He wondered what might have caused the anguish and sarcastically commented, "I didn't know New Eden meant that much to everyone." As soon as he said it, he shook his head, knowing that he shouldn't have made the remark. The news anchors weren't reporting another regular story; many people had died, and that could never be something trivial.

It wasn't until the satellite images came up that he was in complete shock. What was once the United States was now mostly under a massive body of water. The only sections of visible land were the Rocky and Appalachian Mountain ranges. The Rockies were now an eerie isthmus between Canada and Mexico, and the Appalachians had become a broad Canadian peninsula.

Live feeds from military airplanes confirmed the utter ruin of the country; everything was gone. A few animals were saved here and there on the mountain ranges, but no human soul was found.

Just like the star above Bethlehem, which many witnessed at the Anointed One's birth, these modern miracles of healing and retribution were the remains of an ancient battle for all to see.

Horror filled Rafe's mind. He had been right there when it had happened, and he didn't realize the full gravity of it. The entire country had been decimated by the hand of God, like a modern-day Sodom and Gomorrah destruction, because of racism.

The 700-mile radius wall that surrounded Sacred Sodium and the land of New Eden acted like a dam, and when it finally gave way, the water quickly flooded the region.

After more than 500 years of inequality and vicious brutality in the country, the land was made clean again through baptism. New Eden was an example of the worst of humanity, and it was a constant reminder for the rest of the world to be kinder in speech, help others who are down, and love one another.

RAFE STILL FREQUENTED HIS WIFE'S CEMETERY, eating cereal and reading the newspaper by her tombstone every morning; he was home. After the New Eden mission, it was helpful to have a routine, as the simple things seemed to keep the trauma at bay—sometimes.

While he was close to her, he often pondered the vision he received while sitting on a golden sidewalk panel by the pit of the dead. *Who or what was the woman supposed to represent, and what did her healing mean?*

It had become a Sunday-school parable equation he had to solve. Unfortunately, he never found an answer and resolved that whatever it might have been, the vision pushed him forward, and maybe, that's all that mattered.

"Thank you for watching over me and encouraging me to do what you would've done," he whispered to his wife one morning. He then placed a white daisy on her tombstone and gave her a peaceful smile.

A FEW MONTHS LATER, ONCE RAFE'S MOTHER had been released from the hospital, Merlot came over to meet the woman who had raised his friend. She had completely healed, both on the inside and outside.

It was a beautiful spring day. Rafe poured a glass of lemonade for him as they both sat on the porch and watched his mother and Martin play in the apartment yard. She was in perpetual happiness and could not lower her smile. At one point, while tickling the young boy, she hugged him tight.

"You're a man of God," Rafe stated to his friend as if he were about to dive into another friendly Biblical discussion.

Merlot chuckled a little and returned, "Yes, from time to time."

"I wonder why God made us so different. Couldn't we all just look the same? There wouldn't even be something called racism. We would all get along just fine."

Merlot stroked his gray beard and said, "Well, I'm not sure about that. People will always find something that angers them. There are plenty of things that make us different, and I guess that's one of the beauties of it all."

He admired the grandmother and grandson throwing a ball back-and-forth and continued, "If I were to peek into God's mind to understand His reasons for creating us the way He did, I'm sure I would be very baffled. What I do know is that He's trying to help us be more like Him, a loving parent. And maybe that means teaching us to be a little more loving regardless of what we look like, how we act, what culture we may come from, or who we are. We all just need to learn how to walk in other people's shoes, and I guess that having us look different helps us learn that a little better."

"You're probably right," Rafe agreed, and with a loving smile, he teased, "When did you get to be such a wise old man?"

They both chuckled and continued enjoying the family playing in the yard.

Epilogue

The Life of the Land

When the water—or *Mikvah*, as many called it—finally receded a few hundred years later, much was changed. Cities were completely buried, mountains and hills were moved, and the land was covered with trees and streams. To walk in the woods and smell the clean air was like experiencing the earth as God intended it to be.

Many came from around the world to be a part of this new land, as there were no immigration laws; all were accepted. Over the following decades, cities were built, roads were laid, and places were named.

After thousands of submissions, the name that was finally agreed upon by popular vote for the new country was *Philadelphia* because of its meaning in Greek: *brotherly love*.

One young citizen submitted a motto for the entire country, as she had been studying a little Hawaiian history: *Ua Mau ke Ea o ka ʻĀina i ka Pono*. When a Canadian reporter asked the girl to repeat the translation, she said, "It means *the life of the land is perpetuated in righteousness*. If we're just nice to each other, the country won't be taken away from us again—whether by God, nature, or karma."

The reporter smiled and commented, "*Out of the mouths of babes.*"

Most importantly, the citizens didn't want to repeat the same political mistakes from the previous country. Of course, they knew that imperfection was a part of any system, so those appointed to draft the new constitution looked at both historical and modern forms of government for inspiration.

They realized that divisiveness and tribalism had ruined the United States, so the first sections of the Philadelphia Constitution outlined that only independent candidates could run for office. The party system was outlawed. Sure, like-minded people could form groups to further a cause, but the ballots could not contain party affiliation. Voters had to research and align themselves with a candidate that shared their positions and ideals. And, of course, elections were by popular vote only. Every single vote mattered.

It was also evident from McKendrick's *reign* of a presidency that one person could destroy an entire nation. Even though the founding fathers provided for checks and balances of power in government, no one could have foreseen the anomaly that was McKendrick.

Volumes were written about the man, but it wasn't for adulation or reverence. They were written as a warning for all future generations. Most of them were free to read; it was that important for all to know the truth.

As he played into the divisiveness and cultural diversity of the vast country, pitting people against each other on everything from religion to fiscal responsibility, the Framers of the Philadelphia Constitution devised a solution.

Instead of voting for a president or an executive officer over the entire country, citizens elected provincial legislative representatives, who would then, in turn, vote for the Philadelphia president among themselves. The Framers couldn't allow the election of one office to divide and dismantle a country.

This person had to have tenure as a legislative representative and could only serve one term. The Framers felt that a president should not dedicate any time toward any type of re-election.

Special interest groups and commercial entities could not lobby or influence any elected official in any way, and all election donations had to be made anonymously. The Framers wanted to ensure that policies were made for the public interest instead of personal or business gain.

Since the Philadelphia president had the duty of serving each citizen to the best of their abilities, the check on their power rested with citizens. Citizens could cast a semiannual approval or disapproval of the president's performance. If the disapproval reached a certain threshold, they were replaced by another from the group of legislative representatives.

One of the Framers and an actual author of the Philadelphia Constitution, Talia Shui, alluded to a flock of birds to explain the system. "There always needs to be a bird in front that takes the brunt of the wind," she said, "And once they tire, the flock quickly reconfigures with a new leader so that the old one may rest. That is how it is with this presidency."

She then sat down as her remarks were the last on the docket at the assembly hall before the final votes were cast on the Constitution's legal adoption.

Progress was the key. The country needed to fly together in a singular direction, taking into account different points of view and ideas. Everything was debatable as there are two or more sides to every political argument. The point, though, was to consider each without prejudice and go forward together.

IN THE MIDDLE OF THE NATION'S CAPITAL, PHILADELPHIA CITY, is a statue of Talia Shui reading to her son. On the base, written in gold lettering, is her famous quote: *Our differences, our races, and our collective histories make us one. Silencing a single voice weakens the whole. So, I ask you, Patriot, will you stand up to someone who argues the contrary?*

Today, elementary schools from around the country visit and take holographic captures with her. Any of them could recite the famous line, but it's not because it's required memorization. It is because they believe it.

THE END

*If you have enjoyed reading **A Country Called Philadelphia** or were moved by the story, please consider submitting an honest review. Not only do reviews help other readers make an informed decision about the novel, but they also make it more discoverable.*

Creating this story for everyone has changed me as a human being, and I am anxious to read how others feel about it. With all that's going on in the world, I believe that spreading a little love and peace can make a difference.

For the latest news on my journey as an artist and storyteller, please visit 1820studios.com.

Thank you for reading my novel.

—Nathan

Acknowledgements

First and foremost, I need to thank my mom and dad. I am eternally grateful for the indescribable amount of love and support they have given me throughout my life. They both helped me to come closer to God and have a love of the scriptures. I will never forget my mom's sacrifice of waking early every morning to teach me about the Old Testament before school and that she typed my first real story in one night because I didn't know how to use a typewriter. I am grateful that my dad inspired me to write poetry and so many short stories and that he watches over me from above.

To my brother, who was my best friend growing up, I am truly indebted for millions of wonderful memories. My life's ambition to make feature films is a direct result of watching many movies together and being able to correlate everything in life to the stories we experienced.

To my children, I am grateful for your patience and love—especially in my trying times. I am thankful that our home was full of discussions about story structure and analysis. The characters, situations, and plot points of various films and books always seemed to sneak into everyday conversations.

I want to thank Dan Ronyak, who helped me focus on marketing aspects of the story, suggested valuable edits, and inspired a new scene. I am grateful to my editors, **Katie Elliott and Ana Joldes**, who polished the manuscript with countless improvements. You are my superheroes!

There are many more people that have inspired me over the years and have contributed to making this story happen, and I am forever in your debt.

Lastly, I want to tell my wife, Jelaine, how thankful I am for her support in chasing this crazy dream of telling stories. She has given me a second life, and I am so grateful that she is always by my side.

—Nathan Merritt